# LINCOLN

Lincoln



Editor:
Hot Tree Editing

Cover Design:
CT Cover Creations

Proofreading:
Judy's Proofreading



Lincoln/ S. Nelson. – 1st edition

ISBN-13: 9781734302387

# LINCOLN

KNIGHTS CORRUPTION MC SERIES - NEXT GENERATION

S. NELSON

*For all of you who are excited to dive back into their world*

# Prologue

## Lincoln

“Rip his head off!”

The crowd cheered around me; their enthusiasm at watching two men trying to kill each other was enough to make anyone think twice about fighting in this underground world. No one who signed up for these bouts aspired to someday make it to the pro MMA, myself included. I did it because I was a fuckin’ machine. I’d been trained to fight since I was thirteen years old. I was precise. Lethal if necessary. While I’d never killed anyone in the ring and had no desire to do so, I’d take all measures necessary to win. The prize money was nothin’ to sneeze at either. It was my way of contributing to our MC.

Focused on besting my opponent, I ignored the outrageous demands of the spectators. Instead, I honed all my training, steadied my nerves, and calmed my breathing, which was a feat in itself given how quickly I danced around the cage, my arms and legs working together to attempt to take this fucker out so I could be done with this fight and look for *her*.

While I learned never to underestimate my rival, I hadn’t

expected this guy, whose name I didn't care to remember, to last this long. He was at least thirty pounds too heavy, his gut hangin' over the waistband of his shorts. And while his extra weight slowed his movements, he continued to try and best me, even after I broke two of his ribs. If I had the time to care, I'd respect the bastard for his perseverance.

"End this now, Linc," Jagger yelled behind me. He shouted something else, but I didn't hear him, too busy dodging the fist headed straight for the side of my head.

Leaning a few inches to the right, his hand flew past me the same time I hit him with a vicious uppercut, knocking him off his feet. Before he even hit the ground, he was out cold.

There was no time for celebration or showboating the win. I jerked my chin toward Jagger and hopped out of the ring, a flash of dark hair catching my attention in the back of the room.

Before I could tell him to follow me, my feet propelled me toward her, disregarding Marek's warnings and shoving aside not only my safety but the protection of everyone else in the club.

My brain shut down as my body bristled, every step closer warning me of the consequences.

But I didn't care.

I had to save her.

## Lincoln

The metallic aroma of blood infiltrated my nostrils, and while I'd love to say I wasn't used to the scent, I was. Hell, I was even used to the smell of desperation, but this shit was unbelievable. I stood next to Kaden in a cloud of confusion, staring at the circle of men surrounding Tag, who was strapped to the table and unconscious.

"Stop!" Kaden shouted when Cutter raised his fist to strike the guy again. "What did he do?"

Our president moved away from the table and stalked toward us, his eyes focused solely on his son, his hands clenching into fists the closer he approached. The way he glared at Kaden made both of us take a step back. He looked set to explode, and I didn't want to be the one to get hit with the aftermath.

When father and son stood toe to toe, Marek growled, "He's a fuckin' Reaper."

His words penetrated my ears, but my brain refused to

absorb the words. There was no way Tag was a Reaper, part of that cesspool of a club. From what we'd witnessed during our interactions with them, and from the stories we heard over the years, their moral compass had been destroyed long ago, if it ever existed in the first place.

Not only had Tag moved back home to care for his sick mother, but he'd helped us when a fight broke out at Indulge, and again by giving us a detailed description of two members of the Reapers, the ones we thought were responsible for setting fire at that same strip club. If he was indeed one of them, which I still didn't believe, why would he set up his brothers? Why would he say something knowing we'd retaliate against our sworn enemy?

My mind drifted back to what Kaden had told me about the night of the blaze, which was that Tag had gone outside to grab his cell from his truck. Then when he came back into the club, he'd pulled Kaden aside to tell him about two shady-lookin' men he saw come around the side of the building. Not long after, smoke started to fill one of the back rooms of Indulge.

Someone had set a fire, and all things pointed to the Savage Reapers, especially after Tag had described the two guys in detail. They were the same ones we fought after my bout. The same ones who held *her* hostage.

Was it a coincidence Tag had left Indulge right before the fire started?

Had he helped set it?

Or had he truly only gone outside to grab his phone from his truck?

Was his mother even sick?

Did he even have a mother who was still alive?

The more questions I asked myself, the more confused I became, realizing I didn't know Tag all that well. But my gut still told me he wasn't a bad guy. My instincts told me he wasn't a Reaper like Marek believed.

I pulled a breath deep into my lungs before releasing it. "What makes you think he's a Reaper?" I asked, careful to keep my tone calm. Marek was wired to blow, and while I didn't want my simple question to be the reason everything went to shit, I had to ask. The guys were set on killing Tag, their resolve to end his life disturbing. The least our leader could do was give us some sort of justification.

"I know he is."

"How?" I pushed my luck, but I had to in order to be able to live with myself afterward. I'd never been involved in ending someone's life, let alone cold-blooded murder, and I wasn't about to start now. My inner voice screamed at me to shut up, to trust Marek and the other guys, including my ol' man. That they wouldn't do something like this, take such drastic measures unless they felt they had to.

Kaden and I had heard stories about life in the club before the war ended between us and the Reapers, but the tales were edited. I suspected they'd done some bad shit, but whenever we asked them about it, they'd simply say "We handled it" or "We did what we needed to." They never admitted to killing anyone, and while Kaden and I could only assume that's what their coded talk meant, we didn't know for sure.

"Let's get on with it, Prez," Hawke shouted, gathering his dark hair and tying it back, his features more prominent without the shield of his strands, the look in his eyes unwavering. Then I looked at Cutter, who was dressed in all black and wielding a large knife, his stare laser-focused. Jagger stood next to him, a look of worry traveling over his face before he looked to my father. They both glanced in our direction, specifically at Marek, before turning their attention back to each other, sharing a look of apprehension. It was like they feared what our leader would do, but more so for his safety, if that made any sense, which it sure as hell didn't to me.

Kaden grabbed Marek's arm as he moved to turn away from

us. "Dad. What's goin' on?" His voice was eerily quiet, but I had a sense he didn't want to fuel his father's fury. To add to the direness of the situation, Kaden never called his ol' man Dad while in the company of the club members. He either called him Prez or occasionally Marek. I adopted the same habit, only referring to my father as ol' man, Dad or Pops while at home and away from our brothers.

"I told you. He's a Reaper. He infiltrated our club, and you two"—he looked to me quickly before focusing back on his son—"let it happen." There was a shroud of rage in Marek's eyes, but it was more than that. I thought I detected a spark of desperation as well, but I couldn't be sure because he averted his stare and looked to the ground. His chest rose and fell several times before he picked his head up again. "You need proof?"

Kaden swallowed hard, nodding but appearing unsure if that was the right response.

Marek reached into the inside pocket of his cut and pulled out a picture. He unfolded it and shoved it in his son's face, his hand shaking with barely controlled anger.

"This is how I know," he barked, flipping the picture over and jabbing at the words written on the back. I leaned in close to see.

*Mom, Dad, Tag.*

"I'm not gettin' it," I rushed to say, my need to understand this entire situation rushing out of me before I could stop the flow of words.

"Me either." Kaden reached to touch the picture, but Marek snatched the photo back.

He flipped the picture around and pointed to the man. His sandy-brown hair and lean build made him look like any other guy, but when I examined him closer, I saw the expression on his face, in his eyes, and something disturbed me. *He* looked disturbed. He wasn't smiling and stood at least two feet from who appeared to be his woman and baby.

"This bastard right here," Marek yelled, his finger resting over the image of the man, "tortured your mother."

# Lincoln

I didn't have time to react before Kaden ripped the photo from Marek's hand, scrutinizing the man in the picture.

"What the fuck are you talkin' about? Who is this?" he asked, his restraint being slowly plucked apart with every second that passed in silence.

Growing up, Kaden would often tell me that whenever he asked how his parents met, they'd often ignore the question by changing the subject. And on the rare occasion when one of them answered, his mom, Sully, would say she didn't exist before Marek walked into her life, still refusing to give any other details.

"That," Marek said, his voice low and tense, "is Vex." His blue eyes turned to black while he struggled to find an ounce of composure.

"Who is—"

"Vex tortured and abused your mother in every way possible from the time she was fourteen until I rescued her from their clutches." My focus bounced from Marek to Kaden to everyone else in the fuckin' room. Cutter, Jagger, Hawke, and my ol' man shared a look of rage, their body language coiled tightly listening to our leader. Marek removed the picture from his son's hand, and although he held it tightly, he didn't look at it again. "Your mom belonged to the Savage Reapers."

"No." Kaden vigorously shook his head. "It's not true." He took a step away from his dad. "Wh... what does that mean?"

"Her father, Psych, was the president many years ago when our clubs were at war. He'd use his daughter as payment to get what he wanted from other men, even abusing her himself before passing her off to Vex when she was barely a teenager. Whatever awful thing you can think of to do to another human being, they did it without a care for her pain and suffering. She was an object to them, to that entire fuckin' club."

Pain weaved through Marek's voice, the anguish he felt vibrating with every word he spoke about his wife.

"But what does Tag have to do with this Vex guy?" I asked, moving back a step when Marek turned his eyes on me.

"Because he's his son," he growled.

"But he didn't know his dad. The guy left when Tag was a few years old."

"And how do you know that?" Hawke shouted from across the room, his voice vibrating against all four walls. "'Cause he told ya?"

"Well... yeah." My shoulders slumped in defeat because there was a possibility Tag wasn't who he said he was.

"He lied," Jagger chimed in. "Don't you think it's a little too convenient he just so happened to befriend you guys?"

Kaden walked away from me and Marek, heading straight for the guy restrained on the table. When he was close enough, he leaned down and studied him, as if Tag was gonna somehow give him the answers he wanted all without speaking. Hell, all without even being conscious.

"What are you planning on doing?" I asked, aware Marek

planned on killing the guy, but I needed to hear his answer, all the same.

"We're gonna end him like we did Vex and Psych."

"You killed them both?" Kaden asked, turning back to look at his dad.

"We didn't only kill 'em. We tortured 'em first... then we sent them to hell for what they did to Sully." Marek ran his hand over the top of his head several times, and if I wasn't mistaken, I thought I saw a few more gray hairs sprout up.

"Should we wake him?" Cutter asked, reaching for something on the rolling table behind the one Tag was tied to.

"Yeah."

One word from our president was enough to make me nauseous because I could only imagine what was gonna happen as soon as Tag opened his eyes.

Without realizing my feet had moved, I soon stood beside my father, swallowing my nerves as best I could. I'd fought some of the biggest and baddest in the ring, and I never felt the urge to vomit beforehand. But now, looking at the sorry state of Tag, not sure whether he was who he said he was, and realizing the severity of what was gonna happen once he woke up, the bile churned in my stomach. The last thing I ever imagined was being privy to a murder tonight, and never in a million years did I think our club would be the one to commit the act.

Cutter waved something under Tag's nose, and at first, the unconscious man didn't move, but when he moved his hand back and forth under his nostrils a second time, Tag's head moved slightly to the side. I assumed he used smelling salts, a pungent substance often used in the ring to either wake someone up after they'd been knocked unconscious or make them more alert if they'd been hit in the head and were on the verge of passing out.

Hearing Tag groan in protest to the potent aroma tugged at something inside me. Was it nerves? Compassion? Guilt? I couldn't be sure. All I knew was I wanted to be anywhere but here right now.

Once he was alert, Tag's eyes moved to each person until they fell on me. My expression froze because I didn't want to alarm him any more than he already was. I realized the sentiment may seem odd, but God only knew what was runnin' through his head.

If he was, in fact, a Reaper and had infiltrated our club for the purpose of gaining information to later use against us, then I was on board with teaching him a lesson. Killing him, though? I was on the fence about that.

But, if he was innocent, his only sin being related to the man who tortured Sully....

I didn't even know how to complete my thought process on that option.

Marek pushed me aside and moved toward the top of the table, Tag's eyes following him until they were close in proximity.

"We know you're a Reaper and we know who your father was." Marek's voice cracked with a sinister chuckle. "And we're gonna end you, just like we did him." He jerked his chin toward Cutter before taking a step back. In fact, all the men except for me and Kaden retreated as Cutter closed in on Tag, leaning over him with the knife held strategically in his hand. The look in the ol' man's eyes unnerved me. He looked like he was absent, as if a wall had gone up inside him. It was the scariest shit I'd ever seen, although I had a feeling I'd retract the statement in the next few minutes.

Even though Tag was now conscious, when he opened his mouth to speak, no noise escaped. But when the tip of the blade pierced Tag's flesh, separating his skin as Cutter moved the knife diagonally over his torso, Tag's eyes popped open, and a pained groan hurdled through the air, deepening but getting louder with each inch of parted flesh.

His arms and legs thrashed against his restraints, his eyes pleading with me, then Kaden, before Cutter finally lifted the knife. Blood dripped down Tag's side and over the edge of the table. The cut wasn't deep like a puncture wound, but it wasn't superficial either.

"Please," Tag finally mumbled, his hands squeezing into fists while his chest rose and fell faster and faster.

"Please what?" Hawke asked. "Please kill me fast? Is that what you want?"

Tag vigorously shook his head, closing his eyes and breathing deeply through his nose before looking at us again.

"I don't... don't under... stand. Please...."

I turned so my back was to Tag and stared at our president, hoping he would reconsider his plan for disposing of someone I'd come to call a friend of sorts.

"What if you're wrong?"

"I'm not," he said, baring his teeth when he spoke. "He's Vex's son. I have proof."

"So what?"

"So what?" he roared, gripping me up by my cut and pulling me so close the sight of him in front of me blurred. "Did you not hear what Vex did to my wife?" He shoved me back so hard I almost fell on my ass but caught myself at the last second, my arm swinging out and knocking into Jagger. "I'm gonna end the fucker's lineage tonight."

# Three

## Maddie

I huddled in the darkened corner of his room, fearful he'd come back for more once he finished partying with the others. Cowering had become my new normal, a way to protect myself against the blows that would come from either his fists or booted foot.

The turn of the handle and the creak of the hinge pricking my ears made my breath stutter, all while my heart hammered away at such a furious pace, I feared the muscle would arrest any second. Soft illumination from the hallway surrounded his silhouette as he stood in the doorway. I saw his weathered brown boot first, then his jean-clad leg, my eyes traveling upward until his entire form came into view.

He flicked on a light, the obtrusion blinding at first. "What happened this time?" he asked, pulling my arm away from my face. His touch wasn't rough like the others, but I flinched, nonetheless. "What did you do, Maddie?"

"I didn't move fast enough." Pike, whose real name was Cody, although I was warned not to call him that for fear someone might hear, shook his head, the pity in his eyes when he looked down on me enough to make my bottom lip tremble with sadness. The prospect of this club was the only one who was nice to me, when he could get away with it. If his friends were present, he treated me much like they did, without physically hurting me. His words were harsh yet dismissive. He told me he couldn't show weakness in front of them because he'd pay for it, already had when he tried to interfere on my behalf my first night here. They beat him bloody before threatening his life if he ever chose pussy over them again.

While Pike was the reason I was here in the first place, I didn't blame him for what his buddies did to me. I'd met him soon after stepping off the bus, and although his tattoos and leather vest should have warned me he was dangerous, I ignored my instincts when he'd smiled at me.

They didn't have guys like him back home in Oklahoma, not where I grew up, at least. I'd been sheltered my entire life. The mere mention of boys sending my pastor father on one of his tirades about how I was to stay away from them, to never bring shame on our family by acting inappropriately. The entire spiel about saving myself until marriage ran on a constant loop anytime he saw me smile at someone of the opposite sex, whenever I was fortunate enough to encounter a boy at the grocery store or even in our church.

Pike walked into the adjacent bathroom and turned on the faucet before returning and crouching down beside me. "Let me see." I didn't bother to say no because my protest would be useless. He lifted my head upward and placed the wet towel over the corner of my mouth. When he pulled it back to adjust the cloth, I saw the red stain. My tongue drifted over the cut, and I winced, like I'd done right after Griller, who was the leader of these bastards, punched me in the mouth earlier. He placed the towel back on my lip and held it there for a few seconds more. He heard me inhale, the corners of his mouth turning downward. "Sorry."

I looked into his eyes and saw not only pity but a flash of guilt as well. After all, it was because of him I was now a prisoner of the Savage Reapers, his club.

After a few more awkward and silent moments, I pushed his hand away and slowly stood. When he reached out to help me, I slid my palm into his, the warmth of his hand providing a fleeting comfort.

"Do you want somethin' to eat?" he asked, tossing the washcloth on top of the cluttered dresser before shoving his hands in his pockets.

"I'm not hungry."

"You're wastin' away, Maddie."

"So?" A flash of fury wafted over me. "Maybe I'll die sooner than I prayed to." I shuffled toward the bed and sat on the edge, even though resting anywhere near this mattress was the last place I wanted to be. But it wasn't like I could waltz out of Griller's room and flit about the club, or even dare to venture outside.

No, the rules were simple.

Stay put unless otherwise told.

My previously fractured wrist proof of my momentary lapse in obedience.

"I don't know how to help you," he whispered when he edged closer, glancing back toward the door before returning his attention to me.

"You could help me escape." I grabbed his arm and pulled him to sit beside me. Pike didn't make me fear him like the others did. He'd only hit me when forced to do so. While his slap had stung, the force with which he struck me was mild, compared to everyone else's.

He tugged his arm away but kept his eyes steady on mine.

"They'll know it was me." He shook his head. "I'm sorry but I... I can't."

I nodded, understanding that he wasn't gonna put his life in danger for me. A tear fell down my cheek, then another. I turned away from him when he tried to wipe my face with his thumb.

He stood moments later, wrapping his fingers around the handle of the bedroom door.

"Most of the guys are too drunk to stand, so I think you're safe from them tonight."

"But not from him."

"Probably not. But one is better than five," he said, his statement intended to comfort me in a strange sort of way.

Without another word, he left, taking with him any ounce of hope I had, albeit delusional, about forming a plan to escape.

When my eyes drifted closed sometime later, I dreamed of the stifled and bubbled life I'd had back home, and wished I'd known then that my life had been a dream.

Now... it was a nightmare.

# Four

## Lincoln

“We gonna drag this out, Prez?” Cutter shouted, gripping the large knife tightly in his hand, his eyes glazing over as if he enjoyed slicing into Tag.

Marek looked first at his son, then at me. His expression was unreadable, but his delay in answering made the hairs on the back of my neck stand up. If he wanted to give Tag a quick death, he could’ve. He could’ve shot him or instructed Cutter to stab him through the heart. But he did neither of those things. Instead, he wanted to draw out this torture for however long, showing me and Kaden a side of him we’d never witnessed before. And I gotta say, it terrified me.

A nod from our leader was all it took to make Cutter smile, the perverse grin on his face sending shivers down my back. The guy was quiet and kept to himself, essentially not too personable, but I never thought he was twisted.

Tag bellowed when Cutter dragged the blade across his chest once more, this time in the opposite direction, forming an X shape. I couldn’t tear my eyes away from the blood splattering on the ground, each drop tearing away all I thought I knew about these men. Shattering whatever ideals I held dear about our club.

Not only were they set on torturing the guy, but some of them took enjoyment in the act, namely Cutter, Marek, and Hawke, who sported a devious grin of his own as he watched Tag writhe in pain.

When Cutter switched the way he held the knife, gripping the handle with a tight fist, looking like he was gonna plunge it into Tag, I rushed toward him and grabbed his arm.

"You better get your hand off me," Cutter growled, flicking his eyes toward me when I refused. It wasn't until my dad grabbed hold of my shoulder and squeezed that I complied.

The second I took a step back, Cutter drove his knife into Tag's side. The wail of pain that erupted from the guy pierced my ears as well as any sense of comprehension I held up until this point. Even if Tag was indeed a Reaper and had some sort of twisted plan for us, was that enough of a reason to torture him? What kind of war had our club endured in the past that made whatever happened now okay?

"Enough!" Kaden shouted, rushing toward Cutter like I'd done seconds earlier. Only Kaden knocked the ol' man back a step, getting in between him and Tag. "I don't know what the hell you guys used to do in the past, but our club doesn't run like that anymore. Wanna know how I know?" He paused for dramatic effect. "'Cause I've never fuckin' killed anybody," he shouted. "This ends now."

"You better move," Hawke threatened, his shoulders rising to meet his neck. "You have no idea what you're doin'."

"Neither do you." Kaden stood firm, even when Marek approached. Both father and son had their fists balled, and there was no way to predict what was gonna happen because neither Kaden nor I had ever been in anything close to this type of situation. It was apparent, however, Cutter, Marek, Hawke,

Jagger, and my ol' man had been. Probably too many times, judging by their comfort level of what was happening in this basement.

"Is this what you did? Kill people without givin' 'em the chance to tell their side of the story? What if that was me on the table instead? Wouldn't you want the Reapers to at least ask me if I meant them harm?" Kaden asked. "Or are you so hell-bent on exacting revenge for Mom that you're blinded by the need to kill Tag just because he was related to Vex?"

Marek's movements were swift and precise, gripping up Kaden and shoving him against the nearest wall, spit flying from his mouth in his rage.

"Don't you dare trivialize my need for revenge for what happened to your mother. You have no idea what you're talkin' about. You've never seen all the scars on her body from what they did to her. You've never calmed her after one of her night-mares. So don't stand there and lecture me when you're talkin' out your fuckin' ass." He released his son but continued to stand close. "You have no idea, Kaden. None. You and Linc live in a fairy tale. You've never seen what we have, which is the exact reason we went through hell in the first place. We wanted our families to have a better life. But this," Marek said, pointing at Tag, "opens up wounds that never fully healed."

"But what if Tag really is innocent?" Kaden asked, never pulling his eyes from his ol' man's.

"No one's innocent," Hawke interrupted.

"Then why don't we strap you to the table?" Kaden barked.

Instead of Hawke responding, he smiled, enjoying this way too much.

"Please." Kaden's shoulders slumped. "Just have someone do some research. If his story doesn't check out, if he really didn't move back here from Boston after being gone for decades, then..." He gave a half-hearted shrug. "Do what ya want."

Marek stared at his son in contemplation, narrowing his eyes before inhaling a deep breath. Once he released the air from his lungs, he turned to look at our VP.

"Call him," he said before swinging his attention to Cutter. "No more for right now." The ol' fucker looked disappointed, but he threw his knife on the table, the clanking noise enough to startle me though I watched the blade leave his hand.

I didn't know who *he* was, but whoever my ol' man was gonna contact would hopefully put all this to bed, proving Tag was truly innocent.

If he wasn't... then he'd be dead soon.

Marek stepped up next to Tag and leaned over him, grabbing a chunk of his hair and pulling his head up off the table.

"Where did you come from?"

"Boston," Tag garbled, blood seeping from the corner of his mouth.

"Did you really not know your father?" Prez's grip tightened.

Tag winced, but I doubted the pain he felt had anything to do with his hair being pulled and everything to do with the wounds he suffered.

"My mom sent... sent me to live with her parents when I was a little kid. I barely knew my dad. Then he disappeared." Marek released his hold, and Tag's head hit the table with a thump.

"Damn right he did," Marek sneered. He grumbled something to himself, then smacked his friend on the arm. They both ascended the basement steps a few strides later. Hawke followed, but Cutter stayed behind. Although I didn't trust him, he wouldn't blatantly go against what our leader said.

"What about the hole in his side?" I asked, leaning down to get a better look. Blood continued to seep out, although it was slower than before.

Without a single word, the ol' man walked to the other side

of the room and picked up a blow torch. When the fire erupted from the end of it, he grabbed his knife and held the flame against the steel tip. I watched in disbelief when he then held the heated knife over the wound on Tag's side, the sound he made at first contact making me wince.

"What the fuck is goin' on?" Kaden asked. Of course, his question was rhetorical because I didn't have an answer. He knew as much as I did.

But I supposed we were gonna find out if Tag would live or die soon enough.

# Five

## Maddie

"Let's go!" Griller shouted in my face. I was barely awake, and already I was tossed out of his room and dragged down the hallway. Wiping the sleep from my eyes, I focused on the scene in front of me when I entered the main part of the clubhouse.

I wasn't a neat freak by any stretch of the imagination. In fact, my parents used to yell at me all the time to clean up my room or put my dishes in the sink when I was done instead of leaving them all over the place, but I never once lived in utter filth like these guys did.

The floor was sticky beneath my feet, and I cursed myself for not slipping on my sneakers before coming out here, but with the way he pushed me forward, I probably didn't have time for the simple act anyway.

There appeared to be hundreds of beer bottles and cans strewn all around the room, some of them spilling the rest of the contents on the floor, bar, and even parts of the sofa. A fog of smoke lingered in the air, thick enough to offend my senses even though I didn't believe anyone had smoked anything for hours.

"Get to work." Before Griller staggered back toward his room, he shouted over his shoulder, "Hurry up. Don't make me wait too long, or else." I remembered all too well what his "or else" entailed, often resulting in a black eye or sore ribs.

While I looked at the passed-out bodies of the members as well as the half-naked women who accompanied them, I wished again, for the millionth time, for God to save me from this hell. But something told me He was either too busy or just chose not to help me. Maybe He was punishing me for being stupid and going with Pike in the first place, a stranger who disarmed me with his smile. Whatever the reason, I was stuck until one of these guys either killed me or I killed myself—the latter not ideal since I'd been raised to believe suicide was a sin.

As I worked around the unconscious people, I gently placed the trash in a bag, careful not to make too much noise because if I woke up anyone, they'd punish me. Sometimes their cruelty was enough to make my mind drift off to another place, leaving my body behind to do with whatever they wanted. It wasn't like I had a say in the matter, so I learned to adapt each time one of them held me down and thrust inside me. I was thankful they didn't demand I watch them because I needed the darkness to fly away into another realm of reality in order to survive, albeit barely.

Sometimes only one of them would have a go at me, and sometimes it was one after the other. In the beginning, I begged and cried, but they didn't care. The only one who seemed affected was Pike, and the first time he interjected on my behalf, they took turns hitting him before forcing him on top of me.

The torment I saw laced behind his eyes was enough for me to stop struggling... then I gave him a nod, a brief sign of my acceptance for the situation we were both in. I realized he didn't have a choice either, so I closed my eyes and let him push into me. Thankfully, he was fast, groaning when he finished. I thought I heard him whisper, "I'm sorry," but I was so lost inside myself, I couldn't be sure.

Buried deep inside my horrid memories, Pike startled me when he came up behind me, dropping a bottle into my trash bag. The clanking noise made me cringe, but when none of the men stirred, I relaxed.

"I'll help you." I held the garbage bag firm when he tried to take it from me. I knew this wasn't a trick, but I was fearful all the same. Not of him, but of what would happen if Griller happened to come out here and see him assisting me.

"I'm fine." He tugged on the bag once more. "I have to go back to his room when I'm finished." I gave him a pleading look, one he unfortunately understood. A curt nod was thrown my way before he walked out of the clubhouse.

Even though Pike was the one who brought me here and had sex with me in front of the other guys, I saw how my treatment pained him. I didn't blame him for my circumstances. Well... not entirely, at least.

He was as much a victim as I was, more so in a sense because if he tried to leave the Savage Reapers, they'd kill his mom and his sister before ending his life. I found out this information during the rare times we'd been alone. I was grateful I didn't have any more family left, so if they wanted to kill me, I could handle it.

*I say that now because I'm still breathing.*

As I exited the kitchen after tossing the full garbage bag on top of the waste bin, I heard Griller shout from down the hallway.

"Let's fuckin' go, woman!" He knew my name but never used it, a small win I was grateful for. In fact, the only person to call me Maddie was Pike, which I was fine with. There was no malice toward me from him like there was from the rest of the club.

I supposed I took too long because he rushed out of the room and snatched my arm, his fingers pinching my skin as he dragged me behind him, tossing me into the middle of his room.

His nakedness was a blatant clue as to what he wanted from me. And no matter how often he invaded my body, each time was terrifying. He'd forced himself into my mouth, between my legs and even in the place that was forbidden and shameful.

The first time he sodomized me, I cried harder than I ever had in my life, not only from the pain but from loathsomeness, and utter embarrassment. At one point, because I wouldn't shut up or stop trying to get away from him, he choked me until I passed out. When I woke up, I was alone in his room, still face-down on his bed. I ached all over but had been thankful not to have been conscious during the rape. The next time he forced himself there, I hadn't been as lucky, remembering every painful detail as well as his devilish grunts.

Griller gripped my arms and shook me. "Take off your clothes," he demanded, leering at me while he waited for me to do as I was told.

I never understood why he chose to mar his neck and face with tattoos of skulls and daggers. Then again, the ugliness of them matched perfectly with the ugliness of his insides as well as his exterior. He was thin with a receding hairline, the rest of his dark strands cropped close to his head. Sometimes I wished he'd grow a beard, so I didn't have to see so much of his face.

Typically, he was either drunk or high, but right now, his eyes were blank, absent, which terrified me even more.

I put my hands up in front of me and took a few steps back. Why? I had no idea because no amount of distance or silent pleading would make a bit of difference. The result would always be me doing exactly what he wanted.

"I don't feel good," I said, praying he would leave me alone, but my words fell on deaf ears.

"So?" The corner of his lip curved up, but I wasn't dumb enough to think he smiled. No, it was a sneer. A dangerous grin.

"I was hoping maybe I could lie down and rest for a bit." Every word I spoke was wasted, and even so, I continued. "Please." I retreated until my back hit the wall, the sudden stop startling me because I couldn't focus on anything but Griller and the terrifying look in his black eyes.

"When have I ever cared how you felt?" he asked, cocking his head slightly to the side, his eyes lecherously roaming over me. "I don't know what's gotten into you, but if you don't get your ass on the bed in two seconds, you're gonna regret it."

I would've liked to have said I stayed put and that my noncompliance annoyed him, so much so he left the room. But that outcome didn't happen. Instead of testing his lack of patience, I moved forward until I stood in front of the mattress, stripping off my clothes before he got the chance to do it, which would've made him angrier.

Lying down on my belly, I buried my face in the dingy colored pillowcase, the smell of smoke and beer pungent, but inhaling the scent was better than facing him. He'd only forced himself on me once while looking at me. Every other time, he was behind me, which meant I didn't have to watch him as he violated me.

He smacked the back of my leg. I parted my thighs and waited for the pain. Because my body wasn't ready to accept him, every inch he thrust into me sent a shockwave of pain rippling through me. But once he was fully inside, the pain subsided some.

The entire time he grunted, my mind drifted away, but unlike previous times when I'd been able to conjure a safe place, a man I'd seen several times before drifted in.

His warm brown eyes were filled with concern when they

landed on mine, and although he'd never spoken to me directly, he'd asked about me, had even gotten into a fight with Griller because of me.

Why couldn't I have met him instead of Pike? Would he have mistreated me as well? Did he only ask about me because he wanted to enjoy my body, or was he genuinely concerned for my well-being?

While I didn't know anything about him, other than he belonged to a different club, there was something about the way he looked at me that made my heart stutter, but in a good way.

Perhaps I was simply conjuring feelings that didn't exist because fantasy and delusion were better than my actuality. Even so, I looked forward to the next time I'd see him. But after the last brawl between their clubs, I wasn't sure whether Griller would take me along to the fights any longer. I was surprised he let me outside at all, let alone around a bunch of strangers. He threatened to kill me if I ever attempted to escape and I believed him, so I never tried.

He climbed off when he finished. He never lasted long, which was a blessing. The clink of his belt buckle made me flinch, but then I heard his zipper and realized he wasn't gonna use his belt on me this time.

"I'm tired of you," he said nonchalantly, kicking the side of my leg with his. "Get up." He grabbed my arm and pulled me from the bed, leaning in so close the tip of his nose touched mine. "I won't be fuckin' you anymore." For a moment, my heart burst with elation, but it wasn't to last. His next words slammed into me, shredding any hope I held that I wouldn't suffer any more abuse. "I'm givin' you to Dutch."

"Please... no." My body shook in fear. "I'll do anything." I reached for his arm when he turned to walk away. The second I touched him, I realized my mistake, but I had to try to convince him not to give me away. For as bad as Griller was, Dutch was worse. I'd seen what he'd done to the women he'd been with. They left with not only bruises but scars. He liked to use knives on them, and while Griller had broken my wrist, punched, kicked, and raped me, he was still better than Dutch.

The man before me was the devil I knew.

He rushed toward me, knocking me to the ground with a swift backhand. "You wanna stay with me?" he asked, leaning over me, kicking me when I took too long to answer.

"Y-yes," I cried, clutching the side of my face and scurrying back as far as I could, fearful he'd kick me again.

"What are you willing to do for me if I keep you?"

I looked up into his hateful eyes. "Anything."

"You already do anything I want." He shrugged. "Nah... I think Dutch will enjoy you from now on. Besides, he'll owe me big for the favor. But don't worry, he won't be back from Mexico until tomorrow, so you'll only have to deal with some of the other brothers until then."

I parted my lips to beg him to reconsider, but he walked out of the bedroom before I could utter a single word.

Closing my eyes, I said a silent prayer to a God I wasn't even sure existed anymore.

*Please end my life before anyone else can.*

# Lincoln

"I still can't wrap my head around what the hell is goin' on, man," I uttered, following Kaden up the front steps to his porch. After Cutter told us to leave the basement, we decided the only place we could go to hash shit out was back to his place. Some of the guys may have gone back to the clubhouse, but Kaden and I needed to attempt to wrap our heads around the debacle with Tag before we talked to anyone else again.

After we entered his house, he headed straight for the kitchen to grab two beers. I made myself comfortable on his couch, glancing around and wishing I had a place of my own for once. Before tonight, I'd been perfectly content living at home, but discovering my ol' man seemed perfectly fine with ending someone's life put a damper on wanting to live under his roof.

I tried not to judge my father, Marek, or any of the other guys in the club, but it was hard not to after witnessing what I had a couple hours ago.

Granted, Kaden and I didn't understand the severity of life

in the club from decades ago, but whatever happened between us and the Reapers had ended when we were babies, so why were they still acting like we were at war with them?

The coldness of the bottle Kaden thrust into my hand brought me back from my wandering thoughts. He sat at the other end of the couch, propping his feet up on the edge of his coffee table.

"What the fuck?" was all he said, before draining a hefty portion of his drink. Kaden ran his hand over the top of his dark hair, then down his face, looking over at me when I remained silent. I didn't think he expected me to respond, but he wouldn't be opposed to my opinion either, I was sure.

"I'm still tryin' to figure out how Tag got all mixed up in this shit," I mumbled. "I mean, I know *why* he's involved, but if he is a Reaper, he fooled me."

"Me too," Kaden added. "I'm always such a good judge of character. I don't see how I missed this one. There was no indication whatsoever he was anything other than what he showed us."

I nodded, unable to add anything more because he hit the proverbial nail on the head.

"Do you think Marek will really have someone check out his story?"

He took another long pull of his drink. "Yeah. If anything, my dad is a man of his word."

"How long before we know anything?"

"I dunno. But it's not like we can leave the guy strapped to a table for a week, so something's gotta happen soon," he answered, swallowing the remainder of his beer before placing it on the table.

I opened my mouth to ask him another question when my phone alerted me to an incoming text. Kaden received one at the same time, and when we looked at each other, a gloomy feeling settled over us. I wasn't ready to dive back into the situation yet, and I would bet Kaden wasn't either.

He released a whooshed sound of relief when he said, "It's Riley," before typing back a response.

When I looked at my cell, I saw the message was from my ol' man, asking if I was coming home. I didn't want to reply at all, but instead of making him worry, especially after what happened earlier, I told him I was stayin' with Kaden.

"What does my sister want?" I leaned over, pretending to read his text. He shook his head before pulling the device closer to his chest.

"You don't wanna read what she wrote." He half laughed, typing something else back to her.

"Gross. Don't tell me that shit," I groaned.

"Then don't ask."

I still didn't know how I felt about Riley and Kaden being an item. On the one hand, Kaden was like a brother to me. I trusted him with my life, but being lied to, by both of them, had pissed me off. But more than that, I was offended neither of them felt they could confide in me. On the other, I understood their need to keep their secret for fear my dad would find out.

I wondered if my ol' man would've reacted the same as he did if they'd told him when they first got together. I believed a part of his anger came from them hiding it all these years, even after it was over. Then add in that she got pregnant at some point, it had been what pushed him over the edge, the proof now a faint mark on Kaden's face.

"Where is she?"

"At Chelsea's," he grumbled, his lip curling up after he answered.

"Why is that bad?"

"Because I told her I wanted her to move in here with me, but she won't do it. She said it's too fast." His fingers flew over the keyboard quicker than I thought he could type.

"She's right."

He stopped what he was doing to glare at me. "Not you, too."

"You guys just got back together. What's the rush? Besides, Riley is a pain in the ass to live with. Trust me, I know. She's always yammerin' on about cleaning up, and she constantly stole my stuff, especially my razors." I gave him a half-grin when he frowned at me. "You also shouldn't throw that in my dad's face, either. He doesn't like you as it is right now. There's no tellin' what he'll do if he knows you two are shackin' up." My shoulder bounced after my warning.

"I've wasted enough time apart from Riley. I'm not doin' that anymore. I don't care who has a problem with it." His phone dinged again, only this time he cursed before standing. "Let's go." He walked toward the door, his stern expression making me realize it'd be pointless to ask where we were goin'.

Sometimes it was better to blindly follow.

Sometimes, being the operative word.

# Lincoln

We arrived at Chelsea's place in eight minutes flat when it should've taken at least twenty, Kaden driving like a lunatic, all while only giving me bits and pieces of information.

Apparently, Chelsea had invited Ace over, but the more alcohol they drank, the more volatile the night became. I wasn't sure what happened, but Chelsea started throwing shit at Ace, and he then had to tackle her to the ground in order not to get pummeled with whatever it was she kept throwing at him.

That's when Riley texted Kaden to come and get her. She'd been drinking as well, although not as heavily, otherwise, she would've driven her Jeep to his house.

"This is exactly why she needs to live with me. This wouldn't happen at my house."

"Not unless Riley is the one throwing shit at you."

He gave me a half-hearted smirk. "True."

Once we pulled up to the house, Riley was waiting outside on the porch. Both of us exited the truck and rushed toward her. She looked a little shaken up but otherwise okay. I squeezed her shoulder right before Kaden grabbed hold of her.

I didn't need to ask if they were still inside because I could hear them.

Once I entered, I saw Chelsea on one side of the small living room while Ace was on the other. There were items strewn all over, from books to a lamp, to glass scattered in several places.

The moment she saw me, she rushed over and threw her arms around my neck, the alcohol emanating from her making my eyes burn. I was surprised she could walk, let alone run toward me. Her blonde hair was tied back in a ponytail, but most of her strands had come loose. The strap of her tank top had fallen down over her shoulder, and if she moved the wrong way, it looked like the top part of her shirt was gonna come down.

"What's goin' on with you two?" I asked, preparing myself to be caught in the middle of their drama. It was apparent to everyone who knew them that there was something between them, but neither would commit to anything or each other. Offhanded remarks, from both, left everyone guessing as to what the true nature of their relationship was. Since I had my own stuff to deal with, getting mixed up in their spectacle of a relationship, and I used the term loosely, was the last thing I wanted to do. But because my sister had been affected by this shitstorm tonight, I felt it was my duty to at least find out what went down.

"She's drunk... and crazy!" Ace shouted, a spot of blood trickling from his temple. He swayed on his feet, apparent he'd had as much to drink as Chelsea, if not more.

"He said he was gonna fuck Natalie," she shouted in my ear before she pulled back.

"Fuck," I grumbled. "Did you have to yell so loud? I'm standing right here. I can hear you just fine." I pushed her away from me but kept my hands on her shoulders until she steadied herself so she didn't fall.

"I didn't say any such thing, woman," Ace retorted, taking a few steps toward us while tugging on his hair in apparent frustration. "What I said was..." He took a longer pause than normal, breathing hard and closing his eyes briefly before looking back in our direction. "I bet Natalie wouldn't mind tellin' people I'm her man."

"It's the sa... same thing." She stumbled toward him, but only after snatching up a book that was lying on the entertainment stand. When she pulled her arm back, I grabbed it from her before she whipped it at him. The hardback was thick, and if it hit him, I was positive it would hurt like hell.

"Who's Natalie?" I asked, determined to get to the bottom of this and have them calm the fuck down so I could get out of here.

"She works at the salon with her," Ace said, pointing toward the volatile woman.

"Oh, yeah, that's right," I muttered, more to myself than to either of them. Deciding enough was enough, I glared at Ace. "Do you like Natalie?"

"Not like that," he answered, daring to take another step toward Chelsea, scratching his jaw. The man needed a shave.

"Do you wanna fuck Natalie?" My second question made Chelsea's body bristle, her hands finding their place on her hips. I sure hoped Ace answered no because she was gonna explode otherwise.

Instead of answering right away, though, Ace edged closer, his eyes narrowing into slits, his own anger toward Chelsea borderline explosive.

"Well?" My patience for these two had officially run out.

"He does," she yelled, her face turning an even darker shade of red than moments ago.

"No. I. Don't," Ace hissed, the vein in his neck thickening in fury. "All I said was I bet she wouldn't deny me as her man."

"What the hell does that mean?" I asked, placing a hand on her shoulder to hold her back.

"It means she," he said angrily, pointing at my sister's best friend, "won't agree to be with me but gets mad when I talk about other chicks."

"You don't know what you want," she said, calmer than I expected, and it was then I noticed her eyes filled with unshed tears. And as soon as Ace saw the same, he seemed to calm a bit.

"Ace, you need to come with me and Kaden. Nothin' good is gonna happen if you stay." He opened his mouth to either protest or agree, but before either response escaped, I added, "You've both had way too much to drink and should stop right now before someone says something that changes everything... for the worst."

I turned to face Chelsea, griping her shoulders. "Riley is comin' back inside to be with you, okay?"

She nodded.

Then I looked at Ace. "Go outside."

He didn't argue as he walked past me and out the front door.

I led Chelsea to her couch, careful to not trip over the mess on the floor. "Stay here." She didn't respond or even look at me, her attention on the front door. "Do you hear me?" I raised my voice enough for her to tear her eyes from the door and land on mine.

"Fine." One tear rolled down her cheek, then another. I hated it when women cried, and because her sadness made me uncomfortable, I rushed outside to find my sister.

All three of them were on the porch, Ace leaning against the railing probably so he wouldn't fall the fuck over.

"She needs you," I said to my sister. "I think you should stay."

"I will." Riley looked up at Kaden as he was about to protest, I was sure. "Ace is going with you guys, so I'll be fine here with Chelsea." She gave him a quick kiss, and he seemed to relax a little.

"All right, enough." I grabbed Riley's hand and pulled her toward me. "You need to go in there now before she comes out here."

"Yeah, okay." She looked back at Kaden before finally going back inside.

Kaden, however, was not happy, not in the slightest. He shot Ace a disgusted look before he stomped down the steps and toward his truck.

"Come on, man." I was next to Ace in a few strides, slapping him on the back before we followed our buddy.

"Bitch is nuts," he grumbled next to me. "But I think I love her anyway." He said the last part more under his breath, but I heard him. Although whether he remembered what he said once he slept off his drunken state was a different matter.

# Eight

## Lincoln

Kaden stepped over Ace's stretched-out legs. The second the drunk bastard sat on the sofa, he leaned his head back and passed out, his shirt torn on the bottom and sprinkled with his blood. He was gonna have one hell of a headache tomorrow, and to make matters worse, I could bet that Kaden was gonna read him the riot act for what happened back at Chelsea's earlier. Too much alcohol had been consumed, and typically, I didn't give a shit what happened between people, but for Riley to call Kaden to come and get her, well, let's just say I didn't want my sister to be involved in anything like that ever again.

"Have you heard anything more about Tag?" It was close to four in the morning now, and I wasn't under the assumption we'd be kept in the loop every step of the way, or if anything at all had even happened after we left that house, but I asked the question regardless.

"Nope." Kaden blew out a strained breath. He looked exhausted, but he'd probably say the same thing about me. "I'm headin' to bed. The spare room has an inflatable mattress if you wanna use it." He jerked his chin at me before disappearing upstairs, his steps heavy, indicative to the weight on both our shoulders.

After finally settling in for the night, I stared at the ceiling, willing my overcharged brain to shut down. But I had no such luck. From the fight between Ace and Chelsea to Kaden wanting Riley to move in with him, to wondering what was gonna happen with Tag, I couldn't seem to quiet my mind. It was only when my thoughts wandered to a certain brunette that I started to drift off, imagining a scenario where I could make good on my internal promise to myself and save her from them.

---

"HOLD UP," Ace groaned, righting himself against the couch before leaning forward. His eyes were bloodshot, and sections of his dark hair stuck up in places. His shirt looked like a crumpled mess, matching the rest of his appearance. "Run through that again. I wanna make sure I heard everything right."

"Kaden and I were texted an address, and when we showed up, Jagger led us into the basement. That's when we saw Tag strapped to a table." I gripped the back of my neck, the strain of the past twelve hours making my muscles ache.

"Tag?"

"Yeah."

"And why does Marek think he's a Reaper?"

"'Cause he found a picture in the guy's wallet, and apparently Tag's father was a Reaper," I said, blinking a few times because I hadn't gotten enough sleep and my vision was still hazy.

"This Vex guy, Tag's father, was someone who did unspeakable things to my mom when she lived with them," Kaden interjected, taking a seat next him on the sofa.

"Sully was part of the Reapers?" Ace asked, his brows knitted tightly together while trying to piece all the information together.

"Apparently. Her father was the president of the fuckin' club." Even as I said the words, it was hard for me to associate Sully with any part of the Reapers, let alone being the daughter of its leader.

"So, she was involved with their shit?" After asking another question, Ace stood, his fingers pressing the sides of his temples. He groaned and closed his eyes. "Why the fuck did I drink so much?"

"Who knows," I replied, not sure if he remembered much from last night at this point. Before either Kaden or I jogged his memory, however, we finished telling him about our latest issue, to put it mildly.

"My mom wasn't involved with them the way you think." Kaden leaned his head against the back of the couch, his shoulders tense, and his expression deflated. "I was told her father abused her as well as allowing the other members, specifically Vex, to do so."

"Okay... okay. But because your mom was treated how she was," Ace said, slowing his words toward the end because he was probably uncomfortable saying such things about Sully, "Marek thinks Tag is just like him?" Before either of us could answer, he said, "I thought Tag didn't really know his ol' man. That he left when he was a kid."

"That's the information we have, too," Kaden answered, blowing out a breath because now Ace could somewhat understand our frustration. "I really don't think Tag is a Reaper, but it's hard to try and convince the other guys of that."

"Well, what now?" Ace took to pacing, stopping after several steps to clutch his head again.

"Marek said they would research his story before they did

anything else. How long it'll take, we have no idea." I looked to Kaden, and he nodded, agreeing with every word I spoke.

"Now," I started, turning fully to face Ace, "about last night."

"Yeah," Kaden chimed in, rising from the couch. "The next time Riley has to call me to come get her because she's nervous to be around you while you're drunk, we're gonna have a problem." Kaden stepped closer to Ace, but surprisingly, the guy didn't flinch. Maybe his hangover consumed too much of his good sense.

"First off, I didn't do a thing to Riley. I wasn't the one throwing stuff, and I sure as hell wasn't the one screaming bloody murder. If anyone was uncomfortable last night, it was me." His expression hardened when he looked back and forth between me and Kaden. "I'm sorry Riley felt some type of way, but I didn't have anything to do with that."

"You were drunk, and you engaged in Chelsea's bout of crazy." I reminded him he wasn't as innocent as he liked to believe.

"Riley said you tackled Chelsea. Is that true?" Kaden asked, his jaw clenching while waiting for the answer.

Ace closed his eyes, and just when I thought he wasn't gonna say anything else, he nodded, reaching around to grab the back of his shoulder.

"I fucked my arm up, too." His nonchalant words made both me and Kaden bristle with anger.

"Are you serious?" I shouted.

By this time, Ace realized we were both pissed, and he backed up a few steps. "Listen, I didn't tackle Chelsea to hurt her." He reached up and touched his temple once more. "She started throwing shit at me. She even hit me in the head with somethin' heavy. I had to get her to stop, so I rushed toward her in self-preservation." His attention bounced between us. "I'd never intentionally hurt her or Riley."

"You were drunk," I repeated. "You should've left when it got heated."

"You're right," he said, conceding to my point.

"I don't care what you do. But when my woman is present, you better act accordingly."

Ace and I simultaneously grimaced.

"What?" he asked, confused by our expressions.

"It's still weird to hear you call Riley your woman," I said.

"Yeah, it is," Ace agreed.

"Get used to it," Kaden shouted over his shoulder as he walked out of the room.

The vibration of my phone in my pocket drew my attention. When I swiped the screen, I saw a text from Rico, the guy who helped run the fights.

"Fuck," I grumbled.

"What?"

"I got a fight tonight."

"So?"

"So, I got enough on my mind right now. I was hoping it'd be a couple days before I had to get in the ring again. That's all." Once I typed out a response, tellin' him I'd be there, I asked, "What were you two really fightin' about last night anyway?"

Ace shook his head, looking more defeated and disheveled than when he first woke up.

"I wish I could tell ya."

"You don't remember?"

"Bits and pieces but not enough to wrap my head around why Chelsea got so crazy."

"Women," I laughed. "Can't live with 'em..."

"...can't gag 'em," Ace finished, his lips twitching before drawing downward.

# Nine

## Maddie

Sandwiched between Griller and Pike, I could barely catch my breath, and while I wanted to escape, to run out of the building toward freedom, I realized I was trapped. To add to my heightened nerves, I was surrounded by people yelling and screaming for two guys pummeling each other in the ring. Violence seemed so freely accepted by everyone here, something I couldn't wrap my head around. And maybe that was because I'd been thrust into the midst of violence myself.

The sight of blood and bruised skin made my stomach flip, but those same images made everyone else excited. I chose to keep my eyes closed for the duration of the fights, the sound of fists hitting flesh, making me choke on my rising bile.

But then I heard his name and my unsteady breaths evened out, and my lids opened slowly, searching the crowd for the one the announcer called Lincoln Crosswell.

From attending several fights with my captors, I'd learned this guy was undefeated. He'd enter the ring, fight quickly and either knock out his opponent or make them tap out. But I wasn't the least intrigued by his fighting skills, although they were noteworthy. Instead, I was curious about his odd concern for me.

I didn't know him.

I'd only seen him among hundreds of others, yet the first time his eyes connected with mine, I swore he tried to tell me something, all without speaking.

He never wore a leather vest, but I deduced he was also in a motorcycle club, his friends who showed up at his fights wearing theirs. And while I didn't know anything about him, other than his status in the ring, something told me he wasn't like the men who held me against my will. Granted, it was my inexperience that landed me in this mess in the first place, so I proved I wasn't such a good judge of character. But the last time I saw him, I literally ran into him coming out of the ladies' room, his hands landing on my shoulders to steady me in my surprise. His touch warmed me, but I was ripped backward before I could lose myself to him, no matter how silly that sounded.

While the president and a prospect from the Reapers flanked me on either side, I was still able to see the throngs of people part as someone walked down the narrow path toward the cage, their shouts and eagerness to be near the fighter reaching a deafening level.

I watched every step Lincoln took, his eyes straight ahead, focused. He was graceful when he entered the ring, floating about like he owned the place, and I supposed to a point, he did.

He wore black shorts, his chest bare, his muscles stretching beneath his skin as he swung his arms in front of him, then out to the sides in a stretch. There was a man in his corner who pulled him back and talked into his ear. Lincoln nodded once, then again, shrugging away from who I assumed was his trainer. The dark blond stranger looked to be in his late thirties or early forties. I wasn't good with ages, but he appeared much older than Lincoln, who seemed to be closer to my age of eighteen than not.

Lost to the sight of the man in the ring, I was startled when Griller yanked me to the side.

"If he comes after her again tonight, we'll be ready," he muttered to Pike, raising his shirt to reveal the handle of a gun. I didn't need to ask who he referred to, not that he would answer me even if I did, because he was talking about Lincoln.

I didn't want any harm to come to the fighter, so I wrapped my fingers around Griller's arm and tugged. When he looked down at me, I hesitated in speaking, expecting to be struck for my brazenness. But if it meant keeping Lincoln safe and out of their crosshairs, I had to try.

"You don't have to hurt him."

He yanked his arm from my feeble hold and snatched a fistful of my hair, roughly pulling my head back. "I know I don't have to," he sneered, his grip intensifying and bringing tears to my eyes. "But I wanna. It's finally time he learns his place. I'm gonna wait till he's done, though, 'cause I have some money riding on this fight." He winked, as if he'd told me some sort of joke, my heart skipping a beat when, a few moments later, Lincoln was declared the winner.

It was only a matter of minutes now before something awful happened to him. I searched the crowd, looking for his friends, hoping I remembered what they looked like, although it wouldn't be hard to notice them because they should be wearing leather vests. And if their enormous friend was here tonight, there was a chance Lincoln wouldn't be killed.

But I'd learned not to hold my breath over certain situations because I'd only end up dead.

Griller shoved me toward Pike. "Watch her," he growled. "I see Rock and Cosa back there. We're gonna need everyone for this." Again, he didn't need to talk in code because I knew he planned on going after Lincoln and, most likely, his friends.

Pike steadied me so I didn't fall. "I got her," he replied, nodding before his president walked away, leaving the two of us together.

I was under no assumptions Pike would free me, but as his hold on me relaxed, his expression morphed from hard to concerned.

He really was a handsome guy with his light brown hair, flecks of blond streaked throughout, and his hazel eyes, which had brown specks toward the iris. The softness in them was something I believed he only showed to me. It was how he initially enticed me to throw caution to the wind and go with him back to his club that first night.

"I don't want Griller to hurt him," I said, leaning closer, realizing he wouldn't punish me for speaking my mind. He was kind to me when none of the other members of his club were present.

"There is nothin' I can do about it."

While I didn't want to admit it, I realized Pike couldn't speak up. He was one of them. Therefore, he had to follow along, no questions asked. Besides, if he did open his mouth, they'd beat him, like they'd done before. And I didn't want him to get hurt either.

Relishing in the time I had left before the other men came back, I looked toward the ring, but I didn't see Lincoln or his trainer. My eyes trailed over the crowd, but there was only so much I could see, my five-foot-three frame not tall enough to see everyone.

"Come on," Pike said, grabbing my hand to pull me behind him. "We're being summoned." But I resisted with a slight tug, the need to use the ladies' room coming out of nowhere. My urge to pee had nothing to do with nerves, however. For the past couple of days, I had to go quite often, and it was only yesterday that I felt a twinge of pain when I urinated.

I tugged on his hand again, and he looked back at me. We were now in a hallway, and although we were far from being alone, there were fewer people surrounding us.

"I need to go to the bathroom."

"Can't you hold it?" he asked, looking ahead before back at me.

I shook my head and bit my bottom lip, my leg crossing over the other with the urgent need to use the toilet.

He huffed. "Fine."

He guided me further down the hallway until we came to a door marked with an image of a toilet. He pulled me inside, not a care there were other women present. If I had to guess, they didn't seem to mind Pike was in here with us. In fact, two of the girls at the sink looked him up and down, licking their lips in appreciation.

*If they only knew.*

"I'll be right outside. Hurry up or he's gonna be pissed." He let go of my hand and walked out, leaving me to wait in line behind one other person. Even though I relished in the time away from all of them, each second reminded me I had people waiting on me. I wasn't free. I didn't think I'd ever be free again, not until I was dead. Such morbid thoughts for someone my age, but they were all I had. If I wasn't wishing to leave this world, in whatever way that happened, then I was dreaming of nonsensical things, like going to the movies or hanging out with my friends from back home, all scenarios which would never play out again.

As I flushed and exited the stall, I heard shouting coming from outside the door, more and more voices joining in. Something told me the noise had nothing to do with the earlier excitement of the fight and everything to do with Griller's plan to go after Lincoln.

I didn't know what got into me because I wasn't a brave person by nature, but I yanked open the door and rushed outside, only to run right into the middle of an all-out brawl.

# Ten

## Lincoln

"Who the fuck you lookin' for? Huh?"

Griller stood directly in front of me, a few members of his club surrounding him. There were four of them total, like last time, only there was one guy I hadn't seen before. A prospect.

I made sure to keep my attention on the volatile bastard in front of me, though, because out of all of them, he seemed the most amped up. Not that the others weren't, but this was on another level. He had what we called crazy eyes. Wide pupils with a blank stare.

I'd known guys like him before. They loved the thrill of the challenge, even got off on inflicting pain. Granted, most of those guys I'd met were in the ring, but I recognized instability and sadism when I saw it staring me right in the face.

"Is she here?" I couldn't stop the question, even though I'd been warned to stay away from the girl and out of the Reapers' business. But tonight was different. They'd come up to me, so I sure as hell was gonna inquire about her whereabouts. Every second I didn't see her made me think the worst. Did they leave her behind tonight or had they killed her?

Jagger and Ace stood to my right, surprisingly not saying a word. Any other time Jagger would've tried to pull me away, but after the scuffle last time and then the fire, I believed there might be a part of him that wanted to settle a debt.

"It's none of your business." The comment came from one of the guys I'd only seen once before. He had long brown hair, which he kept back in a ponytail, and if it wasn't for the burn scar on the right side of his face, he might've been able to pass as nonthreatening. He was shorter than my six-foot frame by several inches, and didn't look like much of a fighter, in case things popped off again, but I'd learned not to underestimate anyone, not to make assumptions.

Hell, we had a man strapped to a table in a house an hour from here because I'd presumed he was a good guy. Jury was still out on Tag, and I prayed the research came back proving me and Kaden right.

"Why you so interested in her anyway. You can't get your own pussy?" Griller asked. I'd never wanted to punch someone in the face so badly before, the smirk twisting his mouth like a red cape to a bull.

"I know you're holdin' her against her will," I spat, taking a daring step closer. "And I know you hurt her."

"So?"

"It's a fuckin' coward who puts his hands on a woman." The warmth of my rage flowed through me with every word I spoke.

"No, it's a real man who takes what he wants from all these whores, even when they don't want it. In fact, I'm gonna take it from her over and over again."

"Then I'm gonna have a go," the Reaper with the burn scar said.

"Then me," Rock chimed in. Unfortunately, I'd seen that

guy way too many times in my life. The sight of him alone made me want to knock him the fuck out.

I glanced toward the prospect, but he didn't say anything. He just stood there and stared at me, almost as if he was too busy studying me to add his response.

"Then when we're done with her tonight, I'm passin' her off to one of our guys who gets off on cuttin' up bitches. He calls it art and shit." Griller smiled, pleased with himself when he saw my eyes pop wide. "That's right. We're gonna get our fill tonight because there won't be anythin' left of her once my guy gets his hands on her."

Right before my fist connected with his face, I saw the prospect's mouth drop open before turning to look at his president, and even though I only saw his expression for a millisecond, it was enough to tell me he was as shocked as I was with who they were gonna pass the poor girl off to.

There was an explosion of fists flying all around, the narrow hallway where we fought barely wide enough for the seven of us to go at each other. The limited space didn't do anything but propel us from one guy to the other.

Then I saw a blur of dark hair to my left from the girl in question. She'd walked out of the ladies' room and right into the middle of the fight between our clubs.

Ace threw a wicked uppercut at the prospect, hitting him on the jaw, and while he staggered backward and hit the wall, he didn't fall. Instead, he grabbed the girl and held her in front of him like a shield, an action which only served to intensify my anger.

He moved her slightly to the side before he came at me. Swinging his arm back, he pushed her forward, and in the span of a fleeting moment, I heard him say, "Take her." I was so confused by what he said that I hadn't been paying attention, and it was during my lack of focus that he managed to strike me in the face, although his hit wasn't as hard as I was sure he could manage.

The prospect went back after Ace, and while they threw down, Jagger had pinned Scarface on the ground, continuously striking him until he stopped moving. I had no idea if he'd killed him, but before I could even think to ask, Jagger shot to his feet, reached behind his back, and pulled a gun from his waistband, pointing it directly at Rock. I craned my neck and saw the handle of a pistol showing from underneath the Reaper's shirt. As Jagger reached for the man's weapon, I tucked the girl behind me, shielding her from the turmoil going on around us as best I could.

Then I heard a shot.

Then another, followed by an eruption of screams from the crowd. Behind us, throngs of people rushed toward the exit, and it was because of the commotion I barely had time to register the flash of heat that whizzed by the side of my head. Seconds later, Jagger pointed both guns at the Reapers, who were still standing. "Go for it, and it'll be the last thing you do," Jagger shouted. The three of us walked backward with the girl directly one step behind me.

My arm instinctually reached for her. I thought perhaps she'd either run toward the Reapers or in the other direction altogether, but when her hand slid into mine, I turned to face her.

The moment my eyes landed on hers, an ache pumped through my chest but was gone when she tugged on my arm, breaking me away from whatever feeling I'd lost myself in and thrusting me back into the direness of the situation.

Against the warning of our president, we'd engaged in yet another fight with the Reapers, resulting in someone getting two shots off. I still didn't know if they fired or Jagger did, and on top of all the uncertainty, I'd taken the one person who'd started it all, even though she was innocent in blame. I accepted the fault wholeheartedly, but I doubted my acceptance would do any good once the rest of the club found out what happened here tonight.

## Maddie

I sat quietly next to Lincoln as he drove. When we first made it outside, his trainer asked if they were all okay. Once they acknowledged they were, everyone dispersed quickly, much like the rest of the people who'd showed up tonight to watch the fight. In the distance, I heard sirens, and they were getting closer as we rushed toward his truck. His friends sped off on their motorcycles, one of them almost hitting the side of a car who'd cut him off on the way out of the lot.

I had no idea what was gonna happen now. Would he hold me prisoner like Griller had, or would he return me to them, realizing he didn't want any trouble with their club after all? A whirlwind of thoughts raced through my mind, and I couldn't settle on any one in particular.

"Are you okay?" My body twitched at the sound of his voice. "Sorry. Didn't mean to scare you." From my peripheral vision, I saw him glance over at me, but he turned away as quickly as he looked, touching his temple. "Fuck," he mumbled, switching on the interior light when we stopped at a red light. He leaned over and looked in the rearview mirror, turning his head to get a better angle and look at the side of his face. His skin was flushed, but I couldn't yet determine if the coloring was due to the adrenaline of the fight or if the reddened skin would start to discolor, turning into a bruise from where he'd been punched. As my eyes cascaded over him, I noticed blood near where his fingers had been.

"You're bleeding," I said, pointing to his right temple.

"I know." He pressed his fingers against the cut again before turning to look in the back seat. Reaching behind me, he snatched a towel before holding it over the wound. "Close call tonight. If I'd moved even an inch, the bullet probably would've gone right through my eye."

"Bullet?" I'd heard gunshots but hadn't seen who fired or where those bullets had gone.

"Yeah. Seemed it just grazed me." He seemed so calm about the whole thing. If that was me, I'd be freaking out.

"Are you okay?"

"I think so." The light turned green and we were on our way. Where? That was yet to be determined.

A few miles later, when he lowered the towel to his lap, I turned my head in his direction, praying he didn't yell at me for looking. Griller would often remind me with his fist to keep my eyes down whenever he was around, and I wasn't sure if that was because he might feel some sort of remorse for what he did to me if he looked into my eyes for more than five seconds at a time, or if it was another way to control me. My guess was it was the latter.

If Lincoln noticed me staring at him, he didn't make it known, a small act I was grateful for. Other than Pike, I hadn't been able to gaze at someone in quite some time, and although the sentiment might seem like an odd indulgence, I was grateful for the freedom to do so.

Head-on, Lincoln was gorgeous, yet there was something

strong and regal about his profile. His straight nose and strong jawline gave him the air of sophistication even though he was young. His short, dark brown hair was mussed, sections toward the crown of his head not lying down like the rest. His gray T-shirt was torn at the neckline, and there were spots of blood on the shoulder.

He gave off a sense of calm, even though after what happened back there, he had to still be amped up. Hell, my heart was still thrashing inside my chest, and I wasn't even the one engaged in the altercation.

"Are you hurt?" he asked, and it was then I realized I never answered his first question.

"I'm fine." My voice came out as a whisper, but he nodded, telling me he heard me. I hadn't physically been harmed during tonight's fight, and while I was far from fine, it was the only word that came to mind.

I was scared yet at ease. My feelings didn't make a bit of sense to me because, for all I knew, Lincoln could be every bit as bad as Griller.

"Are you hungry?" I watched as his eyes swept over me, my T-shirt and shorts hiding my frail body underneath. My physique was thin by nature, but I'd lost a significant amount of weight since being held captive. There were times I'd go two days without eating because they'd devoured everything in sight. And when I was lucky enough to get some scraps, the amount wasn't much. Maybe a leftover chicken wing and a day-old biscuit. Pike had snuck me food whenever he could, but it wasn't enough to keep my weight sustainable. At least I was able to get my fill of water, though, a gift I'd come to appreciate because most days, the overabundance of liquid kept my belly semi-full.

"No," I replied. Even though my stomach rumbled, my nerves wouldn't allow me to consume anything without the fear of retching it back up.

I glanced out the window at the world whizzing by. None of the sights looked familiar, but I didn't know my way around any parts of California, so every city and town would look foreign to me.

Close to fifteen minutes later, Lincoln pulled off the highway and on to a dirt road. There were no streetlights anywhere, his truck's headlights the only illumination in an otherwise black night. The ride had gone from smooth to bumpy, the gravel beneath the tires crunching so loudly I could hear the sounds even though all the windows were rolled up.

"Where are you taking me?" There was a realm of possibilities in the silence that ensued.

Was he taking me to a police station to report my being held prisoner? This option was unlikely because I assumed all police stations were in town and not off some hidden, beaten path.

Was his interest in me solely for profit? Did he see something in me that would interest someone else? Was he selling me to an even more terrible person than the leader of the Reapers?

Was he taking me to the woods to kill me? Had he realized his mistake after he took me from Griller and didn't want to deal with me any longer? If that was the case, wouldn't he just return me to them?

So many questions rattled around inside my overactive brain, but they were the only thing I had to hold on to during the time it took for him to answer, which was only a few seconds.

"The only place I can," he answered. "Our clubhouse." I squirmed in my seat, shifting further toward the window. Words failed me, but my fear was on high alert. Lincoln reached over and gently squeezed my knee, but when I flinched, his hand found the wheel again. "No one's gonna hurt you." I wanted to believe him, but he'd given me no reason to trust what he said was the truth.

*Had he?*

We pulled up to a large black metal gate, and after he pushed some sort of remote, it finally clicked open, the creak from the hinges unnerving me more than I wanted to let on. Shortly after entering, he parked beside a large white building and turned off the engine, shifting in his seat and looking at me, but not saying anything at first. Was he gonna lay down the rules, telling me what he expected of me once I was free of his truck? Would he demand I service his buddies after him, like Griller had?

Finally, he spoke. "What's your name?" His voice was deep, his tone assertive.

"Maddie." I learned not to hold back my answers, so I responded quickly.

"Maddie what?"

"Shaeffer."

"Maddie." He parroted my first name. "I like it."

I didn't dare look at him because if I saw he was toying with me, my brief sense of serenity, however misplaced, would be shattered. And who knew how long it'd be before I felt such a thing again.

Lincoln exited his truck, appearing next to me in no time. He pulled my door open, reached in, and took my hand, his touch gentle. No words were exchanged as he helped me down, catching me when I stumbled, misinterpreting the height difference from his vehicle to the ground.

He led me toward the door to the building, and I tensed as we drew closer, trying to tug my hand from his.

"It's okay." He tried to assure me, but I didn't trust him. I tugged again, but he refused to release me. "I promise nothin' bad is gonna happen to you again. Not while I'm watchin' over you."

With the darkness surrounding us, I couldn't look into his eyes, but I heard the sincerity in his voice and after several deep breaths, and my inner voice working to soothe my anxiety, I was able to believe that what he told me was true.

When he stepped forward again, I followed.

# Twelve

## Lincoln

As soon as I entered the clubhouse with Maddie, I knew I was in a world of trouble, but I couldn't leave her with them any longer. And when one of their own told me to take her, I didn't think twice, no matter the consequences.

While my ol' man and Marek wouldn't have an issue with me helping someone, this was an entirely different situation. I'd been warned to stay away from the Reapers because of the possible blowback. We assumed they were the ones who set the fire at Indulge, which was payback for the initial fight, and even though we weren't positive it was them, yet, I could only imagine the repercussions for taking Maddie. After witnessing the scene in the basement with Tag, an issue that was still in limbo and had me on edge as it was, my understanding about the old war between us and them was clearer.

Walking toward the bar, I motioned for Maddie to take a seat. "Are you sure I can't get you something to eat?" She looked undernourished, no doubt a result of being with those bastards. Her coloring was pale, her hair, which reminded me of rich dark chocolate, was lifeless, and the clothes she wore were too baggy for her frame, even though they were meant to fit snugly.

"I'm fine."

"Are you sure? I make a mean grilled cheese." The faintest of smiles flashed across her face but was gone a second later. There were so many questions I wanted to ask her, but if I bombarded her with everything running around inside my head, I would no doubt scare her, and she'd had enough of being afraid. "You stay here, and I'll be back in a few minutes."

Her eyes widened. "Where are you going?"

"I'm gonna make you that sandwich."

"I'm not—"

I glanced over her from head to toe. "You need to eat somethin'." My words came out more direct than I intended, but when she didn't argue, I rushed into the kitchen, hoping we had bread and cheese.

Rooting around for a clean pan to use, I hadn't heard anyone enter the kitchen because of all the damn clanking.

"Is that who I think it is out there?" Jagger whisper-shouted, walking up next to me and grabbing my arm. The pan I held dropped and hit the top of my foot, right on the bone.

"What the fuck, man?" I reached down and grabbed the pan and tossed it in the sink to wash it, but not before rubbing my foot. "You scared the hell outta me."

Jagger ignored my outburst. "Is that her?" he repeated, glaring at me with a look of disbelief. He knew the answer before he asked the question.

"Yeah, it is."

"Mind tellin' me why she's here?" Before I had the chance to respond, he grabbed my chin and turned my head roughly to the side. "Christ!" He touched my temple, and I jerked away from him. "One of the bullets grazed the side of your head," he said, as if I hadn't already figured that out for myself. When he lowered his arm to his side, his expression changed from anger to fear to concern all within seconds. "Stone and Addy are gonna kill me."

"Why? It wasn't your fault." The bleeding had slowed enough I didn't need to continually press anything against the scrape.

"It was. I'm the one who pulled my gun first, but that was only because I saw Rock's, and I knew shit was escalating fast."

"Did you fire first?"

"No. Griller did when I reached for Rock's gun."

"Did you hit anyone when you returned the shot?" I asked, the memory of the encounter twisting and fading too much for me to remember exact details.

"I don't know. Everything happened so fast." He looked down briefly. "And now I'm gonna hear about it."

"I wouldn't worry too much. I'm fine. Besides, Marek is gonna be so pissed at me when he finds out, no one will be worried about what you did, which was to defend us and get us all out of there alive."

I turned on the water and rinsed out the pan that had fallen, giving Jagger a perfect opportunity to start questioning me again, now that we got all that other stuff out of the way.

He leaned his hip against the counter and crossed his arms over his chest. "Now, back to the girl." He raised his brow and cocked his head, wearing his impatience all over his face once more. It was only when his tongue swept over his bottom lip, did I notice the corner of it was starting to swell.

"Uh…." I stalled, continuing to wash the pan. I was almost finished when Jagger reached out and slapped the back of my head.

"You better tell me right now."

"Uh…," I repeated, glancing over at him, hoping he'd get frustrated with my lack of explanation and walk out of the kitchen. No such luck. After shutting off the water, I turned to face him, expelling the air from my lungs in frustration. "Where else was I supposed to take her?"

"How about the bus stop? You could've given her some money and sent her on her way." He grabbed the counter and bowed his head. "I can't believe you took her in the first place," he said, anger raising his voice.

"Technically, the prospect gave her to me."

"That's the story you're goin' with?"

I looked away briefly, reining in my apprehension as well as my nerves. "Yes. It's the truth. But I don't think the others knew that he told me to take her. Just a feeling."

"Either way, it was a bad move." He held up his hand when I opened my mouth to argue. "Listen. I saw her. It's obvious she was in a bad way with them, and it's obvious she needed help, but..." He trailed off, looking upward toward the ceiling to gather his next thoughts before making eye contact again. "It's not like we can give her back." He shook his head several times. "We gotta tell everyone what happened. But until then, you stay here where you're safe. You and her both. I'll call Prez and tell him we gotta have an impromptu first thing tomorrow."

Jagger pushed off the counter and mumbled something to himself before leaving the kitchen. The entire time we'd been in here, I'd forgotten that Maddie was all by herself out there, probably terrified. I rushed into the other room, but instead of finding her alone, Hawke and Brick flanked her on either side. At first glance, she looked scared, peering over at me with wide eyes, but the closer I stepped, I noticed her body language was more relaxed than I assumed it would be.

"Are you sure you're okay?" Brick asked, touching her shoulder, but when she jerked away, she bumped into Hawke, who instead of stepping back put his hand on her other shoulder.

I stepped in front of her and reached for her hand, which she gave willingly. She huddled close to me.

"They won't do anything to you," I said. "They're good

guys." What I didn't mention was that I was still unsure about Hawke. After what I saw in that basement, and his reaction and willingness to kill Tag, I didn't know what his intentions toward any stranger would be, women included. Not that Marek would let him get away with harming a woman. That didn't fly in our club. We once had a prospect a couple years back who beat his wife. He bragged about how he taught her a lesson, and Jagger, in turn, taught him one before we tossed him out, telling him if he ever laid a hand on her again, he'd end up six feet under. It was only now that I realized the older guys would've made good on that threat.

"Come on. I'll let you get settled while I make you some food." I led her away from the other two and toward the last bedroom at the back of the clubhouse, neither of us saying another word. Once inside, I turned on the light and closed the door. Checking the bathroom, I made sure there was a towel and soap. "There's plenty of hot water for you to take a shower." I opened one of the dresser drawers and pulled out a plain black T-shirt long enough to cover her, which wasn't hard to do given her height and stature. "There's a knob under the faucet. Pull it down, and the shower will come on." Maddie didn't move a muscle. She just stared at me. When I licked my lips, she focused on my mouth, her attention both unnerving and thrilling. "Okay then," I rushed to say, disappearing from the room before I did or said something inappropriate.

Halfway down the hall, I heard arguing. I rushed toward the noise to find out what was goin' on, only to find Hawke and Brick toe to toe, Brick towering over him like he did everyone else.

"Are you out of your fuckin' mind?" Hawke shouted, shoving him in the next breath. The nomad's eyes widened when Brick didn't move an inch.

"What's goin' on?" I asked, tentatively walking up to them.

Hawke directed his anger toward me now. "I'll tell ya

what's goin' on." He pointed toward the hallway. "You bring that Reaper bitch into our clubhouse, and you think that's okay?"

I didn't know what came over me, but before I could stop myself, I rushed toward him and tackled him, the both of us tumblin' toward the ground. The rule of not putting my hands on the older guys in the club flew right out the motherfuckin' window the second he insulted Maddie. I didn't care if he'd been around for decades. I didn't care if he was Tripp's younger brother. I didn't care about anything right then except for teaching him a lesson.

Because I'd shocked him, Hawke never had a chance to react. I seized the opportunity to pop him in the mouth right before he managed to scramble to his feet.

"What the fuck is wrong with you?" he asked, wiping the blood from his lip. "You're the one who brought the enemy here, and this isn't the first time you let them in." His reference to Tag hadn't gone over my head.

"She's not a Reaper," I shouted, ready to run at him again, but Jagger appeared out of nowhere and stepped between us. Brick hung back, watching with an amused look on his face. I didn't think he cared much for the guy and seemed fully on board with me clockin' him.

"Hawke," Jagger said in warning, shaking his head before leaning into him, telling him somethin' I couldn't hear. Whatever it was made Hawke glare at me as he pulled his hair back off his face.

"You assholes are soft. You don't have the balls to do what it takes." What did Jagger say to him?

"Why? 'Cause we're not killers?"

Hawke didn't respond; instead, he arched his brow, the corner of his lip curling upward. I couldn't tell if what I said offended him or proved his point. He mumbled something to Jagger before he turned and walked out of the clubhouse.

"What the hell is wrong with that guy?" Brick asked, taking a seat at the bar.

"Hawke remembers all too well, like I do, the life we had to defend years ago. He doesn't want us to invite that back in."

"Coulda fooled me. Seems like he longs for the good ol' days," I said sarcastically.

"He doesn't. None of us do. Which is why tomorrow Marek is gonna be furious about that girl."

*Shit!*

For a moment, I forgot all about Maddie. I rushed down the hall without another word and barreled into the room I left her in, only to be stunned by what I saw when I entered.

# Thirteen

## Maddie

I couldn't remember the last time anyone treated me kindly, and even though I wasn't sure yet of Lincoln's motives, I relished in the warmth of the shower, biding my time until I found out for sure what my new life was gonna entail.

Once I finished drying off, I stood in the middle of the bedroom completely naked, ready for what came next. My only hope was that he wasn't as rough as Griller or any of the other guys.

As soon as I heard the click of the door, I lowered my head, keeping my eyes on the ground. Oddly enough, one of my first thoughts, other than what was to come, was how clean the carpet looked and felt against my feet. It was weird what the human brain concocted when in survival mode.

The shouting from moments before was a noise I was unfortunately used to, but what I wasn't familiar with was the unnerving silence surrounding me right now.

Lincoln stood ten feet from me, the heat of his stare burning through me.

The click of the door sounded again, but this time it was louder, Lincoln having shut the door with more aggression.

"What are you doin'?"

"What I'm supposed to," I answered softly, hoping he heard me because I didn't wish to repeat the words.

"What do you mean?" He moved closer. "Look at me." Shaking my head, I refused. "Maddie." He said my name softer this time, and there was something laced in his tone that made me raise my head. Up… up… until I met his soul-searching eyes.

"What do you mean you're doin' what you're supposed to?" He studied me, but he wouldn't find any answers plastered on my face. I'd learned how to hide my emotions behind a mask. It was the only way I survived as long as I had.

"I'm thanking you for helping me." I'd often had to thank Griller and his friends for the simplest of things, such as being allowed to use the bathroom, or for the necessary act of eating. It was their way of controlling me, demeaning me, and because I couldn't fight back physically, I surrendered emotionally.

"What exactly are you offerin'?"

"Me."

Realization dawned, and he nodded slowly before his gaze perused my body. I kept my stare straight ahead, but seconds later, he was gone from in front of me, reappearing with the T-shirt in his hand, shoving it at me before he gave me his back.

"Put it on."

I scrambled to pull the fabric over my head, the hemline falling less than an inch below my knees. A soft noise erupted from my throat, and that's the moment he turned to face me again, looking over me from head to toe, his expression flat and unreadable.

"I'm sorry you don't find me desirable," I mumbled, a tear drifting down my cheek. None of the other guys had told me to cover up before. In fact, there'd been a time when I wasn't allowed to wear any clothes at all, nothing to shield me from their lecherous stares, invasive groping, and worse.

"Is that what you think?"

I gave him a curt nod, another tear falling down my face.

He reached for my hand and pulled me toward the bed, motioning for me to take a seat on the edge. The mattress dipped with his weight when he sat next to me.

"I find you very desirable."

My head shot up. "You do?" I didn't know why I sounded surprised... and pleased?

"Yes. But that doesn't make a difference. I won't touch you like that. No one here will. You can trust me. You're safe here with us."

"No one will force me to have sex?"

"Of course not." He sounded offended. "Is that what they did?" He nodded before I even had the chance to respond, as if he'd answered his own question.

"All the time. Sometimes only one of the guys would make me... and sometimes it was one after another." My mouth wouldn't stay shut, the words flowing from my lips effortlessly. "I told Griller I was a virgin, naively thinking he would spare me, but all my confession did was excite him."

There was something about Lincoln that, although I didn't know him, made me want to tell him every sordid detail, my embarrassment falling to the wayside in exchange for someone's compassion for my situation. It was the first time since I'd followed Pike into his club that I felt seen by another human being.

A tense-filled moment passed before he asked, "How did you come to even be with them?"

Dipping my head and saying a silent prayer for my deceased parents, I started telling him about how I ended up in California to begin with.

"Two years ago, when I was sixteen, my mom went into the

hospital to have her gallbladder removed, and she ended up getting an infection and dying three days later." I thought I'd cried an ocean of tears for my mom, but apparently, there were more, several leaking from the corners of my eyes. I pulled myself together as best I could before continuing. "My dad didn't deal well with her passing. She was the love of his life for nearly twenty-five years. He lost his faith and eventually his church, where he was a pastor. He started drinking more as the months went on until one night, nine months ago, he was driving home from the bar when he crashed into a tree. The police told me he died on impact. There weren't any skid marks or any evidence he swerved to avoid something in the road." Several tears escaped for my dad. "I don't think he wanted to live without her."

"I'm so sorry, Maddie." Lincoln rubbed my back in small circles. "I can't even imagine how hard that must've all been."

"It was. It is," I corrected, stalling for time because the next part of my story involved my imprisonment. "I was eighteen, a legal adult, when he died. My dad drank up whatever money was left after my mom was buried. Then when he passed, his life insurance policy was all I had, which was enough to bury him, leaving me with five thousand dollars afterward. I have one aunt, whom I haven't seen in years because my father didn't agree with her lifestyle, her being a lesbian, so I didn't have anything tying me back home. I decided to come here, to California, and start over. Maybe go to college. I've always had an interest in photography." I shrugged, the dreams I once had seeming like they belonged to someone else now. "Once I got off the bus, I walked into a nearby diner, and that's where I met Pike."

"The prospect?"

"Yes." I didn't know why I was hesitant to tell the rest of my story. I'd already revealed what those men did to me while they'd kept me against my will. "I thought he was handsome and charming. I'd never met anyone like him before." Lincoln's nostrils flared at my admission. "I was naïve, trusting him when he told me he wanted to take me to a party. A party that just so happened to be back at his club." Lincoln closed his eyes and took a breath, but because he didn't tell me to stop, I kept speaking. "Pike told me he liked me and wanted to spend some time with me."

"Then he should've taken you to a fuckin' movie." Lincoln hopped off the bed and started pacing.

I held this need to stick up for the prospect. "He was nice to me when he could be, when no one else was around." Lincoln scoffed before continuing to wear a hole in the carpet. "He told me they threatened him, that if he ever tried to leave, they'd not only kill him, but also his mom and his sister. So, he was as much a victim as I was."

"Like hell he was," he shouted, reining in his temper when he saw me flinch. "He should've devised some sort of plan to get you out of there. He should've killed every last one of 'em." Lincoln suddenly stood still; his eyes cast downward when he asked his next question. "Did Pike ever rape you?"

How did I answer that question? While technically the answer was yes, the situation was muddled. Pike had never wanted to hurt me. They made him do it. So maybe the answer was no? I wasn't sure, and while I racked my brain to come up with the right answer, Lincoln asked his question again, only this time, his tone deepened, restrained anger pricking each word.

"Did Pike ever rape you?"

"Yes," I finally blurted. "Technically... yes."

"What does that mean? Technically?"

"He didn't want to. They made him."

Lincoln crouched down in front of me, grabbing on to my hands when he spoke again. "Maddie, no one, and I mean no one, would ever make me force myself on someone. I'd rather die first."

I pulled my hands from his in a harsh tug. "Then you're a better man." My response was filled with hurt and anger. Even after everything that happened, I still wanted to protect Pike, even if only his reputation. "He did help me in the end, when he pushed me toward you and away from Griller and the others."

He stood back up and continued pacing. I remained quiet for a few moments, allowing him to absorb what I'd told him, while also giving me some time to calm the nerves swirling in my belly from recapping the worst months of my life.

"What else did they do to you?"

My chest deflated. I thought this conversation was over, and while I didn't want to talk about it anymore, I felt like I owed it to him after all he'd done for me.

"Griller would beat me for the simplest things. If I didn't get him a drink fast enough, or if I made his food the wrong way. One time, he threw a full beer can at me, hitting me in the back of the head because... well, just because."

Several expletives fell from his mouth right before he ran his fingers through his hair, flinching when he touched his temple. "We'll make them pay for what they did to you. Trust me on that."

Not knowing what to do with myself, I toyed with the bottom of my shirt, plucking off imaginary pieces of lint in order to have something to focus on other than the tightly wound guy wearing a hole in the carpet.

I sucked in a quick breath when he suddenly appeared back in front of me.

"Sorry." His voice was tense. "I'm gonna make you that sandwich."

"I'm not hungry," I whispered.

"I think you need to eat somethin'."

"I just want to go to sleep, if that's okay." My voice was small, fragile sounding to my own ears.

"Sure." There was a slight pause before he added, "Of course. You must be exhausted." He pulled down the blankets, fluffing the pillow afterward. When he retreated, he gave me a tight grin. "Get some rest. And don't worry. No one will bother you."

I didn't say a word as I climbed under the covers, pulling them up until they rested under my chin. Watching him walk away tore at a piece of me, and even as the odd sentiment took hold, I didn't have the emotional strength to understand the notion.

Right before he opened the bedroom door to leave, he turned to look at me.

"I'm Lincoln, by the way."

"I know."

Whether he was surprised by my admission, he didn't show it, instead disappearing and ending our brief back-and-forth.

# Fourteen

## Maddie

"Hi."

His voice roused me, pushing away the remaining dredges of sleep. As I pried my lids open, I saw Lincoln standing directly beside me, dressed in jeans but nothing else. For some reason, I glanced down at his feet and saw he was barefoot, the sight comforting. Then my eyes roamed back up the length of him, noticing a few scattered water droplets dripping down his finely sculpted bare chest. The muscles of his arms flexed when he raked his hand through his damp hair. He had a tattoo on his upper right arm I'd caught sight of briefly during his fights, but I didn't know what it was until right then. If I wasn't mistaken, the image, which was a skull with flames shooting out from both sides and a large sword slicing through the middle of it, was the same as it was on the back of his friends' vests, leading me to believe it was their club's emblem.

I must've been dead to the world because I never heard him come in or run the water in the adjacent room. Shifting on the bed, I sat up, dropping the covers only when I peeked underneath to make sure my shirt covered me enough to remain decent. Although, I'd exposed myself to him last night, so it wasn't like he hadn't seen me naked.

"Hi," I answered, finally finding my voice. We stared at each other for several moments, a twinge of awkwardness and nerves mixing to form some kind of other emotion I couldn't identify. While I didn't feel like I was in danger in Lincoln's presence, I remained guarded, and unfortunately... ready for shit to go south.

"How did you sleep?" He shoved his hands into his pockets, looking down at me in a way that made my heart speed up. Without realizing, my muscles tensed, and the air I'd drawn into my lungs was released in choppy spurts.

"Better than I thought I would." I tossed and turned for quite a while last night before drifting into a dream I could only now recall bits and pieces of.

"Good." He shifted his feet. "Good," he repeated. "I'll let you get to it, then."

"Get to what?" The expectation of his answer frightened me.

He gave me a half-hearted shrug. "Whatever you wanna do. I found an extra toothbrush in one of the other rooms. I left it on the sink in there," he said, pointing toward the bathroom. "And there's plenty of hot water left if you wanna jump in and wash off. After that...." Lincoln's shoulder bounced once more before his phone vibrated on top of the dresser, flopping around and making noise.

He swiped the screen and held the device to his ear, turning away from me and mumbling something I couldn't make out.

While he was busy talking to whomever, I looked around for a clock because I had no idea what time of the morning it was.

"I'm here," he said loudly, disappearing into the bathroom, but he wasn't gone long. After a few obscenities, he reemerged, this time with a shirt on and his boots in his hands. He sat at the edge of the bed, but before he pulled them on, he rose up and reached into the dresser for a pair of socks. From the angle of his body, his jeans formed around his ass like perfection. I shouldn't be looking at him like that because I sure as hell didn't want to see it. If I never saw another naked man again for the rest of my life, it'd be too soon. But still, there was something innocent in my appreciation of him, a hint of an image I'd keep tucked away in the deepest parts of my brain.

When he finished, Lincoln stood up, craning his neck from side to side before pulling his arms behind his back in a stretch.

"I won't be long." His teeth toyed with the corner of his bottom lip, and my eyes fixated on his mouth because of the action. "Maddie."

I tore my gaze from his mouth. "What?"

"I need you to stay in this room until I get back. Okay?"

I nodded.

"I'll be back in no time." He walked toward the door and reached for the handle.

"What time is it?"

"Seven forty," he answered without looking at me. When he pulled on the handle and I saw the hallway, I asked him another question before he left.

"Where did you sleep last night?"

Lincoln pointed toward the other side of the bed. "Over there, on the ground." He didn't say anything else before he walked out, closing the door behind him. I meant to ask him how his head was but never got the opportunity.

I crawled over to the other side of the bed and looked down, and sure enough, there was a pillow and crumpled blanket on the floor.

Any reservation I held toward Lincoln disappeared with the knowledge that we'd slept in the same room, and he never touched me.

He'd kept his word.

Maybe I was safe, after all.

# Fifteen

## Lincoln

The energy in the room crackled as soon as I entered, but the only thing I could focus on was watching my ol' man hop out of his chair and rush toward me. I had no time to brace for impact before he shoved me against the wall, briefly glancing at the small bandage on the side of my head.

"What the fuck is wrong with you?" he shouted, pulling me forward only to slam me back into the wall. "How many times do we have to tell you not to get involved? How many? Huh? Then I come to find out you almost got killed? Jesus Christ, Lincoln!" If I wasn't mistaken, I thought I heard a level of fearfulness and panic beneath his fury.

I didn't dare play stupid. "It all happened so fast, and before I knew it, she was shoved at me. So I took her with us." The words flew out of my mouth, eager for him to release me so we could talk about this issue with the rest of the club.

"What bullshit is that? They didn't simply hand her over." He lessened his grip but continued to pin me against the wall.

"They did. Well, one of 'em did. Their prospect."

"He just gave her to you?" His brows pinched together while the corner of his mouth curved upward.

"Yeah. But... I don't think the rest of 'em knew he did it."

"You took her. That's what you're saying. You went against what you were told, and you took what didn't belong to you."

"She's a person, ya know," I said, lowering my eyes from his when he grunted at me. The rare occasion happened when I feared my dad, and right now was one of them.

"She's nobody to us, which means she's nobody to you." He finally let me go and stepped back. "You figure this out and do it fast."

His demand was as clear as mud. How the hell was I gonna figure anything out when I didn't know what to do going forward.

I retrieved some of my courage, although not much since he was still too close.

"I can't take her back to them. They raped her. Repeatedly. They might even kill her if they get their hands on her again."

My ol' man glared at me before he returned to his seat. "Not our problem," he answered, pounding his fist on the table before leaning over to whisper something to Marek.

Prez's eyes were on me the entire time, and when our VP leaned back, Marek opened his mouth.

"Where is she?"

"Back in one of the bedrooms."

"Here?" Trigger asked, his voice rising a notch in disbelief.

"I didn't have anywhere else to take her that was safe. I couldn't very well bring her home." I walked to my seat, looking from one guy to the next. I knew where Marek and my dad stood on my interfering and trying to save Maddie. There was no doubt what Hawke and Jagger thought either. Looking to Ryder, then Tripp, all they did was shake their head in disappointment. Cutter was silent and expressionless, as usual, but I could put him in the same category with the rest of them as being pissed I'd gone against what Marek had told me.

While I thought there was a possibility Ace, Brick, and Kaden were like-minded with me, I wasn't about to ask them in front of everyone else.

It seemed I had to go this alone.

"Have we found anything else out about the fire?" Marek asked, looking around the room, obviously done with the issue with Maddie. For now, it seemed.

"Not yet," Ryder answered.

"I haven't heard anything either," Tripp added. "We'll keep at it, though, Prez." He jerked his chin toward our leader before looking down the table at me. "Heard you had a little scuffle with my brother last night. Even managed to draw blood."

"Lucky punch," Hawke muttered, gliding his finger over the affected area, which looked a bit puffy in the light of day.

A snarky comment rested in my throat, but I thought better of voicing it since I was in enough shit as it was. I didn't need to push the envelope.

Brick, however, did it for me. "You're lucky I wasn't the one who decked ya."

Normally, such a statement could be taken somewhat offensively, indicating my hit wasn't strong enough, even though I managed to cut his lip with my knuckles. But it was Brick. The guy was enormous and had knocked out people with a single punch. I'd seen it with my own eyes a few times when he had to break up fights at Indulge, where he worked as a bouncer before becoming a member of our club. Most people got out of his way when they saw him coming. It was the exact reason Marek had made him the club's enforcer. Normally, the person who held that title made sure the club laws and rules were followed by everyone, but Ryder, our sergeant-at-arms, mostly took care of that stuff. Brick upheld the part of the position that required his brute strength, which was coming into play more often recently.

"Yeah, I'm kinda thankful you didn't."

"I would've paid to see that." Tripp laughed.

"Fuck you," Hawke said, smiling right along with his brother.

I couldn't say if the nomad's demeanor was surprising since I didn't know him all that well. I'd heard tales from Tripp about antics his younger brother had gotten up to over the years, though, and while he'd mentioned that Hawke was typically a laid-back kind of guy, joking around and even putting his foot in his mouth more times than not, I hadn't seen any of those sides to him... until right now. Here was a hint of the guy I'd heard about. I'd try not to judge him too harshly going forward, but if he said more derogatory shit about Maddie, I couldn't promise I wouldn't have a go at him again.

I didn't want to bring up a topic that was sure to divide a few of us, but I had to know what was happening with Tag. I opened my mouth to ask the question but didn't have a chance to give my words life before Kaden made the inquiry.

"Any news about Tag?" His stare was on his ol' man. For a moment, I thought Marek was gonna brush over or ignore the question, but instead, he appeared annoyed Kaden brought it up.

"Yeah."

A wash of silence descended over the room, an uneasy tension vibrating around each of us. Marek had given one-word answers to questions before, but this subject warranted more. But I sure as hell wasn't gonna be the one to ask him to elaborate.

"So, are we good, then?" Cutter asked, crossing his arms over his chest and leaning back, the creak of his leather cut against the chair chilling.

"Yeah," Marek repeated, flicking his eyes downward before

they found his son, his expression flat while he waited to see what Kaden would say. I was in the same boat as my friend. I wanted to know as much as he did what was gonna happen with Tag. Was he really a Reaper? Or was he the guy we thought he was, and just the product of a sick and twisted man, having no other ties to our enemy otherwise?

Kaden's hands were on top of the table, and the moment Marek uttered his response to Cutter, his fingers curled into the palm of his hand.

"What does that mean?" Kaden asked, his question coming out harsh and impatient. "What did you find out about him?"

"We'll deal with it," our VP answered, leaning forward and glaring at Kaden. There was so much hostility directed toward him, even I felt uncomfortable.

Kaden turned his attention away from my ol' man and back to Marek. "I think I have a right to know what's gonna happen, what the truth is about Tag."

"You have the right to know?" Marek asked, his brows shooting upward. It was hard to tell if he was genuinely surprised by Kaden's words or pissed off because of them.

"Yeah, as part of this club, I, like everyone else, have a right to know what's gonna be done," he replied, the coloring in his fist paling the longer Marek chose to keep him, and us, in the dark.

"I'd like to know if the guy is really a Reaper," Brick added, shrugging like it was no big deal either way.

"Me too," Hawke sneered, his attitude back in full force now.

"In due time you'll all be brought up to speed," Marek said, staring at each of us like we were bothering him.

"You just told Cutter—"

"I said... In. Due. Time." Prez looked pissed, yet again, but it wasn't like his frown ever disappeared for too long.

Kaden vibrated with anger, but he didn't speak again,

drawing his fist into his lap and pushing away from the table. Marek hadn't used the gavel to release any of us, so Kaden stayed seated.

"Back to the biggest issue we have right now," our leader grumbled, his eyes landing on me. I took a deep breath and swallowed nervously. My ol' man was a force to be reckoned with sometimes, but right then, I didn't like the way Marek looked at me. "Go get that girl."

"What?" I heard him but needed him to say it again.

"Go get her," he repeated.

"Bring her in here?" There was a firm rule that no women were allowed inside Chambers, although I believed there were a couple of times when an exception had been made.

"Of course not. Bring her out to the common area." Marek didn't even ask if anyone had anything else to discuss before he slammed the wooden hammer down.

"Just don't marry her, Linc," Tripp said, a tilt of a smile ghosting across his face.

"Why would I marry her? I don't even know her."

"That doesn't mean anything in this club." Ryder laughed, he and several of the older guys all looking toward Marek.

"Shut the fuck up," Prez growled before rising from his seat. Then he smirked. "I don't regret it for a second." I wanted to ask him what he meant, but Kaden flanked me on my right.

"This is bullshit." He was pissed, and I couldn't blame him. Everything that happened with Tag was beyond our comprehension. Not only was it confusing, but we'd been rocked off-balance the moment we saw him tied to that table, then having to witness what Cutter did to the guy was outside of what we were used to dealing with.

"I know, man. But what are we gonna do?" I genuinely wanted to know because I was at a loss.

"Dunno." He rubbed his hand over his jaw several times before dropping his arm to his side. "You better go get her before anything else goes down." He brushed past me out of Chambers and walked toward some of the others who were at the bar. It wasn't even nine in the morning, yet Trigger handed several of the men a beer.

I caught up to Ace as he took a seat in the corner. "Where'd you go last night after everything went down?" I expected him to come back here, but he didn't show up until this morning.

"I rode around for a bit to clear my head, then stopped at Chelsea's."

"And she let you in?" I asked, remembering their massive fight.

"Only after I sweet-talked her." He smirked but deadpanned quickly, taking a sip of his drink.

I tapped the top of the bar before walking away, apprehension coating my skin as I walked down the hallway. Every step I took closer, heightened my nerves, the beat of my heart picking up its pace at the thought I had to pull her out of the security of the room and into the lion's den. While the guys weren't going to touch her, there was a possibility a few of them wouldn't be their most polite selves. Not that most of them would normally win an award for etiquette.

I rapped my knuckles against the door, counting to three in case she wasn't decent. The memory of her standing in front of me naked last night elicited anger I'd never felt before. Not only from the sight of the fresh bruises scattered among the healing ones, but that she'd been treated so badly, she felt like she had to give me her body in exchange for taking her away from those monsters. Deciding it best to hide my emotions, I kept my expression flat, or at least I hoped I had. Frightening her even more than she probably already was could only do further damage.

I turned the handle and slowly opened the door before peering inside. Maddie stood in the middle of the bathroom in nothing but a towel, bent over the sink spitting out the toothpaste she used to brush her teeth. She appeared to be lost in her own world because she never noticed when I entered the room. It wasn't until I was directly outside the bathroom, did she turn her head and look at me, letting out a small shriek once she saw me.

"I knocked. I guess you didn't hear me." I rested my arms against the doorframe.

"I didn't." She tightened the towel around her chest, her eyes taking on a panicked look. "I… I fell back asleep for a few minutes. I only just now took a shower. I'm sorry." She backed further into the bathroom even though I hadn't moved at all.

"That's fine. No problem." My words came out slower than usual, my tone soft, much like one would talk to a frightened animal who was about to bolt.

Her breaths evened out while she watched me. I must've looked a certain way because she frowned. "Is everything okay?" she asked tentatively.

"Yeah." My cheeks puffed out before I released the air from my lungs. "Uh… I gotta… bring you out there."

She grabbed onto the edge of the sink. "Out where?"

"Out there," I answered, pointing toward the door. "To the common area."

"Why?" Her voice trembled and I wanted nothing more than to give her a hug, to assure her that nothin' was gonna happen to her.

"The president of our club asked me to."

"Will he… will he force me to have sex?" A tear coursed down her cheek. My heart broke right then, and if it was the last thing I did, I'd make those fuckers pay for what they did to her.

"No. I guarantee he won't touch you. No one will." I briefly wondered how many times I'd have to say the same thing before she believed me.

Maddie and I stood staring at each other, and if I wasn't

mistaken, I thought I detected a hint of curiosity shrouded behind her gaze. She didn't seem to be frightened of me, not much, at least.

Taking her all in again, I deemed that her eyes were almost too big for her face, but in the cutest of ways. Her bottom lip was slightly fuller than her top, and her nose was small and in perfect alignment with the rest of her face.

Maddie was beautiful, and while I tried not to focus on her physical attributes, I couldn't help but picture her in various positions on the bed behind me. My thoughts were in bad taste, but as long as I didn't voice them, no harm, right?

She watched me intently, her eyes never leaving my face, and for the first time in my life, I felt scrutinized, but I couldn't say if it bothered me one way or the other.

Finally, she shifted her feet and looked downward, clutching her towel as if she feared the material would suddenly disappear.

"Oh, sorry. I should let you get dressed." I turned and moved to walk away.

"Can you wait for me? I don't want to go out there by myself."

With my back still to her, I said, "Of course."

Her plea disturbed me. I hated that she thought I would make her fend for herself in a place she didn't know, around men who were strangers to her.

Although... I was a stranger to her.

A fact I wanted to rectify and soon.

## Maddie

Fully dressed back in the clothes I arrived in, I stood in front of the mirror, staring at the shell of the person looking back at me. I barely recognized myself. My chocolate-brown hair was dull and lifeless, much like my pale green eyes. My skin was pasty and slightly sunken in, blotches of discoloration painting my cheeks and neck, the sight of bruises a common thing for me to see on myself.

"He said you'll be fine," I muttered to my reflection, breathing in and out to calm my rising nerves. My vision blurred with unshed tears, and for a second, I contemplated locking myself in this bathroom, refusing to go with Lincoln out to the common area where his president was waiting on me.

I'd trusted before, and it hadn't worked out for me. Why would this time be any different?

Lincoln rapped twice on the bedroom door before entering. "You ready? They're waiting." *They?* I shook my head so fast I was surprised I didn't fall over.

He was next to me a few strides later, placing his hand on my upper arm. Leaning down so he could look me directly in the eyes, he said, "Maddie, don't be frightened. Our club is nothin' like theirs. We don't treat women like they do." I heard his words, but they weren't registering. Fear tore through me, and before I knew what happened, I'd bent over the sink and threw up.

Lincoln quickly grabbed my hair and held it away from my face as I continued to dry heave, rubbing my back in small circles to try and soothe me.

"Please don't make me go out there," I sobbed, holding on to the vanity for strength.

"It'll be okay. I promise." His tone was calm and filled with compassion, pity even. The sentiment didn't offend me, because if someone pitied me, then maybe they wouldn't be inclined to hurt me.

Groaning, I clutched my lower belly, the discomfort I'd been experiencing recently only getting worse. And throwing up didn't help my overall situation.

"I have to pee," I said when I straightened up, Lincoln's arms falling to his sides.

"Uh... okay. You take care of what you need to, and I'm gonna go see if Marek will come back here instead. Would that make you feel more comfortable?" I nodded, relieved I didn't have to leave the confines of the room.

Once he left, I closed the bathroom door and sat down on the toilet, an odd sensation erupting before a small trickle of urine finally came out, the stinging pain making me scrunch my face until I finished. It felt like my bladder was full, but it wasn't, the urge to go to the bathroom plaguing me more than was normal.

I was one step back into the bedroom when the door opened, two guys walking in behind Lincoln.

"Maddie, this is our club president, Marek," Lincoln

announced, pointing toward the man directly behind him, "and this is Stone. He's the club VP and my father."

Both men looked to be in their late forties, if I guessed at their ages correctly. Marek had short dark hair with a bit of gray on the sides and the most brilliant blue eyes I'd ever seen. For an older man, he was handsome, his trimmed beard adding to his ruggedness. At first glance, he appeared to be serious, a hard man, but when he stepped closer, closer than was comfortable for me, I watched his eyes soften, his expression relaxing while he captured me with his stare.

Surprisingly, I didn't fear Marek like I thought I would. He oozed strength but compassion toward me, for now at least. Or was this his ploy? Would he play the sheep until the wolf decided it was time to emerge?

Marek motioned for me to sit on the bed. Once I rested on the edge, I counted every breath that left my body. Lowering my head, I didn't dare look at any of the men standing so close for fear of what I'd see. I waited in silence with my hands clasped in my lap, my muscles becoming sore with the anticipation they'd shove me back on the bed and have their way with me.

"Maddie." A tear trailed down my cheek at hearing my name, and I couldn't pinpoint if it was because I heard a trace of compassion in Marek's voice or because I still feared what may happen. "Look at me," he said, his tone firmer than seconds before.

I lifted my head but closed my eyes, my bottom lip trembling because I didn't want to see their expressions, especially Lincoln's. Had he handed me over to his president and VP? Would he get special treatment for bringing in a woman they could do with as they saw fit? Even though Lincoln told me no such things would happen, I didn't believe it. Not fully. Not yet.

The bed dipped beside me, and my lids opened. Lincoln's hand covered both of mine, and he whispered, "It's okay."

"Fuck," Marek shouted, making me flinch. "What did they do to her?"

"Unfortunately, this looks all too familiar," Stone added, a statement I thankfully didn't understand, and didn't want to. When I glanced over at the club's VP, I saw the resemblance between father and son, although Lincoln's hair was much darker than Stone's dirty-blond strands. They had the same shape eyes, nose, and mouth, and while Lincoln was clean-shaven, his dad wore a long beard, giving him an edgier, more hardened appearance.

Stone stood off to the side while Marek moved until he stood directly in front of me and extended his hand. "Let me get a look at ya."

"It's okay," Lincoln murmured next to me when I hesitated to stand. How many times did the guy have to assure me no harm would come to me before I believed him?

Looking into his soft brown eyes, I gave him a curt nod before slowly rising from the bed, standing in front of the president of his club like the frightened girl I was.

I trembled like I'd been standing in the cold for too long, my teeth chattering while my muscles twitched.

"I need to inspect you, okay?"

"Why?" Lincoln asked, and I had to admit I was curious as well. Did he need to inspect me to prove I was worthy enough to be in their company? What kinds of things would meet his approval? I didn't understand anything that was happening, and while I tried to mentally escape my surroundings, every time I glanced over at Lincoln, he brought me right back.

"Because he needs to see what he's dealing with," his father answered, leaning casually against the door like this was an everyday occurrence, and for all I knew, it could be.

Marek placed both his hands on my upper arms and pulled me closer, looking into my eyes for what felt like forever. I wasn't sure what he expected to find behind my stare, and I sure as hell wasn't about to ask.

"How are you feelin'?" he asked, moving my hair over my shoulders so he could look at my neck.

"Fine."

"Are you injured?"

*Only my soul.* "No." My answers were short and to the point, something I believed he may have appreciated.

"I wanna take a quick look at you." He lifted my shirt, and I took a deep breath, my eyes widening the further he raised the material. "I wanna see your rib cage and then your back. Okay?" he asked tentatively, which I was sure he didn't often do with anyone. He looked like he commanded a room with his presence alone, not by asking permission for anything, which was why I relaxed a fraction when he turned me around and inspected my back.

When he lowered my shirt, he looked over at Stone and shook his head. I wasn't sure what he was looking for, but apparently, I didn't have it. I would've been fine with allowing my curiosity on the subject to flit away, but that wasn't the case for Lincoln.

"Why did you shake your head, Prez? What are you lookin' for?"

Marek's brow dipped in aggravation, but he answered, nonetheless. "Burn marks and stab wounds."

"Why would—"

"Never mind," Stone griped at his son, shaking his head when he thought he was gonna push, which he didn't.

"Can you tell me how long you've been with the Reapers?" Marek asked, gritting his teeth when he said their name.

"Eight months."

"And how did they treat you when you were with them?" He took a step back and flexed his hands at his sides, the repeat motion distracting me while I figured out the quickest way to tell them what I'd been through.

"Uh, maybe I can fill you in on that later," Lincoln said, saving me from another round of shame and embarrassment.

"Fine." Marek drew a breath, then released it quickly, turning his eyes to the guy next to me. "While you went against me, and the situation isn't ideal by any stretch of the imagination, I get it. If you hadn't interfered on her behalf, who knows what would've happened to her."

What was he talking about? Had Lincoln mentioned me before? I was aware he'd asked Griller and Rock about me because I'd been right next to them, although I always made sure to keep my head down and my mouth shut. But I was under the assumption the undefeated fighter wanted me for himself. I never thought he wanted to help me.

"I know."

"Well, she can't stay here for much longer," Stone said, looking like he'd rather be anywhere else but in that room with us, his patience seemingly gone from the time he walked in.

"Where am I gonna take her?" Lincoln asked, his teeth harassing his bottom lip.

Before I could stop the words from pouring out of my mouth, I clutched on to Marek's arm in desperation. "Please don't make me go back there," I pleaded. "Griller was gonna give me to Dutch, and I've seen what he's done to girls." Unshed tears blurred my vision. "He uses knives." I hiccupped on my last word, fear bubbling up inside me at what the evil bastard would do to me if he ever got his hands on me.

All three men vibrated with anger, and I wasn't sure if it was directed at me or not. They remained silent while I was left to stew in uncertainty. Leaving me to my thoughts wasn't always a good thing. I'd lose myself to the infinite possibilities of outcomes, dashing any hope I might've had because that wasn't my reality. Hope was for the delusional, and I stopped walking that path a week after being with the Reapers.

Marek removed my hand from his arm and flashed me a sympathetic grin. "We would never send you back to them. Don't worry about that." He looked back at Stone. "Call your wife. Tell her we need her to look over Maddie." He then turned back to face me. "Linc's mom is a nurse. She'll make sure everything is okay." I nodded, relieved I'd be able to talk to someone who might be able to help me with the issue I'd been experiencing when going to the bathroom. And while I'd been uncomfortable the entire time all three men were closed in here with me, I had to admit I'd felt safer in the past twenty minutes than I had in the past eight months.

Question was, would I ever find a sliver of peace again?

# Seventeen

## Lincoln

After telling Maddie I'd be back shortly, I followed Marek and my ol' man down the hall and into Chambers, shutting the door because I didn't want any of the other guys to overhear what I was about to reveal about Maddie's time with the Reapers. Not yet, anyway. I was sure eventually they'd find out and be as angry as I was right now.

They took their designated seats, but instead of me sitting in mine, which was at the other end of the table, I sat in Tripp's seat, to the right of Marek.

There was a brief silence while I figured out what I wanted to divulge, feeling protective over Maddie and what she'd been through. I realized both of them wouldn't downplay her trauma, but I wanted to shield her, nonetheless.

"So, what has she told you about them?" Prez asked, leaning back in his chair, his calm expression the opposite of how I felt on the inside. Simply forming the words in my brain made my blood boil. That anyone would do such vile things to a defenseless girl was beyond the scope of what I could wrap my mind around. Zander and I'd been raised to never lay our hands on a woman, no matter what. Walk away if the situation went sideways because we were the physically stronger sex. Besides, women were to be cherished and adored. Maybe that was the more sensitive side of me sneaking out, a side I didn't show many because I didn't want to hear the comments, but for the right person, I would toss all reservations aside. *Could Maddie be that person?* Even as the question formed, I thought it was ridiculous. I didn't even know her.

"Not much other than the prospect, Pike, the one who told me to take her, was the one who brought her to the club in the first place. She said he told her he didn't know his prez would take her from him, but I think that's bullshit. Anyone who spends five seconds with those fucks knows exactly what type of scum they are." I had to stop and take a breath because my heart started to thump too quickly inside my chest. "She told me they passed her around, but Griller abused her more than anyone." I tried to keep it as vague as possible while still answering.

"Dutch would've killed her for sure," my ol' man said, looking at his friend, then me. "That guy is fucked-in-the-head crazy. We've had some run-ins with him in the past."

I didn't know anything about the guy, so I'd take his word for it, thankful now more than ever I'd been able to finally save Maddie from them.

"See if you can get some info out of her about their dealings. Find out if she knows anything else." Marek leaned toward me. "Maybe she knows if they were behind the fire at Indulge. Since they had control over her, I doubt they'd hold their tongues in front of her, thinking she wasn't a threat to them in any way because she was their prisoner. Plus, those assholes are stupid."

"I'll ask her if she knows anything." While I understood our conversation was important, all I wanted to do was get back to the room and be with her. She was frightened, and I wanted to do everything I could to comfort her.

Both men rose from the table and I followed, but before we walked out of the room, I stopped Marek by grabbing his arm. "Is it all right if she stays here for a bit, until I figure something else out?"

"Yeah" was all he said before he left.

My dad stopped next to me on his way out. "Your mom is gonna be here soon, and she's bringing Sully with her. If anyone can relate to that girl, it's Marek's wife."

Agreeing with a nod, I had something else I wanted to ask. "Does she know about this?" I pointed to the small bandage on my temple.

"No, so you better downplay it."

---

NOT ONLY DID my mom and Sully show up, but so did my sister. All three of them bombarded me with questions as soon as I met them outside.

Grabbing my face, my mom turned my head to the side. "What happened?" She sucked in a lungful of air when she pried the bandage away from my skin. "Oh my God! Who shot you?"

"Shot you?" Riley parroted, stepping up next to our mother and leaning over her, both so close I had to take a step back to breathe.

"Uh... nobody. We just got into a scuffle."

"Bullshit. Not only are you a terrible liar, Linc, but I know what it looks like when a bullet grazes the skin. I've seen too many of these in my time."

After spending five minutes toning down what really happened, and reminding them that I was fine and still breathing, I turned the conversation around to the reason they were here.

I explained the situation with Maddie, and after having heard what Sully had gone through when she was in the Reapers' clutches decades ago, I agreed that if anyone could reassure the girl she would be safe with us, it would be her.

I wasn't sure if Marek ever told her that we now knew what happened to her at the hands of her father and Vex, but I sure as hell wouldn't bring it up. Kaden and I had discussed this new information about his mom on the ride home that night, and for a full hour, he was inconsolable. It was one of the few times I saw him break down and cry, and his anguish tore at my heart.

"Where is she?" my mom asked, walking past me and into the clubhouse. I followed, as did Sully and Riley.

"Last bedroom."

"Is she okay?" Riley asked.

Our mom had filled my sister in on what was going on. "Physically, she's bruised up, but emotionally... that's a different story."

Riley shook her head, her fallen expression something I expected. She was tough, stubborn to a fault, but she had a big heart and hated to see anyone suffer.

"Linc?" I turned to look at my mom, who stood in the middle of the hallway. "You wanna go in first so we don't scare her?"

"Good idea." Maddie knew she was coming, but she didn't know about Sully or Riley, and I had no doubt she'd feel overwhelmed and nervous if all three women waltzed in there unannounced.

I rushed ahead of them and knocked on the door twice before entering. Maddie was looking out the window. The only view she had was of the lot, but she seemed entranced because I unknowingly startled her when I walked up behind her.

"Sorry. I thought you heard me knock." She just shook her head. "My mom is here, and she brought her friend. My sister is also with them." She looked worried and scared, the emotions weaving not only into her furrowed brows and wide eyes, but in her posture as well. Her shoulders rose right before she backed up, but because she was so close to the wall, she didn't have anywhere to go. I reached out and gently touched her shoulder, and she recoiled, the gesture infuriating me. I wasn't upset with her. Instead, my anger continued to be heightened with every reminder of what she'd endured.

"I know it's a lot to deal with, but my mom is a nurse, as you know, and her friend Sully, who is Marek's wife, can relate to what you've been through, and my sister, Riley, wants to make sure you're okay." I wasn't going to provide Maddie with any personal information about Sully because I didn't want to overstep, but if she chose to tell her, that was her business. Although to be fair, I'd just indicated the woman had been through something similar.

"Why do they all care?" Maddie closed her eyes briefly before reaching for my arm. Her slender fingers wrapped around my wrist, the heat of her touch causing a reaction—desire mixed with something unfamiliar.

"Because *I* do." My admission caused her to relax enough for me to guide her toward the center of the room, which was only several steps from where we stood.

They must've been listening at the door because they all entered the room without me asking. My mom was first, her smile big and inviting. She had a calming way about her, making me believe with a simple grin that everything was going to be okay, even when I was unsure myself.

"Hi, honey," she said, setting her black medical bag on the bed. "I'm Addy, Linc's mom."

"Addy?" Maddie asked, her tone bordering surprise.

"Yeah." My mom nodded before opening her bag and pulling out tubes for blood and a pee cup.

"Your name rhythms with mine." A shy smile crept across Maddie's face. "Addy and Maddie."

"That's because we're cool," my mom responded. I saw the tension evaporate from Maddie's frame right before my eyes, which in turn made me relax.

"So, tell me, Maddie. How are you feeling? Any issues? No matter how small, you should tell me so I can make sure there isn't a bigger problem." She placed her hand on Maddie's arm in comfort. "Okay?"

Maddie looked to me, then back to my mom, biting her lower lip but not saying anything.

"Linc, can you wait outside?" It wasn't really a question but instead a command. I abided without giving her an issue. Whatever Maddie wanted to tell her was obviously private, and because I wanted her to be as comfortable as possible, I left them to it.

## Maddie

The moment I sat down with Addy, a calm washed over me.

"Now that it's just us girls, how about you tell me what's wrong." I opened my mouth to start, but she interrupted me. "Sorry, how rude of us." She pointed toward a pretty dark-haired woman who looked to be about her age. "This is Sully, Marek's wife. And this," she said, gesturing toward the younger female who was probably several years older than me, "is my daughter and Lincoln's sister, Riley."

Both women smiled and said hello. The young blonde shared a strong resemblance to her mom, which even included a similar shade of hair color and a family resemblance to Lincoln.

"So, what's goin' on?" Addy asked, her eyes on me as she sat on my right, tucking a strand of hair behind her ear.

"For the past few days, it hurts when I pee. And sometimes I get dizzy." I looked down at my hands in my lap, feeling embarrassed. Had one of those men given me a disease? Would these women and Lincoln, if he found out, think I was dirty, unworthy to remain with them?

"All right," she said, pulling a thermometer out of her bag. "I have everything in here." She laughed. "You wouldn't believe how many times I had to take care of these guys back in the day." Her laughter reminded me of my mom's, and before I could stop myself, my eyes welled up. "It's okay, honey. You'll be okay. We'll make sure of it." I nodded because I couldn't find my voice. "What you're describing most likely sounds like a bladder infection or a UTI." I frowned. "Urinary tract infection."

"Oh," I finally uttered, looking to my left when Sully took a seat beside me, sitting close while still not encroaching on my personal space. Riley remained standing, leaning against the dresser, smiling at me when I looked at her.

Addy put the thermometer under my tongue. "Pain during urination is a symptom, as well as dizziness from the infection." She handed me a small plastic cup with a lid. "I need a sample of your urine so I can test to be sure." I looked at the cup, then back to her. "When you're done, I'm gonna take some blood and test for STDs as well as pregnancy." Her words didn't even register before she asked, "Is there a possibility you're pregnant?" She pulled the thermometer out of my mouth when it beeped.

I would've loved to answer her question with a resounding no, but I couldn't. Every time one of them forced themselves on me, not once did they use a condom, and I wasn't on the pill.

"They never used anything when they..." I took a moment to try and compose myself. "And I don't know when I had my period last. They've never been regular." Any other words I was gonna say got stuck in my throat, a lone tear coursing down my face.

"Maddie, I'm so sorry for what you've been through," Sully said, patting my hand. "If anyone knows what it's like to live with those bastards, it's me." I turned my head so quickly toward her I almost gave myself whiplash. She lived with them, too? At my widened eyes, she continued speaking. "It was a long time ago, but my father was president of that club. But he never treated me like a daughter. He never protected me. He never loved me. He used me, in every way possible, then he passed me off to a man who was as bad, if not worse." For Sully, a stranger, to tell me something so personal, to rehash memories that appeared to still be raw and difficult, meant a lot.

"How did you come to be here?" I asked, hoping I wasn't overstepping by asking for more details.

"Marek took me from them."

"Like Lincoln took me?" I found it hard to breathe while I waited for her to answer. Never wishing the torment they put me through on anyone, an odd, messed-up sense of comfort drifted over me knowing I wasn't the only one who suffered at their hands.

"The situation was a little different, but the result was the same. He saved me, much like Linc saved you."

"He saved me," I repeated, nodding rather vigorously.

Addy tapped my leg and grinned. "Why don't you get me that sample, and then we can proceed?"

"Okay." I stood up and disappeared inside the bathroom. As I awkwardly held the cup between my legs while sitting on the toilet, I grimaced and blew out a breath when the pain came, praying like hell it was only an infection and nothing worse. Once I was finished, I sealed the top, washed my hands, and opened the door to the bedroom, stopping abruptly when Lincoln stood directly in front of me. I almost dropped the cup in surprise.

"Linc, I told you we weren't done yet," his mom chastised, and while I loved that he seemed to be concerned about me, I loved it even more that his mom appeared to be protective of my privacy.

"I know. I just wanted to see if she was hungry." He responded to Addy but never took his eyes from mine.

"I could eat something."

"Like what?"

"I'm not picky."

We stood there staring at each other for a moment before Riley walked up behind her brother. "Are you gonna stand here all day or get the poor girl some food?"

"I'll get her some food." Again, while he spoke to someone else, he kept his gaze locked on me. Only when she tugged on his arm, did he seem to break out of some sort of haze and turn to leave.

"I think someone's got it bad," Riley joked once Lincoln was out of earshot. I flushed at the comment before quickly taking my seat back on the bed.

"Stop teasing her," Addy scolded, but her smile indicated she wasn't upset with her daughter. She took the cup from me and placed it on top of the dresser before returning to stand in front of me. "Have you ever had blood drawn before?"

"When I was a kid."

"Good." She didn't say another word as she pulled out a small pad of gauze, a needle, wipes, gloves, and a stretchy band. "Straighten your arm for me." Wrapping the band around my arm above my elbow, she tied it tightly but not enough to hurt. She pressed on the creased area of my arm a few times before wiping a wet pad over the area. When she was done, she hooked up one of the tubes I'd seen to a needle and placed the tip of it against my skin. "You'll feel a pinch, but that's it." I didn't want to watch, so I closed my eyes and waited, and before I knew it, she said, "All done."

"What?" My lids popped open. "But I didn't feel anything."

"That's 'cause she's good," Sully said.

"That I am. I like to warn people in case I have an issue drawing their blood. But you were easy." She untied the band, put a white piece of gauze where she drew the blood, and folded my arm upward. "I should have the results back later today. It would be sooner if we were in the office, but I have to take the samples there." After Addy gathered the rest of her things, she pulled me to my feet and gave me a hug. "Don't worry, honey. We'll help you as much as we can."

I didn't know how much I needed to hear those words until she said them, and unlike any reservation I had when Lincoln tried to reassure me, I believed her.

Maybe because she was a woman.

Maybe because she was a mother.

Or maybe it was because her friend had been through what I had.

Whatever the reason, I trusted every word she said.

## Lincoln

Every second they were in there with Maddie was a second too long. While I understood my mom needed some time alone with her for privacy, and that my sister and Sully were offering their support, I wanted to be present to offer Maddie whatever comfort I could.

What sorts of questions was she asked? Would Maddie offer me that same information at some point? I took to pacing in the common area before Ryder shouted at me to either sit the hell down or go outside because I made him nervous with the back and forth.

I glared at him and he laughed, and when I opened my mouth to say something to him, although I had no idea what, that was when I saw my mom, Riley, and Sully walking down the hallway. I looked around them, but I didn't see Maddie. Of course, she wouldn't follow them out here. What was I thinking? The girl was scared. She would probably never voluntarily come out of that room.

"Well?" I asked, rushing toward them.

"I'm gonna go to the office and find out why she's having the pain."

"What pain?"

"Because I can see you're worried about her, I'll tell you this much. She probably has either a bladder infection or a UTI. If it's either, I can get her some antibiotics, and she should start to feel better soon."

"And if it's something else?" I asked, worried there might be something wrong with her we couldn't help with.

"Then we'll see what the options are." She leaned in and kissed my cheek before walking away. Sully followed, but Riley lingered behind.

"Hey, have you seen Dad?"

"Yeah, earlier. Why?"

"Because Kaden doesn't know I'm here yet, and I don't want to be the reason something happens. I figure if Dad sees us separately, he'll contain his anger, but if he sees us together, that'll be a whole other story."

"Well, Kaden just walked out of the kitchen and is headed this way."

My sister turned around as Kaden strolled right up to us. "Hey, babe. What are you doin' here?" He leaned in to give her a kiss. That shit was still weird to see, but I kept my comments to myself. I had more important things on my mind.

"I came with my mom and Sully to check on Maddie." Kaden raised his brows. "The girl Linc stole," she clarified, shoving my arm when I shook my head and scowled.

"I know who you're talkin' about. What I can't understand is why you would need to see her." He sounded irritated at the thought of Riley getting involved with the situation with Maddie, and while I would never put my sister in a scenario that would endanger her, I didn't see the harm in her visiting our new guest within the confines of our clubhouse, which was the safest place any of us could be.

"I thought she could use some female energy around her. You guys can be too much sometimes."

"You're not wrong." He flung his arm over her shoulder and kissed her temple.

"Where's my dad?" Apparently, my answer wasn't good enough.

Before Kaden could tell her the same thing I did, I saw the man in question headed toward us, his steps faltering when he saw his daughter next to Kaden.

"Fuck," I muttered before I could tell them to separate. My ol' man managed to walk up behind Kaden and Riley, shoving himself in between and forcibly splitting them apart. Kaden's arm fell to his side on a curse, Riley taking a step back out of surprise.

"What are you doin' here?" he asked Riley, completely ignoring Kaden, even going so far as to step in front of him to block him from her view momentarily. Kaden tried to move around him, but our VP moved with him.

"I came with Mom and Sully. I was just leaving."

"Good." When Riley didn't move, he quirked his brow before pointing toward the exit. "Go."

They weren't quite back on speaking terms. He was still upset about the entire situation, and she was stubborn, not conceding to him or any of his crazy demands she not be involved with Kaden.

"Can I say goodbye first?" she huffed, throwing her hands on her hips.

He stared at her, his expression one that would make anyone wary of him. When Riley tried to walk around our dad, he stepped to the side, much like he'd done with Kaden.

"I'm not messin' around, Ry," he grated. "Go with your mother."

"Just go," I told her, not wanting anything to happen right here in the hallway. Not only did I not want my ol' man and Kaden to get into it, although Marek had told him that nothing will happen between them within the confines of the clubhouse, I didn't want them to start yelling and causing a commotion near the room where Maddie was staying. She was frightened enough. I didn't want anything added to her stress level.

"I told you I'm not hiding us anymore," Kaden said, moving past our VP before he could block him. The second I saw Kaden grab my sister's hand and pull her toward the front of the clubhouse, I knew somethin' was about to go down, the growl from my father making me close my eyes briefly and draw a breath. I prayed whatever was about to happen would end as quickly as it would start.

"You gotta lot of nerve, you little shit," he shouted, catching up to them in a few long strides. He forcibly removed their hands and shoved Kaden so hard he stumbled back a step. "Don't touch her."

"Dad!" Riley shouted, catching the attention of our mom, Sully, Marek, and a few of the other guys who were milling around. "Enough. We're together, and there isn't anything you can do about it." It took courage for Riley to say that to him. It wouldn't change the way he'd react, but at least she was able to speak her mind, something she'd been afraid to do for years when it came to her and Kaden.

"I'll never allow this," he yelled back, keeping his eyes on Kaden and not his daughter.

"Stone, come on." Addy suddenly appeared next to him and reached for his hand. She wanted the situation to deescalate as much as the rest of us did. Two members in the clubhouse goin' at it was never good, but a fight within a family was even more stressful.

He finally tore his eyes away from Kaden and looked at his wife. "Take her and go." Addy didn't respond or move a muscle, and apparently, her stubbornness was the catapult to the man losing his mind. "I'm not fuckin' around here, woman. Take Riley and go." Every word he spoke was clipped. His shoulders were tense, and his neck and face flushed a tinge of red the longer our mother stood there glaring at him.

Then she spoke, but not before pointing her finger in his face and flashing him a snarl of her own.

"You're drivin' a wedge in this family because of your anger." She took a step closer. "I get you're not happy about Riley and Kaden, but get over it." My ol' man opened his mouth to respond, but my mom threw her hand in front of his face before he could say anything. "Don't bother comin' home until you get your head out of your ass."

"What? Are you serious?"

"You're goddamn right I am. You need to stop this. Stop acting like an ass before you do or say something that tears this family apart for good. And I swear to you, if that happens...."

There were only two other times in my entire life I saw my mom this upset with him, and right now might take the cake.

She walked away and took Riley with her, forcing my sister in front of her when she tried to break away and go to Kaden.

I glanced over at my dad and studied him as he watched the two of them leave, the look of disbelief and anger on his face mixed to form some other kind of emotion altogether.

He cursed under his breath and stalked off toward Chambers, disappearing inside our meeting room without saying another word to anyone. I could imagine that while he was enraged at what just happened, he had to be somewhat embarrassed as well. To have his wife chastise him like that in front of his club had to be emasculating. I wasn't gonna say I didn't blame my mom, but I was sure he felt whatever way he did, regardless. Or maybe I was projecting how I would feel if something like that happened to me.

"Always a fun time around here," Hawke mumbled, shoving his hands in his pockets and leaning against the bar. "I miss this shit."

# Twenty

## Lincoln

“Everybody back in Chambers,” Marek shouted, and while he didn’t sound angry about what just went down, his tone was filled with impatience.

“Can I check on Maddie quick to make sure she’s okay?” I asked as I walked up in front of him, hoping he would at least let me see how she was doing.

“Hurry up.”

I rushed off without another word. If anything, I wanted to tell her I’d be in a meeting and for her not to worry. I hated that I had to be separated from her for who only knew how long. She’d consumed my thoughts, my worry for her physical and emotional well-being something I wasn’t used to.

That’s not to say I was a self-centered person. If anything, people who knew me would say I cared about others as much as the next compassionate person, but to worry so much about a relative stranger was new for me.

My knuckle hit the wood of the door once before I entered. Maddie lay in the middle of the bed with her eyes closed and her arm thrown over her face. When she heard me enter, though, she scrambled to sit up but didn't quite make it. She clutched her head and eased back down, blowing out several quick puffs of air.

"Are you okay?" I was next to her two steps later.

"Just dizzy." She averted her eyes, looking everywhere else but at me until I cleared my throat. Only then did her gaze land back on me. "Your mom... she said I might have a bladder infection or a..." She shrugged, looking puzzled, clearly not remembering what the other option was, but I wasn't gonna fill in the blank because I didn't want her to think my mom said anything to me about her possible situation. "She said dizziness could also be a symptom."

"Well, she should know what's wrong soon. Then she can give you some meds." Silence ensued after I spoke. I wanted to ask her what she was thinking, but I wasn't sure I wanted to know the answer. If she mentioned the Reapers, I'd be pissed off. Not because I didn't want her to be able to confide in me more about her awful time with them, but because I wanted to kill every last one of them as it was, I couldn't imagine how much more furious I'd become if she elaborated on her time there with them.

"Can I take a nap? I'm not feeling very well." She tucked her dark hair behind her ear and looked up at me with such innocence all I wanted to do was wrap her in my arms and promise her the world.

"Of course. I actually came in here to tell you that I have to go to a meeting. If you change your mind about the nap, you can either hang out in here, or if you get hungry, you can always go to the kitchen to fix yourself something to eat. I think there's stuff for sandwiches."

"Okay" was all she said, pulling on the bottom of her T-shirt.

I stood next to her for another ten seconds without speaking. Out loud, that was. Internally, each of my questions mixed with the next until I didn't believe I was even forming coherent thoughts.

"Lincoln!" Ace shouted from down the hall. "Let's go, brother!"

"That's my cue." I smiled at Maddie before slowly turning around, leaving the bedroom and wondering if she'd ever get to a place where she trusted me implicitly. There was no time to dwell on such things now, however. Marek had called us all back into Chambers.

Dropping my phone on the table outside the room, I walked in and took my seat. I was the last one to sit, and both Prez and my ol' man didn't seem to appreciate it much.

"Now that we're all here," Marek started, "there's some stuff we need to discuss, and although I never intended on bringing this up ever again, I now see it's a necessary evil." I heard the older guys grumblin' under their breath, but their words weren't coherent enough for me to understand.

Leaning toward Brick, I whispered, "Have any idea what he's talkin' about?"

He shook his head, replying, "I'm as confused as you are." We were far enough down the table, Marek couldn't hear what we said, but when his eyes landed on me, I straightened in my seat and acted like I wasn't having a side conversation, no matter how brief it was. Whatever reason he called us all back in here, I was smart enough to know it was important.

Our leader rubbed his hand over his bearded jawline, his expression flattening. He appeared to be conflicted over whatever was about to come out of his mouth, but he continued regardless.

"When most of us weren't much older than you guys," he said, jerking his chin in the general vicinity of us younger members, "our club was run completely different." *Oh... more generalities.* "We were involved with running drugs for the Los

Zappas cartel." I wasn't gonna lie. I almost choked on my spit when I heard him say that, not used to him giving specifics, other than the small bit he spewed in the basement about Tag's father and what he did to Sully. "At one point, we were responsible for two-thirds of the cocaine supply smuggled into central Cali. And even though we had many people in our pockets to help keep the profits high and the risk low, there was still a risk, which came back to bite us every now and again. The stress of it all became too much, too many of our lives at risk to justify continuing for much longer. The head of the cartel, Rafael Carrillo, owed me a favor for saving his life once, so after some negotiation, he allowed us to walk away without repercussion. But it wasn't easy to cut ties and go legit. We had to take care of some stuff before everything finally fell into place."

I saw Tripp and Hawke shift in their seats, seemingly uncomfortable with Marek's retelling of the past. Or was I reading them wrong?

"The war between us and the Savage Reapers dated back to when Stone and I were kids, when our fathers were in charge, and it seemed to all come to a head a few years before we finally ended it for good."

"What happened?" Ace asked, and at first, I wasn't sure if Marek was gonna take offense to the question or not, but I had to admit that I was just as curious. Thankfully, our prez answered without reservation.

"Those fuckers were gettin' greedier and more careless. They'd show up at our establishments and threaten to take us out one by one. They wanted to replace us and take top position with the cartel, but what they didn't know, and what we would never tell them, was that we planned on exiting anyway. And while we dealt with them here and there..." He stopped speaking, blew out a breath, and elaborated. "And by dealt with, I mean killed. We ended them before they could end us, although sometimes we weren't as lucky." His eyes found

Cutter briefly before continuing. "The breaking point for us, the moment we knew we'd have to end as many of them as we could, came when they left Tripp for dead outside our gates. Shot four times and clinging to life."

"Seems like only yesterday," Tripp said, a half-smirk appearing on his face. "Thank God Addy was there to watch over me." He looked to Stone, and his grin widened, but instead of my ol' man barking at him because of his comment, he simply shook his head.

"Mom helped?" I asked, looking at my dad before Marek. I'd heard comments here and there, but no one ever went into any details, and because I knew they'd never elaborate, I figured it was pointless to ask, after the first ten times, anyway. Come to think of it, it did seem like my mom and Tripp had a special relationship, nothing inappropriate, but if she was the reason Tripp didn't die, then I could see why they appeared to care for each other.

"Your mother helped us out a lot back then, patching up these bastards whenever shit went down," Prez responded, looking surprisingly comfortable in revealing all sorts of details now. "She was a godsend for sure." I leaned forward in my seat, eager for more information, every question I ever had about what our club dealt with before I came along on the precipice of being sated. "When we finally decided to hit back, and hard, we raided their club, killing whoever we could before kidnapping Psych's daughter." Marek looked at Kaden. "Your mother. Then I married her the next day, essentially sending the biggest 'fuck you' I could to the Reapers. Integrating one of their own was one of the worst kinds of insults between clubs, so to wed the rival president's daughter was highly offensive."

I couldn't help but think about the similarities between what happened with Sully and what I'd done by taking Maddie from the same club, albeit different members. It was only then that Tripp's comment of "just don't marry her," made a lick of sense.

"I can imagine that didn't go over well," Brick said, eager to hear more, just like me, Kaden, and Ace.

"Not at all," Cutter responded, something that took me off guard because the man didn't say much. But the look on his face told me whatever happened next, he wasn't opposed to. Maybe even enjoyed? I remembered the coldness in his eyes when he stood over Tag.

"While Sully adjusted quickly to our club, and to me, her father wanted her back. Most likely so he could kill her. I wasn't gonna let that happen, especially after I'd fallen in love with her, and she with me." Marek lowered his eyes to the table, gripping the edge so tightly he lost most of the color in his hands. "The things they did to her while she lived with them...."

"You don't have to rehash that, brother," our VP said, placing his hand on Marek's shoulder as a show of support.

"No, I have to. To make these guys understand why we did what we had to. Exacting justice for someone changes you, gives you purpose. To right the wrongs is the only outcome that's acceptable." I didn't need to ask him what he meant because his words resonated deep in my soul, the image of Maddie infiltrating my brain. "That piece of shit Psych raped and abused his daughter before passing her off to Vex when she was fourteen. He took over making her life as miserable as possible. Sully bears the reminders of what they did to her, physically and emotionally. They burned her with cigarettes, stabbed her, raped her, passed her off to Carrillo's righthand man, Yanez, as an offering. Everything horrible you can imagine... they did to her." Marek looked at his son again. "Vex is the reason your mother could never have children of her own." For a moment, Marek's breathing became shallow, a pained look crashing over his face. The rest of the resident members hung their heads. "During one of his tirades, he violently raped her with a bat after he could no longer do it himself, leaving her tied up for a day to bleed out. There was too much damage afterward for her to ever bear a child of her own."

My eyes flew to Kaden, wanting to say something, anything that might lessen the impact of what his dad just told him. The two of us knew Vex abused her, but we didn't know the severity until now. Hearing what his mother went through made me want to hurt someone. I could only imagine how Kaden felt. His shoulders tensed right before he gripped his hair, leaned back in his chair, and briefly raised his head to the ceiling.

Oddly, Cutter was the one who placed his hand on Kaden's shoulder, much like my ol' man had done with Marek moments ago.

"She's okay now," the old guy said. "Sully is one tough broad."

"That she is," Jagger added. His lips thinned into a tight smile. There was a brief moment of silence, and I wasn't sure if it was because the conversation was uncomfortable for everyone present, or if Marek tried to gather his next words. Maybe it was a combination of both. Either way, he soon continued with specifics from the past.

"We tortured and killed Yanez, Vex, and Psych, sending them to hell where they belonged, and each one of them knew exactly why. The one connection they had between them was what ended their lives in the end." As if feeling his confession wasn't enough, he rose from his seat and walked up behind Kaden. "I made them all pay, son." He rested his hands on Kaden's shoulders. "I made sure they suffered till they took their last breath." Kaden's eyes glassed over as did Marek's.

His ol' man cleared his throat before retaking his seat.

"After hiding this from us all these years, why now? Why is it okay we know everything that happened?" I asked, my curiosity getting the better of me.

"Because we didn't want you guys," he said, referring to me, Kaden, Ace, and Brick, "to be tainted with what we had to do back then. We did it because we wanted to end the war between us and the Reapers, to stop looking over our shoulders every time we left this compound, to stop losing members of our club at their hands. We wanted a better life for our kids, and whoever else came into the club well after that shit was done and over. The only things you had to worry about were school and girls. You didn't have to wonder if at any point during the day your life would either be snatched from you or you'd be the one to end someone else's. I now see we did a disservice by not telling you. If you'd been armed with the details, you would've known the detriment of what could happen if that war started back up."

"Which we think it has," Ryder grumbled.

"Because I took Maddie," I said, a declaration and not a question.

"Yeah," Marek answered. "After looking at her, I understand why you did it, but I have no doubt they will retaliate. They'll either want her back or—"

"I can't hand her back over to them," I spit, my anger doing a shit job at staying hidden, erupting before I could control myself.

"No one is sayin' that," my ol' man interrupted just as hurriedly. I relaxed, but only a fraction.

"If they were the ones who set the fire at Indulge because of a scuffle, what the fuck do you think they're gonna do knowing we took their plaything from them?" Hawke asked, his reference to Maddie as a *plaything* fueling my anger even more.

"Exactly. And when I spoke with her, she mentioned Dutch," Marek said. Jagger, Trigger, and Ryder groaned while Cutter and Hawke sported an odd grin I didn't understand.

"That fucker's nuts," Tripp mumbled, but we all heard him loud and clear.

"Who's Dutch?" Brick asked.

"He's one of 'em, but from a different charter," Marek replied. "Although he's been spending more time here than back in Tucson. He rivals Psych in delusion and amusement with torturing women. If he hadn't been mentioned, I wouldn't be as worried but now... now we gotta prepare ourselves, which means making sure you four are carrying from now on."

We all knew how to shoot, had been visiting our makeshift range behind the clubhouse for a couple years, but we never had a reason to carry before today. In fact, we were forbidden to have our guns on us whenever we left the clubhouse lot. To be honest, I didn't mind because while I was a damn good shot, I didn't care much for the weapon. I could give or take it, preferring to use my fists. But now I'd be sure to follow the change in instruction and be strapped from here on out.

Marek cleared his throat and sat up straighter. "On to the issue with Tag." My ears perked up at the mention of the guy who could possibly be a Reaper. Last I knew he was still tied up in that basement, but things could've changed.

"We don't believe he's a Reaper, even though he comes from one." Our leader spewed out the words as if they pained him, and after hearing the details of what Tag's father, Vex, did to Sully, I could partially understand his distaste for Tag. But, like he just said, he wasn't a Reaper.

"Are you sure?" Hawke asked, tucking his hair behind his ear and leaning forward. He looked pissed at the news, and from what I remembered of how he acted in that basement, I could guess the nomad wanted to revisit old wounds.

"Yeah. We had guys we trust dig into his past to see if the story he told Kaden and Linc was true. These same guys have been keeping an eye on the Reapers for years, and none of them have ever seen Tag before, indicating he hasn't been around the rest of them. He did check out as having a job back in Boston, attending grade school, then high school there as well as college. We even went so far as to visit his mother, and while she didn't know us personally, she knew who we were. She confirmed she wanted to get him as far away from his father because he was a bad man."

"Did she wonder why you were there to see her?" Ace spoke that time.

"Yeah, she did. We told her he wanted a job with us, and we liked to vet everyone who applied."

"She didn't think that was weird?" I asked.

"No, but then again she was high. She told us about the cancer and how she needs to smoke because of the chemo treatments. This actually works to our advantage because she doesn't even realize her son hasn't been around. She told us he came by the other day for a visit, which is obviously impossible since we have him."

"Okay, then we can let him go," Kaden rushed to say, glossing over everything Marek just said.

"Well... that's where it gets tricky," my ol' man added. "We didn't exactly treat him well, and we basically admitted to killing his father, so..."

"So... what?" I asked, hoping to God he didn't suggest killing Tag because they fucked up.

"Read between the lines, man." Jagger leaned forward and stared at me. "If we let him go, he can cause an issue for us."

"So, you're gonna kill him?" I looked to Jagger, then to my ol' man, then to Marek, my pulse loud and thrumming in my ears.

"We don't know yet."

I ran my hand over the top of my head, releasing the air in my lungs before forgetting how to breathe for a moment. "Can you at least tell us if he's still strapped to that table? He's been there for days."

"I'm fully aware how long he's been there," Marek answered, irritation pouring out of him and toward me, but I wasn't the one who jumped to conclusions, and I certainly wasn't the one who beat the poor guy before divulging our club had killed his father. Although, the latter part I doubted he'd care much about. But what the hell did I know? "Nash, Miles, and Rez are here. They're taking turns making sure Tag doesn't go anywhere until we decide what to do with him." I didn't need to ask if Tag had been released from his restraints because Marek's statement answered my unasked question. My guess would be that they had him contained to one of the bedrooms.

All three men were members of our Laredo charter. I'd met Nash and Miles many times, and I could attest that both men were loyal and the epitome of what a Knights member encompassed. Rez, on the other hand, I'd only met once, so I couldn't properly form an opinion about him yet. He was younger than the other two, somewhere in his early thirties, I believed.

I'd continue to be on edge where the issue with Tag was concerned, praying for a resolution that didn't result in his death. If Marek decided to go down that road, however, could I live with knowing that I had a part in killing an innocent man, even if I didn't commit the act myself?

## Lincoln

"I think that's enough for today," Marek announced, slamming the gavel down before anyone could say anything else.

I could only imagine how hard it was for him to tell us the details of what happened to his wife. From the pained look on his face and the tension in his form, revisiting that sordid past was the last thing he wanted to do, but I was happy he stopped keeping things from some of us. Okay... happy was the wrong word, but I felt empowered having the information because I now knew what types of people we were up against. And while I was fully aware that the Reapers were soulless bastards, and the club that existed today didn't have the same members from long ago, they seemed to carry the same morals, or lack thereof.

Everyone had left Chambers except for me, Kaden, Marek, and my ol' man. While I wanted to rush to check on Maddie, I needed to make sure my friend was okay first.

Kaden slowly rose from his seat, Marek coming to stand next to him. "Your mom isn't volunteering today. Go see her.

You'll see she's okay." Kaden nodded, a solemn expression twisting his features. "Don't let her know you're aware of all the details. I don't want her thinkin' about what happened or worried about you now that you know. She's been through enough."

Sully volunteered at a domestic violence shelter, her need to help people who had been abused unfortunately making perfect sense to me now.

"I understand," his son replied before turning toward me. "Go with me?"

"Of course. Let me check on Maddie first."

"Okay, I'll meet you outside."

"Grab your gun before you go," Prez shouted after him before he was out of earshot.

"I'll make sure we have them before we leave here." I walked out to the common area and while I didn't want anyone in the room with Maddie—my protectiveness over her becoming stronger all the time—I didn't want to leave her isolated back there until I returned because I had no idea how long Kaden wanted to spend with his mom. And I wasn't gonna rush him. "Ace, can you come with me?"

He jogged up next to me. "What's up?"

"Can you check in on Maddie while I'm gone with Kaden?"

"Yeah, I can do that." He stopped walking while I continued down the hallway. When I noticed he wasn't beside me any longer, I turned to search for him.

"Are you comin'?" He looked at me like I was a stranger. "I know she's seen you before, but I don't need you scaring her if you were to go in there by yourself later." He frowned but didn't move. "Just come on," I yelled, frustrated he wasn't making this any easier on me.

"Jesus, Linc. What the fuck's up your ass?" He was behind me several strides later, but I ignored his question. I should, in fact, ask him the same thing, but I had an idea. Not only was he probably trying to digest everything we found out, but he had his own issues with a certain female.

Knocking on the bedroom door like I'd been doing, I entered shortly after I heard her say, "Come in."

"Hey. How ya doin'?"

"Fine." She looked from me to Ace and back again, swallowing before parting her mouth. I tried not to, but I stared at her lips a little too long. Ace made a noise beside me, winking when I glanced his way. *Fucker.*

"Turns out I have to go somewhere with Kaden, but until I get back, Ace here is gonna check on you from time to time to make sure you don't need anything."

Maddie forced an awkward grin at the news, but at least she didn't appear frightened. Her beautiful green eyes roamed over Ace from head to toe, her attention on him innocent but pissing me off all the same, a feeling I kept quiet.

"I won't be long. You can come out to the common area if you want. There's a TV out there, a bar, kitchen if you're hungry. Or you can stay back here. Your choice." I gave her a faint smile, all the while hoping she chose to stay in this room alone rather than out there with Ace and whoever else might be hangin' around.

"Okay" was all she said, no definitive answer on her plans either way.

"Okay," I repeated before turning Ace around and pushing him out of the room, closing the door behind me. I grabbed his arm before he took another step. "Don't scare her. Don't touch her, and don't let her out of your sight if she comes out here."

"That's a lot of instructions. You wanna write 'em down?"

"I mean it, Ace. Just don't."

He threw up his hands. "I get it, man. She's yours. No one's gonna mess with her in any way."

"She's mine?"

"Obviously," he answered, disappearing before I could argue.

Did I even want to?

## Maddie

"Hey, pretty lady. Wanna join me for a drink?" The man who asked me to consume alcohol with him at two in the afternoon was the biggest man I'd ever seen. The stool he sat on looked like it was a miniature piece of furniture under his weight. Muscular, broad, intimidating, all these words described him well, and even though he was sitting when I walked up, I had no doubt he was extremely tall.

He was handsome, his dark hair short and styled close to his scalp, his beard neat and trimmed. And while his brown eyes were nice, they didn't compare to Lincoln's, which were soulful. I realized I sounded ridiculous thinking such a thing, but when Lincoln looked at me, I sometimes forgot where I was or how I came to be in his company.

I made brief eye contact with the man but then looked down at the floor. And that's when I heard what I could only assume was him slapping the top of the stool next to him.

"I don't bite." I wanted to engage him, but my fear of strangers urged me to remain quiet. When I eventually picked my head up, he winked at me before turning his attention to an older man who walked behind the bar. "Trigger, can you get her a shot?"

"I can't drink," I blurted, taking a single step toward him, placing my hand on the edge of the bar top. "I'm only eighteen." I'd only had a drink a handful of times in my life, all with girlfriends of mine at school, and learned quickly hard alcohol by itself wasn't for me.

His hearty laugh and big smile made me relax a fraction, some of my nerves from having decided to come out of the room fading away.

"I don't think anyone is gonna tell on ya, sweetheart," he said, patting the stool next to him once more. After a few more controlled breaths, I finally moved forward and sat down. He shifted his stool over a bit to give me more room before extending his hand "I'm Brick."

I stared at his palm for a few seconds before I placed my hand in his, the warmth of his touch melting away the rest of my reserve.

"I'm Maddie." My voice wasn't as loud as I wanted it to be, but he heard me all the same.

"So how about that shot?"

"I don't like hard liquor." Was I gonna upset him with my refusal? Fumbling over my next words, realizing what I said would probably be construed as an insult, I added, "It makes me sick. But if you want me to drink it, I will."

"Why would I want you to do something you don't want to?" Brick genuinely looked confused, the pull of his eyebrows creating an indent in his forehead. This was so far outside my element I didn't know how to answer his question, but luckily, he threw another one at me before the interaction between us became any more awkward. "How about one of them fruity drinks, then? Do you like those?" I shrugged, not remembering ever having what it was he was talking about. He flicked his attention back to the gray-haired man. "Can you make her a mixed drink? Something girly?"

"What the fu—" The older guy looked at me and twisted his features. "Sorry 'bout that." He turned his focus back on Brick. "Do I look like I know how to make a girly drink?"

"Well...."

"Keep it up and that's the last beer you're gettin' today." He was in front of me in two steps, extending his hand in greeting like Brick had done moments ago. "I'm Trigger." I shook his hand and told him my name, which I was sure he heard me tell Brick. "Okay, Maddie. I think I can whip up something. Let me see what I can do." He moved toward the other end of the bar and bent down. Not wanting to put him out, I leaned forward to tell him he didn't have to make me anything, and the stool slid back.

"Whoa," Brick said, catching my arm before I fell on my ass. "Careful. If you get any new bruises on ya, Linc is gonna beat my ass."

A couple things about what he said baffled me. Firstly, why would Lincoln be that upset I'd fallen that he'd go after Brick? And secondly... the image made me chuckle to myself. While Lincoln was a trained fighter, besting his opponents in the few fights I'd been dragged to, the sheer size of Brick compared to Lincoln was laughable. Then again, sometimes the big ones weren't coordinated enough and were too slow.

"What's goin' on in that head of yours?" Brick bumped my shoulder with his before taking a healthy sip of his beer.

"You'd squash Lincoln." The words left my mouth before I could stop them. I meant to leave them floating around inside my brain, but apparently, I gave them life.

"What?" He tilted his head to the side and stared at me.

"You said that Lincoln would beat your ass if I got any new bruises." My eyes raked over him. "You're the biggest man I've ever seen, and unless you're oddly clumsy, you'd squash him." I hoped my blunt comment didn't offend him in any way.

"Probably." He raised his head in faux cockiness, or maybe it was real, and laughed. "But I've been in the ring with him a time or two, and the man's got some skills. He got in a few good shots," he said, pointing to the side of his face. Brick finished the rest of his beer at the same time Trigger placed a tall glass of yellow liquid in front of me.

"We don't have much back here. Hope you like this," he said, wiping down the corner of the bar afterward. I stared at the glass but didn't reach for it, the small voice in my head roaring to life and shouting, *What if he drugged it?* I couldn't help it. I didn't believe any amount of reassurance from Lincoln or from the women who visited me, or even from these guys, acting as nice as could be, would ever tear away my reservation completely. "Take a sip," Trigger urged. "Tell me what you think." He folded his arms over his chest, his mouth curving up into a smile. If I hesitated too long, would I be punished in some way?

"I'll taste it first to make sure he didn't make it too strong." Brick grabbed my drink, moved the straw out of the way, and took a gulp. "That might be a bit too much for her." He put my drink back in front of me. "What do ya think?"

I wasn't sure if Brick picked up on the reason for my hesitation, but I was thankful to him for trying to put my mind at ease.

Wrapping my fingers around the cool glass, I brought the straw to my lips and took a tentative sip, the mixture of sweet and tanginess hitting my tongue, then sliding down my throat. After my first swallow, I wanted more, so I took another sip, then another before placing the drink back on the bar.

"That's really good. What is it?" I wanted to have some more but didn't want to seem greedy, so I folded my hands in my lap and waited for Trigger to at least answer me before I attempted to devour the rest of it.

"It's called a screwdriver. Nuthin' but orange juice and vodka." He saw me eyeing up the glass. "I'll make you another when you're finished." Trigger winked before walking away, stopping to talk to Ace before disappearing into the kitchen.

Reaching forward, I snatched my drink again, the clink of the ice cubes sloshing some of the contents forward, but luckily not spilling any over the rim. "This is good."

"Drink up, woman," Brick chuckled. "He'll make you as many as you want." He angled his large body toward me, looking me over but not in a lecherous way. "So, what do you think of Linc? You like him?"

His question took me by surprise. What was the right answer? If I told him that I'd been dreaming about Lincoln every night since he rescued me, would that make me seem more desperate than I was sure they already thought me to be? And if I feigned indifference, would he think me to be unappreciative, passing along his thoughts to Lincoln? Maybe even convincing him I was no longer welcome?

"It's not a trick question, Maddie."

"Um..." I parted my lips, but then sucked down a few hefty gulps of the concoction in front of me before answering. "Yeah, I like him. He's nice and has been so caring. He's sweet."

"He's sweet on you," he replied, smirking when my eyes widened. "He put this whole club in jeopardy to help you, to save you from them." He nodded, like he was having an internal conversation. Brick's demeanor switched from playful to serious in the blink of an eye, but before I could respond—and say what I had no idea—he switched back. "You're beautiful. Why wouldn't he be?"

"Beautiful?" The question popped out of my mouth on a reflex of disbelief. I'd been called cute and pretty but never beautiful, and even though Brick had paid me such a high compliment, I didn't get the feeling he was hitting on me. Although, I wasn't so good at reading guys, the reminder I had to be rescued from the Reapers compounding that notion.

"Who's beautiful?" Ace asked, strolling up behind me, then taking the seat to my left, leaving me sandwiched between two of the members of this club. Two men I didn't know. Two people I oddly wasn't frightened of.

"I was talkin' about Maddie," Brick replied, motioning to Trigger when he came out of the kitchen, pushing his empty beer bottle forward to be replaced.

"You want another?" the old guy asked, to which I nodded emphatically, swallowing the rest of my screwdriver and enjoying every single drop.

"Don't let Linc hear you tell her that." Ace shook his head when Trigger picked up a bottle of beer and flicked his chin toward him.

With my second drink in hand, my eyes bounced between the two men beside me. While I found them both attractive, my thoughts kept reverting to Lincoln. Not only did I think he was sexy, but I felt safe whenever he was around, a notion I hadn't experienced in more time than I cared to admit.

"Hey, let me ask you something." Ace moved his seat closer, bumping my leg with his. "You're a girl."

I looked down at myself, then back at him. "Last I checked." My straw had somehow become glued to my lips, a steady stream of orange juice and vodka disappearing before my very eyes.

"What does it mean when a chick sleeps with you and is clearly interested, but then won't agree to anything more?" I thought he was finished, but he held up his finger and kept going. "And when I mention that maybe I'm gonna mess around with other people since she clearly doesn't want anything more with me, she gets all pissed off and starts screaming about how much of an ass I am and that she should've never got with me in the first place."

Based solely on looks, whoever this girl was he referred to was crazy not to want to be with him. While I couldn't quite figure out what color his eyes were exactly, the mixture of blue and green too close to determine, it was the faint dimple in his left cheek that showed whenever he talked that I was sure drew a lot of attention from the opposite sex. His hairstyle was longer than Brick's, while still being short, the color a shade lighter than Lincoln's.

"What the fuck, man?" Brick asked. He looked like he held back a laugh but also appeared confused by Ace's outburst, much like me.

"What? She's a chick. She knows how they think."

"I have no idea," I rushed to say, slurping the rest of my drink through the straw. "I've never had sex with anyone I wasn't made to." My admission didn't sound as harsh out loud to me as it did inside my head, this yummy drink probably the reason why.

"Fuck," Ace grumbled, scratching the back of his head. "I'm sorry, Maddie. I didn't mean to.... Shit!"

"You're an asshole," Brick shouted, reaching over me to punch him on the arm. Ace nearly fell off his seat, catching his balance at the last second.

"I wasn't thinkin'."

"You're damn right you weren't." Brick's expression softened when he looked at me, clearly pissed at his buddy. But I knew Ace didn't mean anything with his question. How would he know I'd say what I did? I didn't even know I was gonna say something like that. The words just came out.

"It's okay," I said to Brick before turning to Ace. "It's okay," I repeated.

"I'm sorry," he apologized again before accepting that beer from Trigger.

---

An hour and a half later, after two additional drinks and three cold pieces of pizza, I was the bravest I'd ever been. Two hot guys seemed genuinely interested in what I had to say, and for once, I didn't fear they had an agenda or had thoughts for harming me in any way.

The more alcohol I drank, the more curious I became, asking them all sorts of personal questions. I learned that Ace's real name was Jaime, that he grew up in foster care, and he got his nickname from playing poker. Cards was his way of hustling people before he joined this club, his way in being he went to school with Kaden, two years ahead of him to be exact. Ace loved to talk, as was evident with all the information he told me. Brick, on the other hand, refused to tell me his real name. I suspected he didn't like it much. But he did tell me that he used to be a bouncer at one of the strip clubs they owned. Oh, and that he was thirty.

Trigger checked on me from time to time, reminding Ace and Brick to behave themselves, to which they would simply nod, occasionally tossing a wary glance at each other. Or, at least, that was my interpretation of the look they shared.

"My tongue is numb." I laughed, smacking my lips together to make a weird sound.

"That's because Trigger poured quite a few shots for you," Ace replied, shaking his head at me when my mouth popped open dramatically.

"I didn't have any shots."

"What do you think is in your drinks?" When I stared at him like the proverbial deer in headlights, his grin got bigger, that damn dimple popping out. Or should I say sinking in? "Vodka." He answered his own question. I stuck my finger in the remainder of my drink, pulled it out and put the digit in my mouth.

"It's good," I said, draining the rest of the contents. Trigger was back in front of me with another, only this time the color of the concoction was clear.

"It's water. You gotta drink up or else you're gonna have a nasty headache later." The old guy walked away to tend to something else, leaving the tall glass of water a fingertip's reach from me.

"You're not feelin' any pain, are ya?" Brick asked, leaning closer, his scent infiltrating my senses and making my head swoon. He smelled good.

"Nope. And I gotta tell ya," I mumbled, slapping his arm. "It's refreshing."

"At least here, you don't have to worry—"

"Shit!" Ace groaned on the other side of me.

"What?" his buddy asked, never finishing his sentence.

"Linc." Ace pointed toward the door. "He's comin' over here and he doesn't look happy."

# Twenty-Three

## Maddie

"Lincoln's here?" I hadn't realized I yelled my question until I saw Brick jam his finger in his ear as a joke, although the amused look he had on his face disappeared the second Lincoln walked up next to him.

"What's goin' on here?" Lincoln glared at his friends, but his eyes softened when they fell on me. "Maddie? You okay?"

"Never been better." My speech was sluggish, and my vision blurred when I turned my head too quickly, but otherwise, I had no complaints.

"That's good." He looked at the empty glass in front of me. "How many of those have you had?" I couldn't tell if he was upset or curious. After all, he was the one who told me I could come out of the room, even going so far as to remind me there was a bar.

I held my hand in front of me and started counting, my fingers flying up until I hit the total. "Four." Extending my arm, my hand was inches from his gorgeous face, the sudden intrusion into his personal space making his eyebrows quirk upward. I lowered my arm and rested my hand in my lap while I studied him.

Lincoln was stunning, from the style of his hair to his gorgeous eyes, to his full lips, to his amazing physique. And the way he looked after me, first by saving me, a stranger, from their club's enemy, then making sure I was as comfortable as possible, both physically and emotionally. There were no words to describe how much I liked him, feelings that were still unfolding inside me. My attraction toward him was more than his good looks. It might be the alcohol talking here, but I thought I could see his soul.

He lifted the glass and smelled it, then took a sip, although all that remained was ice. Looking toward Trigger, he asked, "What were your givin' her?"

"Screwdrivers. I only put a shot in each."

"She only weighs like ninety pounds, ol' man. Didn't you think that might be too much for her?" Lincoln placed his hand on the bar and leaned toward Trigger, but the moment I grabbed his arm and tugged, he spun his attention back on me.

"I asked him for them. Don't be mad." I pulled on his arm a bit more until he completely faced me, his closeness making my head spin. Or was that the vodka? "He gave me food and water, too. To make sure I didn't get sick."

I could tell he didn't want to, but he smiled and relaxed, rubbing the top of my arm. "I'm happy you got out of the room."

"Me too." I leaned closer to him and said, "Brick said I'm beautiful." I thought I whispered those words, but apparently, I didn't because I heard Brick curse under his breath next to me.

"He did, did he?" Lincoln looked past me and shot his friend daggers.

"Yup." Since I was being brave, I asked him a question I never would have otherwise, but being tipsy, okay... probably drunk, gave me the courage, and nerve, to find out what Lincoln thought of me. "Do you think I'm beautiful?"

I tried to focus on his face, but I saw two of him. I lowered my gaze and waited for his answer, one which hopefully wouldn't completely dash all hope I still had left.

"Of course, I do. You're the most beautiful thing I've ever seen."

I didn't take offense to the word "thing" because that meant he viewed me as the most beautiful of all the females, all the sunsets, and of all the flowers.

"So, you think I'm a flower," I mumbled, dipping my fingers into my glass and pulling out a piece of ice, the frozen water melting some before I even put it in my mouth.

"A flower?" He didn't give it much thought before he replied, "Sure. You're a flower. Now, how about we get you back to the room so you can lie down for a bit?"

"Okay." I didn't resist, because although I had a surprisingly good time with his friends, I wanted to be alone with him.

I shifted in my seat and planted my feet on the ground, but when I stood up, I was a little wobbly. Lincoln held my arm until I found my footing, lowering his hand until he clasped mine in his, leading me away from the others. Before we got very far, though, Trigger stepped in front of him, and because he stopped abruptly, I ran into him. I smelled him like some kind of crazy person, but fortunately, I didn't think he noticed.

"She's not in complete control of her faculties," the old guy said. "Watch yourself."

"What kind of person do you take me for?" Lincoln's voice was low but angry, like he tried to control his tone so as not to frighten me.

"I know you're sweet on her."

*That's the second time someone said he's sweet on me.*

"I'm not an asshole, Trigger." Lincoln huffed, released my hand, and guided me toward the hallway, his hand resting on my lower back and warming me more than any alcohol could do.

"What did he mean?"

"He's worried about you. That's all."

"Are you mad?"

"Not at you," he replied curtly, shutting the door behind me as soon as we entered the room. I headed toward the bed, feeling like I needed to sit down, while Lincoln leaned against the dresser, watching me the entire time.

Every thought I had scrambled into the next. I wanted to thank him again for saving me. I wanted to ask him about this club, about his family. I wanted to hear him say he thought I was beautiful a thousand more times.

"My mom called and said she'll be here soon to check on you." He smiled. "She likes you."

"I like her, too. Did you know our names rhyme?"

His lips turned up in a shadow of a smile. "I suppose they do."

Switching topics completely, I blurted, "Brick smells good, but I prefer you," before getting to my feet. I wasn't as wobbly as I had been when I first vacated my barstool, my legs working much better this time around. Even though I had my bearings, Lincoln reached for my arms, his touch soothing yet exciting.

"You prefer me? Because I smell better than Brick?" His eyes narrowed, but the hint of his smile remained.

Leaning closer, I breathed him in. "Different. Good. Like home." My words didn't make much sense to me, so I could only imagine how they sounded to him, but I only repeated what my brain managed to concoct.

I stepped into him, and he stiffened, lowering his hands from my arms and resting them at his sides. At first, I thought I'd misread the interaction between us and was embarrassed, but then he wrapped me in a welcoming hug.

"Maddie." My name never sounded so good before.

"Do you really think I'm beautiful?" I searched for the compliment even though he'd already told me he thought I was.

Call it insecurity.

Call it low self-esteem.

Call it whatever… I wanted to hear his answer again.

When I looked up at him, he lowered his face, his mouth several inches from mine. His tongue swept over his bottom lip, the sheen of wetness glistening… teasing.

"Yes." I almost forgot I asked him a question, focusing on his mouth before I lifted my gaze and looked deep into his eyes. There was some sort of emotion laced behind them, but I couldn't sort out what it was exactly. Compassion? Desire? Intrigue? Although I would've expected to see pity again, there was none.

Seconds passed with us staring at each other, and under other circumstances, I would've felt awkward under the microscope, but sharing such intimate space with Lincoln fueled my need to connect with him. Unsureness fell to the wayside.

Leaning up on my tiptoes, I pressed my lips against his and at first, he didn't move, his only reaction to my boldness was a quick pull of air. I counted the seconds, and if he didn't kiss me back, I would pull away.

One…

Two…

Lincoln grabbed the sides of my face and pulled me closer, which I thought was near impossible, but he managed to capture my mouth with a firmness I'd only dreamed about. He tilted my head and begged for entrance with the tease of his tongue. Once I opened for him, our kiss turned frenzied. I followed his lead, exploring his mouth as he did mine, breathing his air into my lungs and feeling like if we stopped, I'd cease to exist. But as quickly as our kiss happened, he stopped it, moving back while still holding my face.

"I'm so sorry," he said, shaking his head and looking like he'd hurt me. "You've been drinking. I should've never kissed you."

Hearing what sounded like regret in his voice, I pulled my head back, and his hands dropped. "Did I not do it right?"

"What?"

"That was my first kiss. Did I not do it right?" Sudden embarrassment stole over me, tamping down any shamelessness I'd felt. I'd seen some of my girlfriends kiss their boyfriends before, and I had hoped I'd emulated what I'd seen. But maybe I failed.

"What do you mean that was your first kiss?" Lincoln looked at me like I'd grown a second head.

"I've never kissed anyone before." I thought my words were self-explanatory.

"How is that even possible? How old are you?"

"Eighteen, but my parents were super strict, especially my father. Being the daughter of a pastor didn't do anything for my appeal with the boys. Mix that with I attended an all-girls school, and there wasn't much opportunity for kissing. Then when I met Pike, I thought maybe he would be my first, but that didn't happen." I looked away for a moment when I said, "I prayed none of them would try and kiss me whenever they forced me. I wanted to keep something sacred. Besides, they weren't interested in that stuff. Only the...." Looking back into his eyes gave me a brief amount of comfort that he would understand, but when I saw him tremble, if only for a second, my nerves took over. "I'm sorry." Those two words were the only thing I could think of to say if he was, in fact, upset with me for whatever reason. Hopefully my apology was enough for him not to shut me out, in whatever way that meant.

"You don't have anything to be sorry for, Maddie. You didn't do anything wrong." He cradled my cheek in his hand when he spoke again. "And no, you didn't do it wrong. You were perfect."

He leaned closer, and I thought he was going to kiss me again, so I closed my eyes, but then his lips pressed against my forehead. Releasing a disappointed breath, I took a step back afterward.

"I thought maybe you wanted to kiss me. You said I was beautiful. I misunderstood." I turned to walk away, but he grabbed my wrist to stop me, pressing his chest flush to my back.

His warm breath spanned across the side of my face. "I did want to kiss you. I shouldn't admit this, but I wanna do everything with you, but I can't."

Without looking at him, I asked, "Why?" Was I ready to have sex with Lincoln, a guy I barely knew, simply because I desired him, especially after everything I'd been through? No. But did I see any harm in sharing a passionate kiss like the one we just had? Again... no.

"Because it's not right."

He gave me the answer I feared he would. Because of what his enemies did to me, he no longer saw me as decent, as worthy. My father always told me that if I was to ever have sex outside of marriage, I'd be considered dirty, and no one would want me otherwise. I now see he was right, even though I hadn't chosen to have sex with those men.

"I understand." I tugged my arm away from him. "Because of what happened, I'm no longer clean."

"That's not what I meant at all. I don't think that. I just can't—"

"It's okay. I should've never thrown myself at you." Tears blurred my vision, and I was thankful I wasn't facing him, but I needed to be alone, and I wasn't about to go back out to the common area with his friends, so my only option was the bathroom. I rushed into the small room and closed the door behind me.

"Maddie." Lincoln knocked on the door. "I'm sorry. That's

not what I meant at all. I want to kill every one of them for what they did to you." I heard a thud, but the sound didn't come from his knuckles. Instead, I believed he stood on the other side of the door with his forehead pressed against the wood. "But I'm not any better if I take advantage of you after all you've been through. Never mind you're drunk." Several curses flew freely from his mouth seconds before I heard the bedroom door slam shut.

With my energy depleted and the nice feeling of the alcohol waning, I slid down the wall until my butt hit the floor. Then I broke down and cried, releasing all the hurt, anger, and uncertainty swirling around inside me.

## Lincoln

When I pulled into the lot, Kaden didn't follow me. He rode off, needing to be alone after spending time with his mom, a visit that went better than I thought it would, especially after learning all the disgusting details of what happened to her all those years ago.

While we'd been at Sully's, I tried to be present, knowing my friend needed my support. The conversation revolved mostly around her son and Riley since that was the biggest thing to happen recently. Kaden was careful not to reveal anything about what we'd learned but did ask his mom if she was okay. She smiled and gave him a hug, her short bout of worry disappearing as to why he asked when he apologized for not being around more because of everything goin' on.

On the ride back all I could think about was Maddie, worried about whether she was scared without me there, only to find out she'd been havin' a good ol' time with Ace and Brick.

"Were you hitting on Maddie while she was out here drinking with you?" I stood directly in front of Brick, who continued to consume beer after beer. But because he was so big, the alcohol didn't seem to have much effect on him. I enjoyed a cold one as much as the next guy, but I didn't drink often, or should I say to excess because I was either training or competing in a fight.

"No, I wasn't hittin' on her. I asked her if she liked you, and during our conversation, I told her she was beautiful."

"First off, are we in high school? Asking her if she likes me? Why didn't you just pass her a note? And it sounds like a move to me, you tellin' her she's beautiful."

"It wasn't like that." The corner of his mouth lifted when I didn't have anything else to say on the matter.

I was pissed when I saw her sitting between Ace, who was only supposed to be checking on her, not fucking drinking with her, and Brick. The three of them seemed to be having a great time, and while I was upset I hadn't been able to get her to open up like they had, underneath it all I was happy she felt comfortable enough with them to relax a little.

"Is she feelin' okay? She seems to be a bit of a lightweight," Ace chimed in, reading something on his phone and not even bothering to look at me when he asked about her.

"Have you seen how tiny she is? I'm surprised she was able to drink what she did and still string a sentence together." Four mixed drinks weren't a lot to any of us, considering Trigger only used a shot per glass, but to Maddie, they had obviously had an impact, enough where she felt comfortable enough to kiss me.

Shock flared to life that she didn't shrink away from me, or from any of these guys; it told me what kind of fighter she was. After everything she'd been through, and I was sure I didn't know all of it, to continue to trust anyone of the opposite sex was astounding. Let alone guys who also belong to a motorcycle club, albeit we were completely on a different level than the Reapers, but she didn't know that. Not yet, at least, but she was learning to trust she would be safe with us.

"She's fine." Trigger walked up next to me and put his hand on my shoulder. "She needed a few drinks after the shit she's endured." He took a step back and flattened his expression, looking at me like he was skeptical all of a sudden.

"What?" His scrutiny made me uncomfortable, like I'd done something wrong.

"What'd you do?"

"I don't know what you mean?" Shifting my feet, a warmth traveled through me at the thought he might know what happened between me and Maddie. But how could he, and why had I felt guilty when I stopped the kiss?

"Did you do somethin'?"

"Like what?" I asked, praying he'd stop talking and leave me alone. I had enough guilt consuming me, I didn't need him judging me on top of everything else.

"Ya look like ya did somethin'. Did you take advantage of her?" It must've been the flick of my expression, but Trigger suddenly looked angry.

"She kissed me."

"I knew she liked you. She got all starry-eyed when I mentioned your name." Brick laughed. "But I think it's only hero worship or savior something or other."

"What the hell are you talkin' about?" Ace asked, peering around me so he could see the big guy.

"You know. When someone saves someone, and that person then forms some sort of bond with the person who saved them."

"You mean like Stockholm syndrome?" Trigger involved himself in their asinine back-and-forth.

"What the hell is wrong with you guys?" I hated they knew Maddie and I shared a moment, and I definitely wasn't gonna tell them that I was her first kiss, but what they were spewing only served to piss me off more than I was when I first came out here. "Stockholm syndrome is when you kidnap someone, and then they develop ill-placed feelings toward you."

"Didn't you kinda do that? Take her?" Brick looked too smug for my liking when he asked that question.

"No. Well... yeah, but—"

"Sounds like stalker syndrome to me," Ace said, giving me a halfhearted shrug.

I looked to each of them, waiting for any one of them to tell me they were joking, but all they did was shake their heads, as if they were disappointed in me, like I did something wrong where Maddie was concerned.

"Fuck you guys!" I shouted, walking away from them before I ended up hitting all three of them. Well, two of them. I wouldn't strike Trigger. He was an old man. Okay, maybe only one, since my hit wouldn't do much damage to Brick. *Fuck those guys.*

I thought I heard one of them laugh behind me, but my focus was now on my mom, who had just come into the clubhouse. She told me earlier she'd be back with the test results from Maddie's physical, and while I wasn't sure what kind of scene was gonna erupt with her being back so soon after scolding my ol' man, I needed to know if Maddie was gonna be okay.

As I opened my mouth to ask her what she knew, my dad barreled through the door, his sights set on his wife and no one else. He'd disappeared into Chambers immediately following their fight, but while I was gone, it appeared he'd gone outside somewhere because I hadn't seen him until right then.

He rushed up next to her and reached for her hand, but she stepped away before he made contact. "Addy." His tone was filled with warning, but if he knew anything at all, it was that my mom wouldn't cave because his voice was stern. If anything, he'd probably pissed her off more.

"I'm not doin' this right now. I have to go see Maddie."

He stepped in front of her, blocking her each time she tried to move around him, not a care in the world he had an audience. "I'm not stayin' here just because you're mad at me."

"You don't have to stay here." My attention bounced back and forth between them, my ol' man's expression softening when he heard that. "I'm sure Marek and Sully will let you stay with them for a while."

His eyes popped open, and he looked like he was ready to spit nails. "If you think for one second I'm gonna let you tell me—"

"It's done, Lincoln." She said *Lincoln* with such disdain, it made me feel guilty for having the same name. Then she turned her sights on me. "I need to talk to you." Her tone relaxed when she addressed me. "Come with me." She pulled me into one of the corners of the large room, not once glancing back at my dad to see what he was doing. I didn't dare look because, honestly, I didn't want to get involved.

"What is it? Is Maddie okay?" My pulse quickened at the thought there could be something wrong with her.

"She has a bladder infection, which is what I thought. I have some antibiotics for her, so she should start to feel better soon."

"Is there anything else?"

The way she looked at me made me nervous, but when she responded, "No," I released some of the tension I'd been holding onto. The possibility Maddie could've potentially been dealt more of a raw deal had weighed on me more than I thought possible, and even though I had no idea what those options could've been, my mom's words erased the worry.

Now I could focus on helping her heal emotionally from the trauma she'd suffered.

# Maddie

I heard voices next to the bed, and it took me a moment to realize I wasn't dreaming but instead had company. Prying my eyes open, a more difficult feat than I thought considering I'd only been resting for close to an hour, I saw Lincoln and his mom. They'd been talking low, but when they realized I was awake, they both stepped toward the bed.

Sitting up, I leaned against the wall behind me because there was no headboard.

"Hi, honey." Addy sat on the edge of the bed and patted my hand. She looked up at Lincoln before returning her focus onto me. "So, it was as I thought. You have a bladder infection, but that's easily taken care of." She reached into her bag and pulled out a pill bottle. "These are antibiotics." She handed them to me. "You'll start to feel better within a day or two."

Clutching the bottle in my hand, I said, "Thank you for helping me."

"Of course."

"And, now I have to use the bathroom." Addy stood,

allowing me room to get up. "I'll be right back." I caught Lincoln staring at me as I walked away. I really hoped he didn't hold my earlier boldness against me. I didn't know what I'd do if he started to ignore me, or worse, view me as a problem.

After I reemerged, I noticed the two of them huddled close and whispering, Lincoln's voice stern when he responded to whatever his mom said. I cleared my throat when they continued talking, not wanting to eavesdrop on their conversation but wanting to thank her again for tending to me so quickly.

Addy wandered a few steps closer, resting her hand on my shoulder.

"Is something else wrong?" I asked.

"No. I wanted to tell you that since your periods aren't regular, you can start taking the pill to fix that issue. You can be put on a low-dose estrogen, and if you have any issues, we can always switch you. If this is something you're interested in, you'd have to have an exam first. Have you ever had one before?

While I was naïve in many factors of life, I realized the exam she referred to was a gynecological one. "No, I haven't."

"Well, let me know if you want to go this route and I can set everything up for you."

I nodded before glancing at Lincoln, thinking that the moment our eyes met, I'd feel some sense of embarrassment because of the intimate topic, but I didn't. There was something about him that put me at ease, even while talking about womanly things.

"After everything you've been through, I'm happy you didn't end up pregnant on top of everything else. And you have a clean bill of health. Take the antibiotics and you'll be as good as new in no time."

"Thanks again," I said. My gratitude didn't seem enough for everything she'd done for me, but it was all I had.

"Of course, sweetheart." She turned to face her son. "Walk me out."

They both disappeared, closing the door behind them. Whatever she wanted to talk to him about was to be kept private; otherwise, she would've told him in front of me. But I couldn't wonder about what they were discussing. I wanted to focus only on the good news she'd given me, not that having a bladder infection was positive, but the fact I wasn't pregnant and hadn't contracted any diseases from those animals helped to erase some of the anxiety from simply contemplating the likelihoods.

A few minutes after they left, I heard Lincoln shout, "Mom! I know." They weren't far down the hallway. "Why does everyone think so badly of me?" He lowered his voice toward the end of his question, but his anger was apparent. I moved across the room, curious as to what was going on out there, but the door swung open before I could put my ear against it. And good thing too because he probably would've knocked me over.

Lincoln stood before me, his expression matching the tone I'd heard.

"Unbelievable," he muttered, entering the room before slamming the door. When he saw he'd startled me, he apologized. "I don't know why everyone thinks I'm gonna take advantage of you." He paced, his hand running over the top of his hair before dropping to his side. "I'm not an asshole." I retook my seat on the edge of the bed, watching him as he moved back and forth. His next words were jumbled together, not making a lick of sense to me, but I didn't think they were supposed to.

I didn't interrupt him, but after some time with still no words exchanged between us, my curiosity finally won out.

"What did your mom say that made you so upset?"

At first, he frowned, clearly contemplating on whether to answer my question. Then when his expression relaxed, followed by his posture, he leaned against the dresser and shoved his hands in his pockets.

"She told me that if we do anything, I should cover up."

Tilting my head slightly to the side, I asked, "What does that mean?"

He licked his lips, the corners of his mouth lifting slightly when he caught me staring. "It means that if we have sex, she wants me to wear a condom, which I would do regardless... if ever that happened... if you wanted to."

"Um... I... uh... I'm not sure—"

Lincoln was next to me before my brain could finish stringing my words together to form any sort of coherent sentence. "Maddie, I'm not saying we're gonna have sex."

"Oh. You don't want to do that with me?" I couldn't believe I was disappointed. I shouldn't ever want to think about having sex with anyone ever again. Not that what had happened between me and those bastards was sex, because it wasn't. But still, the intimate act, the vulnerability, the opening of myself to another, both physically and emotionally... it should be the farthest from my mind.

But Lincoln wasn't just anyone.

My heart told me he was someone special.

Maybe even *the* one.

Oh, who was I kidding? I couldn't trust myself to think or feel anything right now, even as my brain and heart battled. And at this point, I wasn't sure which one would come out on top.

"No. I mean, that's not what I'm saying." His chest expanded, the fabric of his shirt stretching over his defined muscles. "Of course, I want to. But after what you've been through, I would never expect you to want to be with me... in that way." Although the topic was touchy, I appreciated that he at least sounded nervous discussing it. I found it endearing. He cared about me, about how I felt, which only made me want to be that much closer to him in any way possible.

*Damn conflicting emotions.*

Thinking it would be safer to change the subject, I lost myself in the way he looked at me for a moment. The rich coloring of his irises drew me in so deeply I didn't want to look anywhere else. An emotion glimmered behind his entrancing gaze, but I couldn't readily decipher what it was. Adoration? Lust? Pity?

"Am I gonna have to leave soon?"

"Leave where? Here?" Before he allowed me to respond, he asked another question. "Do you want to leave?" The bed dipped when he sat next to me, allowing me to stop straining the muscles in my neck from having to look up at him.

"No." When he placed his hand on top of mine, I stiffened. "Sorry," I whispered, having no idea why I reacted like that. He moved to pull his hand away, but I caught his fingers with mine and entwined them. "I don't want to go anywhere." A ghost of a smile pulled at the edges of his mouth before quickly falling when I added, "I'm scared."

He wrapped his arm around me and pulled me into him, his scent calming my erupting nerves. "Don't be scared. I won't let anything happen to you." Part of me was desperate to believe him, but I'd witnessed firsthand how evil the Reapers were, and I would continue to fear them coming after me, even though I had a feeling Lincoln and his friends would do all they could to keep me safe. But in the end, only fate would know the outcome of my future, or lack thereof. "I got you," he continued to say, kissing the top of my head and holding me close. Wishing to escape the depths of my wayward thoughts, I wanted to sink into him, to disappear inside him so I would be safe from the world. Safe from my own mind, but the only thing I could do was to allow him to comfort me.

After several minutes, I pulled back, smiling at him to let

him know I was okay. "It's been a day," I half laughed. There wasn't anything amusing about my situation, but I was grateful I hadn't received devastating news. "I think I'd like to lie back down if that's okay."

"Of course." Lincoln kissed my temple, his lips lingering a few seconds longer than necessary, but I wasn't complaining. When he did finally pull away, he asked, "Can I get you anything? Are you hungry?"

"No. I had some pizza before."

"At least they had the sense to get something in your stomach, other than those drinks." His voice wasn't tense, but I saw the quick tic of his jaw.

"They were all nice to me. I wasn't afraid."

"That's good." He stared at me for a couple more seconds before standing.

"I'll be around if you need me."

"Thank you."

I crawled under the blankets after he left, and as my eyes drifted closed, the oddest question barreled through my brain. If I had the opportunity to go back in time, would I have still accepted the ride from Pike? Would I have subjected myself to the abuse of those men simply for the opportunity to meet Lincoln? A rational person would scream no, but something deep in my soul made me teeter between safety and... hell, I didn't know what the other feeling was. All I knew was that every time I set eyes on him, heard his voice, or felt his touch, my heart ached, and my instincts told me I belonged to him.

# Twenty-Six

## Lincoln

A week had passed and still the Reapers hadn't made a move. Not knowing where or how they were gonna strike only made everyone more on edge than they already were.

On top of everything else, Maddie seemed to be in a funk, not that I could blame her. She was dealin' with a lot, but at least she wasn't pregnant. I couldn't even imagine how devastating that would be for her if the test results had come back positive.

I checked on her often, even bringing her a television so she could stare at something other than the four walls shielding her from the rest of the world. Her appetite picked up, which I was happy about, but just when I thought we were making headway, she shut back down, uttering one-word answers every now and then. No two hours were the same. Sometimes she was sullen, and sometimes she acted like she didn't want me to leave her side. In the end, I took my cues from her moods, reacting accordingly and never pushing her to do or say anything I believed she wasn't comfortable with.

There were many times I thought about that kiss, although I didn't dare mention it for fear she'd tell me she regretted it.

---

"IF YOU DON'T SIT down soon, I'm gonna tackle your ass," Hawke grumbled, sitting on the sofa with a beer in hand. He looked a bit worse for wear, his hair messed, and his clothes wrinkled, looking like he'd been through the wringer.

The jury was still out on what I thought of him, but I had no energy to give to that right now. I needed to think of something to do for Maddie to cheer her up.

Simple ideas came to mind, from watching a movie with her to making her favorite food, whatever that might be. And by making her food, of course I meant ordering the dish from a local restaurant. I didn't want to give her food poisoning. Before I could decide on what would do the trick, my sister's name popped up on my phone... then an idea hit me full force, making me smile.

"Hello."

"Hey, is Dad still there?" she asked. I heard people talking in the background and assumed she was at work.

"I think he left about an hour ago. Why?"

"Can you check?"

Walking through the clubhouse, I checked all the bedrooms, minus the one Maddie was in, the kitchen, Chambers, and the two other rooms that were hardly ever used.

Making my way outside, I checked the garage, then looked around the wide-open space and still didn't see the man. "Nope, doesn't look like he's here. Why?"

No response to me, but I heard her talking to someone else. I waited impatiently while she finished her short conversation, but still, she didn't answer me.

"Riley!"

"Oh, sorry. Is he gone?"

"I told you yes. Why do you wanna know?"

She huffed, and I was two seconds away from hangin' up on her but didn't. "I wanted to stop by and check on Maddie. See how's she doin'. Poor girl is surrounded by male energy. I feel bad for her."

"Me too."

"I think you might feel somethin' else for her." The teasing in her voice irritated me, mainly because I wasn't completely sure of my feelings toward Maddie.

I thought she was beautiful.

I wanted to protect her because I felt responsible for her.

I was definitely attracted to her, as was proven by that kiss.

But did my feelings go beyond that?

Whenever I looked into her eyes, I wanted to grab her and hold her close, cursing the times we had to separate. I wanted to fight all her battles. I wanted to promise her everything would turn out fine, but I had no such knowledge of what the future held. She was safe with us, but could I guarantee she'd never be put in harm's way again? No, and that knowledge tore me up.

"Hello? Are you still there?"

"Yeah," I hurriedly answered, wondering if Riley would say something else about me and Maddie.

"Okay, I have a break between clients, so I'm gonna swing by soon."

"Why didn't you want to come by while Dad was here?" I asked a question I already knew the answer to.

"Because he's bein' a pain in the ass."

"What's new there?" The memory of the blowup last week was still fresh in our minds.

"Kaden's done with whatever it is he's doin'." Her tone dipped, sounding angrier than not. "And he said he'll be back in the garage in the next half hour. I just don't want another encounter like last time."

Instead of focusing on her worry, which was justified, I asked, "What's with the attitude about Kaden?" Typically, I didn't involve myself in their relationship, which I was still getting used to, but she sounded annoyed.

"I hate when he goes to those clubs."

"He has to, Ry. He needs to stop by to check on the status of the reno. The fire did more damage than we thought." I wasn't in the habit of discussing club business with my sister, but this information wasn't a big deal. Besides, it was because of my dumb ass that she'd been there when the fire broke out, so I wanted to give her an update, even though I didn't have to. Silence greeted me on the other end of the line. "He's not doin' anythin' there with anyone."

"I know. I still don't like it."

"I get it." There wasn't anything more I could say to her on the subject. "Hey, can you do me a favor?"

"We both know how well the last favor you asked me turned out."

"You ever gonna stop reminding me about that?" I wasn't upset at the dig.

"Probably not."

"Whatever." She chuckled, giving me the in to ask her what I wanted. "Do you think you can swing by the house and grab Maddie a few things to wear? She doesn't really have anything here."

"Sure. I think I have some stuff in the back of my closet that might fit her."

"And do you think I can bring her by the salon? Maybe you can pamper her a bit, take her mind off things?"

"Of course. I'll let her know when I get there."

"Thanks, sis."

We hung up as I saw Kaden driving back into the lot,

backing his bike into his assigned spot. When he cut his engine, I was next to him. "Ry's on her way over to see Maddie."

"I can only hope she's still not mad at me." Kaden dropped his helmet on his seat. "I can't help it if I have to do my fuckin' job," he grated, plucking his phone from the pocket inside his cut. "I can't pick and choose what I'm responsible for."

"You don't have to tell me."

"I love your sister like crazy, but sometimes I wanna sew her mouth shut." While I hadn't been privy to the details of their conversation, Kaden's comment, although not entirely serious, told me this wasn't the first time they'd argued, and it certainly wouldn't be the last. My sister was hardheaded, as was Kaden, and even though no one knew about their relationship from years ago, the two of them had always gone at it since we were kids. So, to hear him express his annoyance about Riley wasn't new.

"Try livin' with her."

"I am tryin'."

Apparently, no matter how aggravated he was with her, he still wanted her to move in with him. A few people had told him to slow down, myself included. One, because they just got back together and two, he didn't need to throw that in my dad's face so soon. Let the man calm down a bit before springing that on him. But Kaden didn't care. Patience was not one of his virtues.

My attention shifted when another bike turned into the lot. The cut was ours, but I couldn't readily tell who it was until he parked, killed the engine, and took off his helmet.

Rez, one of our brothers from the Laredo charter, the one helping to keep watch over Tag, swung his leg over his ride and strode toward us.

"Hey, guys," he greeted, shaking our hand one after the other. "Is Marek around?"

"He stepped out, but he should be back soon. You want

something to drink while you wait?" Kaden asked, walking toward the clubhouse. Rez followed, as did I.

"Sure. It's been a long fuckin' day already."

The Knights member from Texas had olive-tinted skin, his inky-colored hair long and wavy, a-few-days-old scruff covering his face. He was similar in height to me and Kaden, only an inch or so shorter. His build was thin, but I wouldn't classify him as lanky.

"Plans not lining up?" I was curious how things were going at the house where Tag was being held. Did he have free roam of the place while Nash, Miles, and Rez supervised, or was he confined to one room like I suspected?

"As good as can be expected," he responded, taking a seat at the bar. Trigger came out of the kitchen as Kaden and I joined Rez, the old man leaning forward and clasping his hand. "Haven't seen you in a bit."

"Yeah, not since the ruckus we had a few years back."

"That shit was crazy." Trigger laughed. "I don't think I slept for two days."

"That's 'cause you snagged some crazy pussy." He tied his hair back before accepting a beer from Trigger. "Shocking for an ol' bastard like you."

"Don't underestimate the draw of the gray," he said, sliding his hand over the top of his short hair.

"Did someone say somethin' about a ruckus?" Hawke took a seat two down from me and tapped the top of the bar. Trigger slid him a beer. "I fuckin' miss those."

"What's a ruckus?" I asked. I had somewhat of an idea but wasn't sure.

"A ruckus was the best throwdown of all time. An anything-goes type of party. No wives or girlfriends allowed, only party favors. Wannabes galore," Hawke said.

"Wannabes?" Kaden asked.

"A chick who wanted to be someone's ol' lady. But that

would never happen because ain't none of us givin' any bitch who slept with half the club that title." Hawke took a swig of his beer, wiping the corner of his mouth when some of the liquid came out too fast. "The good ol' days."

"If I remember correctly, you were shit at a ruckus," Trigger chided, throwing a dishtowel at Hawke. "Edana always caught your ass."

"That she did." Hawke laughed, but the sound quickly faded, a hazy look shadowing his eyes before his smile slipped.

"Speaking of," Trigger started. "Where is your ol' lady?"

"In Florida, visiting her sister. When Marek called and told me he wanted me here for a bit, I didn't want to leave her alone, not knowing exactly how long all this was gonna take."

"Well, tell her I asked about her."

Hawke tipped the head of his bottle toward Trigger and nodded. The mood seemed to have switched, resembling something somber, that was until Rez spoke up.

"We still have 'em," he said. "A ruckus is called for every now and again."

"Lucky bastard," Hawke and Tripp responded simultaneously.

"Why did we stop?" I asked, wondering why our club hadn't thrown one since I'd been part of the Knights. Come to think of it, I didn't ever remember the word ruckus ever uttered before.

"Before the war with the Reapers ended, we chose any excuse possible to throw one, realizing our lives could end at the drop of a hat. Live like tomorrow's not promised and all that shit," Hawke answered. "But then after we got rid of the threat, there really wasn't a reason to have one. Besides, all these fuckers," he said, pointing around the clubhouse even though there wasn't anyone else present beside us, "all wound up gettin' pussy-whipped and didn't want to have anything to do with the club whores anymore."

"And boy were those chicks disappointed." Trigger laughed.

"I had to do what I could to keep 'em happy." It was odd and unlike Trigger to talk so freely, and about sex of all things. But I supposed I couldn't fault the guy. He wanted it like the rest of us did.

"I can't listen to your old ass talk about that anymore," Hawke groaned. "Grab me another." He slid his second empty bottle toward the resident bartender.

Lost to idle chitchat, I didn't realize my sister had walked in until I saw Rez turn in his seat and whistle, drawing my and Kaden's attention. When we followed his line of sight and realized he was whistling at Riley, I hopped off my stool and stood in front of Kaden, who had stood as well, glaring at Rez.

"Who is that?" Rez asked, licking his lips and probably thinking some sordid shit about my sister.

"My woman," Kaden growled. When our visitor finally looked at my buddy, he threw up his hands but not before smirking.

"You're one lucky bastard."

"Hey, babe." Riley strode up to Kaden and kissed him, looking at me afterward, then at Rez. "Hi." She extended her hand. "I'm Riley. Kaden's girlfriend and Linc's sister." She seemed to be in a better mood than she projected over the phone. Apparently, whatever disagreement she'd had with Kaden had been put on the back burner or extinguished altogether.

He returned her greeting, thankfully not holding on to her hand any longer than was typical. "Rez. I'm visiting from Laredo." Cocking his head, he studied her for a second. "Wait. Are you the VP's daughter?"

"Yeah," she answered tentatively.

Then Rez's gaze danced over Kaden, and he laughed before he said, "Your pops has a temper. We heard about what happened when he found out you two were shackin' up."

Kaden bristled with anger, but Riley appeared composed.

"You guys are worse than women with the way you all gossip." She shook her head before leaning into Kaden, essentially calming the waters before they drowned in tension. "I have a bag of clothes in the car," she said, looking at me. "Can you grab them? Then we'll go see Maddie."

"Thanks. I'll be right back." The entire walk to her car, all I could think about was making Maddie happy, if only for a little while. And I hoped my gift to her would be enough to make her smile.

## Maddie

What's wrong?"

"I'm nervous."

"Have you ever been on one before?" Lincoln asked, twisting around to look at me, his sunglasses shielding his eyes. He sat on his bike with his helmet in place, so I couldn't readily see if he was upset with my hesitation to hop on behind him.

"Once. When Pike took me for a ride… back to his club." The memory seemed like a lifetime ago, yet gave me the chills because it had been less than a year.

His left hand rested on the handlebar, his fingers squeezing tightly when I mentioned the Reaper. I didn't want to upset him, but I didn't want to lie to him either. If we were going to forge ahead in whatever relationship there was to be between us, I shouldn't be afraid to tell him the truth, no matter how much he might not want to hear it. I was sure there would be plenty of times when I wouldn't want to answer, but if I'd been taught anything growing up, it was never to lie.

Nothing good had ever been born from dishonesty.

"Do you trust me?" He reached for my hand.

"Yes." And I did, without reservation.

"Then come on." I slid my palm into his, steadied myself, and swung my leg over the bike. "Put your feet right here," he said, reaching back and helping me. "Then scoot forward more. Yeah, right there. Now I need you to put this on." He handed me a black helmet, but mine was a full-face one, whereas his only covered his head. Once I clicked the strap under my chin, I rested my hands on my lap. Turning over the engine startled me, even though I saw him switch the position of the key. The deep rumbling both frightened and thrilled me, a mixture of emotions I'd never experienced before. Lincoln reached behind him and grabbed my arms, pulling them forward and wrapping them around his waist. In this position, I was so close to him, my body practically melded around his. "Hold on tight, and when I take a curve, lean into it with me." My entire body tightened at the thought I was gonna do something wrong and cause us to crash. He patted my leg, then gave it a light squeeze. "Don't worry, babe. You'll be fine."

*Babe?*

I didn't have time to dissect why he used that term of endearment before we were flanked on either side by Brick and his other buddy Kaden.

"You guys ready?" he asked, and after a nod from them both, Lincoln patted my hands and took off out of the lot. Once we were on the highway, he picked up speed but didn't go too fast, which I was thankful for. Something told me he would've broken some laws had I not been on the bike with him.

After several minutes, I relaxed, all while keeping a tight grip on his waist. I quickly learned why people loved to ride these things so much. The feel of the open air mixed with the rumbling of the machine beneath me gave me a sense of freedom, something I'd never experienced before. When I'd ridden with Pike, I hadn't experienced this calm, this exhilaration, and it was because I didn't know him. And because of this, I didn't trust him, which only made my ride with him tense. And although I hadn't known Lincoln long, there was an attraction I felt toward him, and it wasn't purely physical.

His stomach muscles contracted every time I moved my fingers, even an inch, and at first, I thought it was because I was griping him too tightly, but every now and again, he would reach back and touch my leg, caress the top of my thigh, and the notion I bothered him drifted away.

When his sister came by the club earlier, she brought some of her clothes for me, a gesture I appreciated more than she realized. I had to wear a belt with the jeans I wore because they were a little too big. But the shirt and sneakers she gave me fit better. Funny how a simple change of clothes did wonders to elevate my mood. On top of her generosity, she told me Lincoln wanted to bring me by the hair salon where she worked. She said he asked her to pamper me because he wanted to cheer me up. Hearing how much he cared about how I felt was enough, but I had to admit I looked forward to getting my hair done.

Whenever I started to think about what happened before Lincoln saved me that night, the vibration from the bike stole my thoughts and redirected my focus to the world passing us by. I wanted to live in this moment for as long as I could, and even surrounded by traffic, I felt a sense of calm. I didn't want our trip to end, but five minutes later, he pulled off the highway, made a few more turns, and pulled into a busy parking lot. His friends pulled up next to us, and the three of them shut off their bikes at the same time. I didn't realize how hard I'd been clinging on to Lincoln until I pried my hands away from his body, a slight ache making me stretch my fingers.

Reaching under my chin, I unhooked the strap and removed my helmet. "Did I hurt you?"

Instead of answering, he motioned for Brick to come over.

"What's up?"

"Can you help Maddie off the bike?"

"Sure, but why?"

*Was he mad at me? Did I do something wrong on the way here?"*

"Because I need a minute," Lincoln answered, practically growling at his friend.

Brick looked at him oddly for a second before chuckling. "Happens to the best of us, man." He picked me up and set me on my feet before I realized he'd even touched me.

"Go inside," Lincoln told me, shifting in his seat before biting his bottom lip. I even heard him huff.

"Are you mad at me?" The thought of him being upset with me for any reason troubled me. If only I knew what I'd done.

Brick placed his hand on the small of my back and ushered me toward the salon, but before I entered the building, I turned to look behind me. Lincoln stood next to his motorcycle, his hand adjusting the crotch of his jeans.

"Your man got a bit excited with you on the back," Brick said, and it was then I understood what happened. I couldn't focus on the fact that Lincoln was aroused, however, because my brain had wrapped around what Brick just said.

"My man?"

"Face it, sweetheart. You're his."

As soon as we entered the salon, Riley stopped what she was doing with her customer and came over to give me a quick hug.

"I'm so happy to see you, Maddie. Take a seat, and I'll be with you in a few minutes. I'm almost done here." There were three empty chairs against a nearby wall. I took the one on the end, closest to the door.

"I didn't know you'd be here," Brick said next to me, and when I looked up at him, I saw he was looking at the woman in Riley's chair. She was beautiful, her hair the most gorgeous shade of red I'd ever seen.

"I needed a trim."

"I'm sure you did." His words were innocent, but the way he said them made me shift in my seat. Brick leaned up against the desk near the door, his gaze on the redheaded woman the entire time. "Whatcha doin' after this?"

"I promised my dad and Braylen I'd stop by for dinner."

"Maybe I'll come with you."

"I don't think that's such a good idea," a blonde-haired woman replied, coming from the back of the salon and walking toward all of us. "You better watch yourself, Brick, or my husband is gonna be one pissy bastard, and I don't need two moody people in my house right now." She rested her hand over her belly before rubbing in a circular motion, and I could only assume from her gesture, and words, that she was pregnant.

While I wished to remain in the moment, I couldn't help but be thankful Griller and his men hadn't been able to steal another thing from me, more than they already had. I'd always dreamed of one day getting married and starting a family, and those options seemed to still be within my grasp.

Riley leaned over her chair and whispered something to her client, to which the woman shrugged before smiling.

"I have plans after dinner anyway. But we can meet up afterward," the redhead said to Brick.

"Zoe," the blonde woman said in warning. She looked back and forth between the woman, whose name I now knew, and Brick. "I hope you two know what you're doin'. You see what happened when Stone found out about Riley and Kaden. These guys don't take kindly to other Knights dating their girls."

"I'm grown. I can hang out with whoever I want." Zoe's brows rose. "Besides, even though my dad won't like it, he won't go after Brick."

"He can't do much damage even if he does," I blurted, slapping my hand over my mouth as soon as I finished speaking. What the hell was I thinking? I wasn't part of their conversation, and I had no right butting in. "Sorry," I said when I saw all eyes were on me.

"Yeah, what she said." Brick laughed, pulling Zoe off to a corner as soon as she vacated Riley's seat.

"Looks like you're up, Maddie."

The blonde woman who told him to watch himself brought me bottled water. "So, you're Maddie. I've heard a lot about you. I'm Braylen." She pointed toward Zoe. "Her stepmother and Ryder's wife." The blank look on my face made her clarify. "Ryder is one of the other guys in the club."

"And he's hot." I turned to look behind me and saw a girl who appeared to be around my age turn the corner. She was pretty, her chestnut-colored hair styled poker straight.

"That he is." Braylen chuckled, not at all seemingly annoyed the girl fawned over her husband. "That's Natalie. And if you haven't guessed already, she's got a thing for my hubby."

"And every other red-blooded male," Riley added, draping a black cape over the front of me before securing it in the back with a snap.

"What can I say? I love a hot guy. Speaking of which...." I turned to see who was in her line of sight and saw Lincoln and Kaden walking toward the salon, stopping outside on the sidewalk for a moment before reaching for the handle. The chirp of the door sounded seconds later, and both guys headed straight for us.

"Hey, guys," Natalie sang out, and even though I didn't know her at all, she rubbed me the wrong way. An inexplicable feeling of jealousy erupted, something I'd never experienced before in my short life, and I had to admit... I hated it.

"Natalie," they replied in unison, but neither of them

looked at her. Instead, Lincoln's eyes were on me, and Kaden's were on Riley.

The small victory of sorts made me smile, which in turn made Lincoln grin at me like he just heard the best news.

## Lincoln

"Hey, babe." Kaden drew my sister in for a hug right before kissing her. A few of the women hooted, but I looked away, not needing to see the display. My focus was on Maddie and no one else, not until I heard Riley ask a question I realized was bound to be brought up at some point.

"What is that?" she asked, patting his lower back. Kaden moved back a step but didn't say anything, and if I knew my sister as well as I thought I did, there was no way she was gonna let this go. She'd press the issue and demand an answer, right here in front of everyone present. She didn't care.

When she reached for him again, he grabbed her hand and shook his head. "Stop. We'll talk about it later."

"Since when did you start carrying a gun?" I supposed later was right now. I didn't think he meant to do it, but Kaden glanced over at Maddie before returning his focus on my sister.

"Since now."

"Why?"

"It's only a precaution. Don't get all bent out of shape over it. I know how to use it, and well, I might add."

"I don't care. I don't want you carrying one." She huffed, her hands finding a home on her waist.

"It's not up to you."

Kaden was out of his mind if he thought my sister wouldn't dive headfirst into this argument. She pulled her eyes from him, and they soon landed on me.

"Are you carrying, too?"

I nodded.

She looked at Brick. "What about him?"

"Everyone is," Kaden answered, shifting her attention back on him. "Nothing is gonna happen. We're fine."

"How can you say that? Something is obviously wrong if everyone was told to carry a weapon when they never had to before." Riley's face flushed, and it was only a matter of seconds before she exploded. Because I didn't want Maddie to be caught in the middle of a potentially volatile scene, I pulled my sister away from everyone else so I could have a few words with her.

"I don't like this one bit, Linc," she muttered.

"I know. I'm not a fan either, but we have to protect ourselves in case something happens."

"What's gonna happen?" Her eyes searched mine for an answer I wasn't allowed to give. Club business was just that... business of the club. But I would give her a tidbit of information to try and put her mind at ease. "The Reapers are gonna come back at us because I took Maddie from them. We don't know how or when, but we need to be ready when they do."

"I don't like it," she repeated.

"You don't have to." I realized how clipped my tone sounded when she raised her brows at me. "This is hard enough for all of us," I confessed. "You would do well to stop giving the guy such a hard time." My sister was stubborn and would argue until she ran out of words, a trait I never found appealing, as I was sure Kaden didn't either. But she had a right to speak her mind, like I did, and I told it to her straight, hoping she'd back off a bit on this issue. "If you wanna give him a hard time, do it later and not in front of Maddie. I don't need her feeling any worse about her situation than she probably already does."

My protectiveness over Maddie grew each day. Strike that, I believed it grew each hour, and I knew one thing for sure. I'd do everything in my power to keep her safe and if that meant killing someone in order to do it.... My thoughts drifted away from me because I didn't want to think about the details, albeit hypothetical for right now. Then again, that was the potential danger I faced, we all faced. My assumed threat could turn real at any time.

"I'll talk to Kaden in private about this," she finally conceded. "Because you're right, Maddie doesn't need any more drama in her life right now." She walked away before I could thank her.

"So, Maddie, what do you wanna do today? Different style? Or only a trim?" Maddie's eyes met mine in the reflection of the mirror, and I wasn't sure if she sought my approval or genuinely didn't have an answer for Riley.

"Um... I've always wanted bangs."

"Bangs would look great on you. You have the perfect face shape to pull them off. Are you okay if I cut off a couple inches as well? You have some dead ends."

"Sure," she answered, her voice timid.

As Riley grabbed her scissors, she turned to look at me, then to Kaden. "Are you guys gonna hover around the entire time? Don't you have somewhere to go?"

"We're not leavin'," Kaden answered before I could. There was no way I'd ever leave Maddie here alone. Not that I didn't trust my sister with her, but if anything popped off while we were gone, I'd never be able to forgive myself.

"If you're so worried, you could have the big guy stay

behind." Riley jerked her chin toward Brick, who was still huddled with Zoe in the corner. God only knew what was goin' on with them, but if Ryder walked in here right now, the situation wouldn't be pretty.

"He's busy," I said. As I inhaled to say something else, Chelsea came barreling into the salon, her face flushed, and looking like she was out of breath.

"'Bout time you got here," Braylen chastised. "Your client will be here any second."

"You know I'm usually here early, but time got away from me." She plopped down in her chair and released a heavy breath. "What are you guys doin' here?" Chelsea looked to all three of us, although Brick's back was still facing the group.

"I thought Maddie could have some fun."

She leaned forward and looked around her best friend. "Who's Maddie?"

"Linc's woman," Kaden blurted, making me cringe. If we were alone, I'd punch him. Then again, if no one else was around, I'd have no reason to be upset. I immediately looked at Maddie and saw her tense, but when Riley whispered something to her, she relaxed, although only marginally.

I could've corrected him and told everyone, including Maddie, that she wasn't my woman, but I didn't want to say such a thing. I barely knew her, but something inside me prohibited the words from leaving my mouth.

Riley moved to the side so that Chelsea could see the person in her chair. "This is Maddie."

"Oh. Hi." Chelsea smiled before leaning back. I could see the wheels hard at work in her overactive brain, and because I didn't want her to spew a bunch of questions or comments at me, or anyone else for that matter, I asked her something which would redirect her attention.

"Where's Ace?"

She shifted uncomfortably, averting her gaze. "How should I know?"

"You two make up from your drunken brawl?" I knew they had, or at the very least she'd let him back into her house the night I could've died, still thanking whoever or whatever saved me that night by only having the bullet graze the side of my head.

"Wha... what?"

"What do you mean *what*?" Kaden asked, taking a step toward her. "Which, by the way, was fucked up. That's the last time you put Riley in that kind of situation."

"Kaden." A twinge of warning sliced through both syllables of his name when it escaped Riley's mouth.

"I mean it," he said, shoving his hands in his pockets before narrowing his eyes at her best friend.

"Then you need to talk to him yourself. It was Ace's fault all that went down in the first place." Chelsea glared at Natalie when she walked past her toward her own station.

"What happened?" Natalie asked, completely oblivious to the aggression wafting toward her.

"Nothing," Chelsea answered, crossing her arms over her chest.

"Fine." Natalie huffed. "Leave me out of all the juicy convo. See if I care." She pulled out her phone, giving the device all her attention.

Even though she and Maddie were only a year apart, Natalie being older, the difference in maturity was astounding. During the times I'd been around Natalie, she came off as self-absorbed, either making comments about lusting after guys or partying. Maddie, on the other hand, had been through stuff no one should have to go through. Her biggest worry in life was safety, not drinking and hooking up.

Consumed with the rampant thoughts firing off inside my

overcharged brain, I wasn't paying attention when Ace suddenly walked into the salon. *Speak of the devil.*

"Hey. What are you guys doin' here?" No one got the chance to answer before he saw Maddie, heading straight for her. "Nice to see you outside the clubhouse." He chuckled, touching her shoulder in familiarity. She smiled at him, and even though I realized he was only being nice, their interaction annoyed me.

But apparently, my feelings toward the two of them were nothing compared to Chelsea's. Fire lit behind her eyes when she saw Ace touch Maddie, her posture straightening right before she unfolded her hands. The chick looked like she was ready to blow.

Ace pulled a phone from inside his cut. "You left this at my place." She snatched it from him, looking at all of us briefly before turning her focus back on him. Her scowling at him should've been enough of a hint that she didn't want to see him, but he didn't turn and walk away. Instead, he poured gas on the fire.

"What's wrong with you?" he growled, stepping closer to her so as not to be so obvious they were about to argue. Little did he know that all eyes were on them.

"You're way too friendly with everyone," she grated.

"What are you talkin' about?"

"First Natalie and now Maddie?"

"You're blowing things way out of proportion like usual."

"Am I?" she asked, shoving him out of the way so she could stand. Chelsea took a few steps away from him, mumbling something under her breath, but she didn't get too far before he grabbed her arm to stop her. His grip wasn't strong, however, because she easily dislodged herself from his hold and briskly walked toward the back of the salon. I thought I heard her say "fucker," but I couldn't be sure.

"Christ!" Ace threw his head back and grunted, and I was positive if he were anywhere but here, surrounded by his buddies and other women, he would've flipped the fuck out. But he restrained himself.

"Maybe you should go," I said, coming to stand beside him with a supportive pat on his back.

"Yeah." He shook his head. "Fuckin' women," he mumbled before walking toward the door. But he stopped when he reached the desk, turning back to look at me. "When's your next fight?"

I shrugged. "I haven't heard from Rico."

"Maybe we should talk to Marek about having you lie low for a bit." His eyes raked over Maddie, but thankfully she didn't notice, too busy paying attention to whatever Riley said to her.

"Yeah." I gave a short answer because I honestly didn't know how I was gonna handle entering a fight so soon after what happened at the last one. I had no doubt the Reapers would show up, and God only knew the outcome this time around.

## Maddie

"Wow! This look certainly fits you." Riley fiddled with my hair before stepping to the side, her eyes on mine in the mirror to see my reaction. When I pried my attention from her and onto me, my mouth fell open. How could something as simple as bangs change my look, almost completely? Even the whites of my eyes looked brighter. She cut a couple inches off, so now the length of my strands hit slightly above my collarbone. Whereas earlier my hair appeared lifeless and dull, it looked vibrant, rich.

"I love it, Riley," I gushed, working to keep my unshed tears at bay. She had no idea what her simple act had done for me, and while I didn't want to make a fool of myself in front of her and everyone else here, I couldn't stop my emotions from barreling to the forefront.

"Oh, please don't cry. 'Cause then you're gonna make me cry, and I don't feel like fixing my face." She laughed, giving me a side hug before motioning for her brother. Every now and again, I'd caught Lincoln looking over at me, smiling whenever our eyes met. He was talking with Kaden and Brick when Riley waved him over. "What do you think?" she asked, moving out of the way when he stepped closer. His hand brushed my arm, a tingle of excitement swirling deep in my belly, and possibly someplace else.

"You look even more gorgeous than before." His voice dipped. "I didn't think that was even possible." The compliment threw me even though he'd previously told me he thought I was beautiful. I'd been drinking then, my boldness pouring out of me before I could think better of it, even going so far as to kiss him.

I looked away for a moment, the intensity in his stare borderline too much. "Thank you."

Lincoln traced his finger over the top of my hand, the touch triggering heat to bloom beneath my skin. I jerked my head up, catching the smile on his stunning face the same time he winked at me.

"You ready?" he asked, holding out his palm to me.

"Yeah." I glanced at my reflection one last time before exiting the seat, placing my hand in his and allowing him to help me stand. He didn't step back, which caused me to bump into him. "Sorry." Only then did he back up enough to give me space, but not enough to allow me to breathe without inhaling his smell. If we were alone, I'd bury my nose in the crook of his neck and never leave. But we weren't alone. We were surrounded by his sister and his friends. If I acted in such a way, they would definitely think there was something wrong with me, if they didn't think that already.

"Thanks again, Riley. I love my new hair."

She leaned in and kissed my cheek. "Anytime." She then looked to her brother. "Don't keep her hidden away in the clubhouse. Bring her by the house for dinner soon."

"Whose house?"

"Mom and Dad's," she replied.

"I'll bring her by there if you invite Kaden, too."

Riley squinted at him, her teeth toying with the corner of her bottom lip. "Yeah. Can you imagine?"

"I can," Kaden interjected. "And that's not somethin' I wanna experience again right now."

Instead of trying to decode their conversation, I focused on the part where Lincoln tried to barter with his sister about bringing me to their house for dinner. Was that his subtle way of telling her he didn't want me there, without blatantly saying it in front of me? Was he embarrassed of me? I thought his mom liked me, so I doubted she was the issue.

Normally, I would keep my mouth shut, but as we walked toward the door, I pulled my hand from his.

"You okay?"

I gave him a halfhearted shrug. Again, I wouldn't typically question anyone's statements, but his resistance to take me to his house hurt my feelings.

"Why don't you want to bring me to dinner?"

With the door held open, he gestured for me to walk outside ahead of him. "Let's go," he said to Brick and Kaden, allowing them a moment to say goodbye to Zoe and Riley. Turning his attention to me, he said, "It's not that I don't want to take you home for dinner, but I don't think it's a good idea."

"Oh." I was right. He was embarrassed of me. "I understand. I thought since your mom was so nice to me, she liked me."

Lincoln pulled me to the side as his friends passed and headed toward their bikes. "Maddie, what are you talkin' about?"

I looked down at my feet. "You're ashamed of me. Which is okay. I understand. I'm just thankful you saved me." I felt the tears brewing, but I didn't want to break down in front of him, especially out in public where I would have no shield whatsoever if things really turned south.

"I'm not ashamed of you." He shifted his feet. "Maddie." I

kept my eyes lowered, my emotions whirling through me faster and faster. "Look at me." Still, I kept my eyes averted. "Please." I didn't know if it was the pleading in his voice or the pain I thought I heard, but I lifted my head. "I'm not ashamed of you," he repeated. "I just don't think it's safe. We don't know what the Reapers are gonna do, so I don't want to take any chances. The only reason I brought you here today was because I have backup with me," he said, pointing toward Kaden and Brick, who were looking at us with interest. "Do you understand?"

"Yes." His explanation soothed my ego. "I do."

"You okay?"

I nodded, taking a step around him and heading toward his bike. Once we stood next to the impressive machine, I touched his arm as he clipped his helmet in place.

"Do you want me to ride back with one of your friends?" I could've been mistaken, but I thought I saw the muscle in his jaw flex.

"Absolutely not. Why would you ask me that?"

"Because I made you uncomfortable."

"When?"

"When I rode with you here." I didn't mean to, but I glanced down at his crotch.

Gone was the flash of irritation I detected from him. Instead, he seemed amused. "Don't worry about me. I love having you on my bike." He handed me my helmet, positioned himself on the bike, then held his hand out to assist me. Once I swung my leg over the other side, I scooted forward and wrapped my hands around his waist, clutching him tightly.

Only this time, I wasn't nervous about the ride.

I looked forward to pressing against him for as long as I could.

# Thirty

## Lincoln

The ride back was challenging. The rumble of my bike would often soothe any apprehension I felt, but as it happened the girl molded to me was the source of my anxiety as of late. If I wasn't trying to make sure she was not only safe but comfortable with us, I was consumed with thoughts of her.

Of her innocence.

Of her ability to distract me with the flick of her eyes.

Of her strength.

I doubted she thought of herself as strong, but she was, in every sense. Most people would've crumbled, withdrawn so far into themselves after what she suffered, but not her. Sure, she was timid and shy, but I saw the fire she tried to keep dimmed behind her gaze.

I saw her.

Plain and simple.

And it wasn't until she uttered that bullshit outside the salon about me being embarrassed of her, that I decided once and for all where she and I stood.

No more messin' around.

No more fighting my feelings for her.

I saw the way she looked at me, at the way she melded into me whenever we touched.

I wanted Maddie to be mine.

Everyone else thought she was already.

Now it was time for me to step up and make sure that's what she wanted as well.

From the outside looking in, it might appear that I was rushing things between us. Especially after what she'd endured. But the pull I felt toward Maddie was undeniable and inexplicable. And if she felt the same way, as I suspected she did, then why wait to make the connection between us real?

Once we arrived back at the clubhouse, all I wanted to do was be alone with her, but as luck would have it, I was called into Chambers upon walking inside. Most everyone else sat around the table. Marek nodded when I asked for a minute to escort Maddie back to the room she'd been staying in.

Leaving her tucked safely inside, I walked back down the hall and toward our meeting room, hating the time spent away from her, even if for only a short while. The image of her bombarded my every thought, and without realizing it, I soon walked right into a wall. Or to be more specific, a wall of a man. Brick grabbed my shoulder when I bounced off him, laughing at my clumsiness.

"I was gonna say somethin' to you, warn you I was standing right here, but I thought it would be funnier if I didn't."

"Nice," I grumbled.

"Whatcha thinkin' about?" Before I answered, he looked back toward where the bedrooms were housed. "Never mind." I thought possibly Maddie had come out of her room, but when I didn't see her there, I realized Brick was fuckin' with me. "She sure does look good." Confused about whether his compliment was innocent or not, I chose to ignore him. I had enough on my mind. I didn't need to add punching the mammoth of a man to it.

"Let's go before Marek sends someone lookin' for us." I walked around him, deposited my cell on the table outside Chambers, and eventually took my seat next to Trigger, Brick following closely and sitting to my left in his assigned chair.

Marek leaned back in his seat, running a hand over his face in what appeared to be frustration. He had a lot on his plate as it was, and me bringing Maddie here had only intensified the situation.

After he came clean about all the past dealings with the club, I felt even worse about engaging the Reapers, but even through my guilt, I wouldn't have changed a thing.

My concern for her, even when I didn't know her, had continuously plagued me, and every time I saw her with them, it was like a knife to my gut. It was a no-brainer when their prospect shoved her at me during our last fight.

"Tag." One word garnered everyone's attention, especially mine and Kaden's. Sitting upright, my focus solely on our leader and shoving the errant thoughts of Maddie to the back of my mind, I listened intently to the words that followed. "I gotta take care of some stuff first, but at the end of the week, I'm goin' to the safe house, putting all this to rest once and for all. And I want you, you, and you there as well," he said, looking at Ace, his son, and me. "Cutter will be there, too. Everyone else will remain behind. We still don't know what the hell is goin' on with the Reapers, and I don't want to pull too many people away from here. God forbid anything go down, we're an hour away."

"What's gonna happen once we get there?" I asked, completely aware I pushed against his patience. He didn't answer, so I closed my mouth, knowing if I continued to ask questions, forcing him to speak more on the subject when he clearly didn't want to, I'd be on the receiving end of one pissed-off man. Not wanting to cause any more upset than there already was inside our club, I simply nodded when he arched his brow at me.

"We should ask Mom what she thinks about all this," Kaden suddenly blurted. Apparently, he didn't mind pushing his ol' man's buttons. And while I was relieved he spoke up, I wasn't looking forward to the fallout. If the change in Marek's demeanor was any indication, we were all gonna feel the hit any second.

"What did you say?" Prez's expression morphed from astonishment to confusion to fury in the span of seconds, his grip on the edge of the table frightening. I had to give Kaden credit for the size of his balls, though. Not only did he have to deal with Stone's anger toward him constantly now that he was with my sister, but he had no qualms about adding his father's outrage to the list.

"Sounds to me like you've made up your mind about Tag, and you want me and Linc to go along with it, possibly even witness his death." Kaden would've continued to vomit his words, but Marek slammed his hand down on top of the table so hard it was a wonder he didn't flinch in pain.

Ignoring his son's ranting, he repeated, "What the fuck did you just say?!" The room became eerily quiet.

"I think we should ask Mom what—"

Marek stood so fast, his chair skidded behind him and hit the wall, the thump causing me to wince even though I was already on edge and paying close attention to what was unfolding.

"I told you what that fucker did to her!" he shouted. "Do you think for one second I'm gonna tell her about any of this? Remind her what happened to her all those years ago? Let her know Vex's son is at our safe house? That he infiltrated our club? That he was close, too close to her?"

"But Tag is innocent," Kaden replied, tripping over his words when his father moved closer to him.

Admittedly, Marek wasn't making a hell of a lot of sense, speaking as if Tag was indeed guilty, that he was as evil as Vex, which wasn't the case. The only thing I understood was that Marek wanted to keep Sully as far from this shit as possible, which I couldn't blame him for, but a man's life hung in the balance. At what point did you put someone's emotional state at risk to save someone else?

"It doesn't matter," Prez yelled, first at his son, then at the rest of us. "I'm not bringing my wife into this. She won't know a goddamn thing about what's goin' on here." He pointed at his son, then snarled. "Don't you even think about tellin' her, Kaden. She will NOT find out about this." This was the first time I'd seen Marek not only enraged but fearful as well. His eyes darkened, but a look of panic flashed over his face. It was brief, but I saw it.

"Remember the last time you hid stuff from Sully?" Ryder asked, leaning back when Marek swung his focus onto him.

"That was different."

"How?"

"It just was. I couldn't tell her that back then, not when I didn't know if it was true or not."

"Yeah, but do you remember how hurt she was? How distraught she became?" Jagger asked. *What are they talkin' about?* "You almost lost her, Prez. Don't make that same mistake again."

"What the hell is wrong with all of you? Do you not remember the vile things they did to her?"

"We do." Trigger replied that time. "But maybe the boy's right," he said, referring to Kaden's request.

Having no idea what they were talkin' about, I spoke up again. "If Tag's life hangs in the balance, all because of what his father did to Sully, isn't it fair for Sully to then weigh in on what happens to him?"

"No!" Marek shouted. "No." He shook his head, hitting the top of the table once more.

"You did promise her," Tripp said.

"Promise her what?" Ace asked. "What are you guys talkin' about?"

My ol' man looked to his best friend before opening his mouth to respond. Marek didn't give his silent approval with a nod, but he gave it when he sat back down and threw his head back, stealing his eyes from everyone at the table.

"Before we killed Psych, he decided to mess with Marek one last time." Our VP took a quick breath. "He told us that the reason the war started between our clubs in the first place was because he'd raped Marek's mother, and that wasn't the worst part. He then insinuated that Marek and Sully were half brother and sister."

"You're related?" Kaden uttered, his mouth dropping open at the shock.

"No, they're not related. It was Sully's father's last-ditch effort to fuck with Marek before he died. But while we waited to find out for sure... let's just say he didn't handle things with his wife so well."

"I didn't," Marek finally spoke up. "And I did promise not to hide anything like that from her again, but I can't... I can't bring myself to tell her about Tag, reminding her about Vex." He shook his head vigorously. "I won't."

"You might not have a choice," my ol' man said, clutching his friend's shoulder in a show of support.

I wasn't sure what was gonna happen once we left this room, but one thing was for sure, whether Sully was told about Tag or not, I didn't believe Marek was ever gonna be the same.

# Maddie

"Are you all right?" Lincoln walked into the bedroom looking tired and beat down, a frown marring his gorgeous face. "Bad meeting?"

"You could say that."

"Do you wanna talk about it?" I moved from the bed and walked up in front of him, reaching for his hand, which he readily gave. "I'm a good listener."

"Thanks, but it's club business. Nothing I can discuss with you." He pulled away from me and disappeared inside the bathroom, reemerging moments later and taking a seat. When I sat next to him, wanting to offer him any support I could, he pulled me onto his lap, hiding his face in the crook of my neck. The action surprised me, but only seconds later, I melted into his touch. He wrapped his arms around my waist and held me prisoner, but I wasn't about to complain. In fact, I preferred this position rather than sitting next to him.

Lincoln didn't scare me.

His touch made my heart skip a beat.

His kiss had made my stomach flip.

The way he looked at me made my soul hurt because it had taken me so long to find him.

"Is this okay?" he grumbled, his words muffled against my neck.

"Of course."

"Of course," he echoed, breathing me in like he was trying to commit my scent to memory. Then he said something I never expected. "I need you."

Our eyes weren't connected, which was good because I was sure I looked odd with the way mine widened at his confession.

"You do?"

Lincoln finally moved back and looked at me. "I do. More than I want to."

"What does that mean?" I had no idea what he was gonna tell me, but whatever his response, I believed there was no going back for me. Not that I wanted to. With my own thoughts confusing me, my brain barely had time to register his response.

"I don't know."

"Oh." Disappointment covered me like a shroud.

Moments passed, and neither of us spoke another word nor made a move. I wondered if he cared for me other than as someone he saved. Did he feel something deeper for me as I did for him? Could I love someone I barely knew? Was it possible for feelings to develop that quickly? Or was I feeling something else entirely for Lincoln?

I didn't dare voice the craziness rattling around inside my head. Instead, I remained as still as I could because I didn't want our physical connection to break. But several moments after he'd pulled me to sit on his lap, he set me on the bed beside him.

"Are you in the mood for some Chinese?"

"Sure." I watched him walk across the small room,

entranced with the simple way in which he moved. His stride was typically confident, sexy, but today his gait was different. I couldn't explain such a thing, but whatever plagued Lincoln affected every part of him. I only wished there was something I could do to help, all without knowing the issue.

"Do you want anything in particular or wanna leave it up to me?"

"You can choose. That's fine with me."

"Okay. I'll be back soon."

The second he was gone, I missed him. I could barely inhale a breath. It was alarming how much I'd become used to his presence that when he left, he seemed to take the air with him.

If what I felt for him was something other than love, I'd hate to know how messed up I'd be if I ever fell hard.

---

"ARE you sure you don't want more?" he asked, sliding the container toward me. I would've been content eating in the room, but he convinced me to join the land of the living, so we sat at the bar. And since most of the guys weren't here, I agreed. That's not to say I didn't like his friends. They'd been nothing but nice and respectful. But I preferred solitary with Lincoln over anything.

"I guess I wasn't as hungry as I thought."

"We gotta fatten you up, woman," he teased, winking at me right before I looked down at myself. I wore one of the maxi dresses Riley had given me, and while it was comfortable, the size was a bit big.

"You think I'm too skinny?" I hadn't meant to sound so self-conscious, but how Lincoln perceived me was important. I know it shouldn't be, but I couldn't halt my inner voice from rambling how he might not find me attractive at my current weight, which admittedly was under what I should be, what I'd been in the past.

"I think you're beautiful, Maddie. Get outta your own head." I reached for the container, but he pulled it away before I could grab it. "If you're not hungry, you're not hungry. Don't force yourself to do something because you took my joke the wrong way." I licked my lips. "Don't do that."

"Do what?"

"Wet your lips."

"Why?"

"Because I want to."

Heat bloomed in my belly. "Oh." I looked at my lap before picking my head back up, his gaze simmering against mine for the longest seconds of my life. "You do?"

"I can't get that kiss out of my head."

"You can't?"

"You only gonna use one or two words to answer me?"

"No." I smiled when he smirked. "I don't know what you want me to say. I think about the kiss all the time, too."

"That's promising." Lincoln finished his beer and slid it forward on the bar. "Wanna go back to the room now?" My mind drifted off, but before I could lose myself to all the different scenarios of why he asked that question, he caressed the side of my face. "I only meant that we could watch a movie or something. In private."

Two of his friends walked toward us as we vacated our seats. "Where ya goin'?" Kaden asked, occupying the stool to my left.

"We're gonna watch a movie," Lincoln replied, resting his hand on the small of my back.

"Why not watch one out here? This TV is huge." Ace was the one talking now. "What movie you got? Maybe we want to see it, too." If I wasn't mistaken, I thought I saw the corner of his lip curve upward when Lincoln shook his head. "Oh, you wanna be alone. Is that it? I can respect that. I'd love to be alone with a certain someone, but I guess she'd have to answer her phone in order for any of that shit to happen."

"Oh, no," Kaden griped. "Linc, don't leave me alone with his sullen ass."

"Fuck you, man. I'm not sullen. I'm horny." Ace flicked his eyes at me. "No offense, Maddie. But it's true."

"Is it Chelsea you're talkin' about?" I asked, surprised I allowed myself to be so forward.

"Yeah." He moved his head up and down before shaking it side to side. "Wait. How do you know?"

"I guessed from the interaction you had with her earlier today. There seemed like somethin' was goin' on with you two."

"Oh yeah. Can you believe she—"

"Okay. That's enough." Lincoln gently pushed me forward. "How did you go from hardly ever discussing anything about you and Chelsea to her being the only topic? Hash it out with her or let it go, Ace. Stop goin' back and forth already. It's exhausting for the rest of us."

Ace mumbled something behind us, but we were too far away now for me to hear what it was.

"He seems like he's havin' a hard time. If you wanna go talk to him, I don't mind." I opened the bedroom door and stepped inside, Lincoln right behind me. I barely made it two feet before he turned me around and crushed me to him, dipping his head low so we were eye level.

"I don't wanna talk to Ace. I wanna hang out with you."

He pressed his lips to mine, and what I thought was gonna be a peck on the mouth turned into something else altogether.

Bunching his shirt in my hands, I yanked him closer and devoured the sweet taste of him. I groaned into his mouth, my breaths stolen the longer we kissed. All sorts of images rushed through my head, mainly of us naked and writhing around on the bed, which was situated only a few feet from where we stood.

I tried to take a step back while continuing to hold on to him, but he broke the kiss and shook his head. At first, he didn't say anything, but when I attempted again to make him move with me, he parted his delectable lips and spoke.

"We should stop." His words crushed me, but I didn't want him to know that, so I nodded, hoping I hid my disappointment well. "I don't wanna start something when I can't finish it. And trust me, I want to finish it... all night. But it's wrong."

I wasn't gonna say anything, but him telling me it was wrong rubbed me the wrong way.

"Kissing me is wrong?"

"No. That's not what I meant."

"You know what, Lincoln? You don't have to do anything with me. You don't have to take me to dinner at your house. You don't have to kiss me. You don't even have to spend time with me alone." Once I started vomiting the words, I couldn't stop. "I like you, more than I've ever liked anyone in my entire life. But I get it. You can't involve yourself with me because of what happened."

By this time, I'd stepped away from him and walked to the other side of the room, needing the distance to calm myself.

Annoyance darted through his eyes. "I told you why I shouldn't bring you to my house. It's not safe. It has nothing to do with anything else." He erased the distance between us, coming to stand directly in front of me again. "And as far as kissing you, Maddie, it's all I think about, among other things. But I know we can't... do anything more."

"Why can't we?"

Surprise contorted his expression. "Because I'd never forgive myself."

"Why would you have to forgive yourself?" I didn't want him to answer even though I asked the question. "What I feel for you scares me. Sometimes I can't breathe when you're not with me. I'm selfish because I want all your time, but I know you can't be with me like that. I thought...." I looked away for a moment, but he didn't like it when I stole my eyes from his.

"Go on," he urged, turning my face back toward him and licking those damn lips of his.

"I thought if you gave yourself to me, I could take back a piece of my heart." A lone tear drifted down my cheek, and I cursed myself for showing my weakness, which was him.

"If I gave *myself* to *you*?" A disbelieving laugh erupted from his mouth as he wiped away my tear. "Where did you come from?"

"Oklahoma," I sheepishly replied, which made him laugh right before he pulled me into his embrace, the muscles of his arms trapping me. But I wouldn't want to be anywhere else.

After a brief silence, he kissed the top of my head and pulled me toward the bed. "How about we relax and watch a movie? I think I can scrounge up a comedy."

"Um... okay."

"I thought I saw a couple movies in one of these drawers. I can't tell you what they are or how long they've been here." Lincoln searched through several of the drawers beneath where the television stood before he pulled two movies from the last one he looked in. It was either *Forrest Gump* or *Reservoir Dogs*. Both were way before my time, but I chose *Forrest Gump*. Although it wasn't necessarily a comedy, I'd seen the film a few times and loved it. He popped in the disc and joined me on the bed, leaning forward and taking off his boots and socks before he grabbed the back of his shirt and pulled it over his head.

"Is this okay? I'm kinda warm."

"Yeah, it's okay."

After he hit the Play button, he scooted back until he lay flat, his head on the pillow. "Come join me, will ya?" His smile brightened my otherwise downtrodden state.

Everything Lincoln had done for me since the night he saved me was to show me he cared. Whether it was for my safety, or my basic human necessities, such as food, he made sure I had what I needed. He was patient with me while I learned to trust that what he told me was the truth. He didn't push me to do anything I wasn't comfortable with, even going as far as sleeping on the ground each night beside the bed.

It was then I realized he wasn't rejecting me.

He was respecting me.

## Lincoln

I tried like hell to concentrate on the damn movie, but all I could think about was her mouth and the feel of her clutching on to me like she was afraid to let me go. Then she hit me with *"I thought if you gave yourself to me, I could take back a piece of my heart."* What the ever-loving fuck?

The girl nestled in the crook of my arm with her head on my chest exhilarated yet scared me.

She was fragile but strong.

Bold but shy.

"I love this part," she said, looking up at me to make sure I was watching. The gleam in her eyes cut right through me, and all I wanted to do was capture her mouth again, but I refrained. My stare flitted from hers to the screen, smiling when the character awkwardly ran from the bullies before his leg braces busted away to allow him to go into a full-on sprint.

"It's a good part," I agreed, pulling her closer.

Everything was going fine. We were relaxed, together, and engrossed with the film, but when Maddie suddenly draped her leg over mine and cuddled even closer, my breath caught in my throat. Then her finger traced over my stomach, my muscles twitching from the contact. If she kept this up, I was gonna be sportin' a hard-on, one I'd barely managed to keep at bay this entire time.

"Maddie." I swallowed and inhaled a choppy spurt of air. "I... that feels...." I didn't even finish my sentence before she extended her arm and placed her hand on the mattress on the other side of me, lifting the rest of her body until she hovered half over me. Her mouth was close, her warm breath fanning over my lips.

"I want you to make love to me, Lincoln." Her eyes traveled from mine to my mouth and back again. She appeared resolved but tentative at the same time.

It took my brain a few seconds to compute what she'd said, and when they hit their mark, I pulled back so I could see more of her face. The flecks of gold around her irises seemed to brighten as she looked at me, and I almost forgot to respond.

"What?" I finally said, pulling myself out of my self-induced trance.

"I want you to make love to me," she repeated. "I've never wanted anything more."

"Are you sure?" What the hell was I saying? There was no way we could have sex or make love as she put it. Fuck, I'd never "made love" to anyone before. At best, I had sex, fucked. Never made love.

Her face lit up as if I'd said yes. "Yes. I know you're worried about me, and I love that about you, but I want to be with you."

She loved that about me? Loved? I focused on the wrong thing, distracting myself from the real issue, which was that Maddie told me she wanted to have sex. Correction... make love.

I could either continue to deny her and possibly compound

any hurt feelings she already had, or I could give in to what we both wanted.

Hard choice. No pun intended.

"I don't want you to do somethin' you're not ready for only because you think I want to or for any reason other than it's really what you want right now. You've been through a lot. More than most. Quite frankly, I'm surprised you're able to function as well as you are."

"My dad was crazy religious, and while I didn't agree with everything he told me, I did believe one thing, and that was that God would help me."

"Help you? How did God help you by allowing those bastards to do what they did to you?"

She shook her head. "No, God helped me by sending you to save me." Her eyes glassed over, and the last thing I wanted her to do was cry, but if we kept talking like this, it was inevitable.

Pressing my lips to hers, I could feel her smile when I kissed her, when I teased her tongue with mine, when I nipped her bottom lip before exploring her depths once again.

Maddie tried to move on top of me, but I needed to be in control. I wanted her beneath me, squirming, begging me. Flipping her onto her back, which was an easy feat since she weighed next to nothing, I spread her legs with my knee.

"You're positive about this? Are you still having any pain? Everything good there?"

"All good," she answered, rolling her eyes, which made me chuckle. My girl was spirited. *My girl?* Yes, she was mine, a possession I needed to announce before any more of our clothes were removed.

"Once we do this, you're mine, Maddie. I don't own you, of course, but you will belong to me and only me."

"And will you be mine in return?"

"Yes."

"Okay." She raised her head off the pillow and kissed me,

anchoring my body to hers when she wrapped her legs around my waist.

At first, all we did was kiss, which was fuckin' amazing, but eventually, she unlocked her legs from around me and pushed me back.

"I need to take off my clothes." Her words were authoritative, but her tone hinted at her slight reservation. I wasn't gonna ask her again if she wanted to go ahead with this, but I would take things slowly in case she changed her mind at the last second.

"How about I take off your clothes for you?" I hopped off the bed and urged her to join me, reaching out to help her up. I turned her around and unzipped her dress, moving her hair to the side as I kissed her neck, sliding the straps off her shoulders. I unhooked her bra, removing both articles of clothing together. Several healing bruises littered her skin, but she looked much better than when she first came here. Forcing a calming breath through my nose, I focused on her and not the evidence of what was done to her. It was hard, but I needed to stay in the moment, more so for her than for me.

Maddie stood before me in nothing but her black cotton panties, the bottoms of her cheeks peeking out from beneath the fabric. Before I could ask her to turn around, she faced me. My eyes drifted down her body, my mouth watering at the sight of her tits. They were small but perfect. "You're gorgeous." Her face tinged pink, and I didn't think I'd ever seen anything so beautiful in all my twenty-one years.

She took a single step closer and raised her arms to link them behind my neck, pulling me down for a soul-searing kiss. All I wanted to do was toss her on the bed and have my way with her. Fast. Hard. All-consuming. But I couldn't. I had to be careful, gentle even, especially for the first time. She wasn't a virgin, but I had to treat her as such because even though she appeared resolute and strong, her emotional status was fragile.

"Can you take these off?" she asked, her fingers fumbling with the button of my jeans.

I extended my hands at my sides. "Have at it, babe." Her eyes lit up when I said babe, and I made a mental note to use the endearment more often.

The sound of my zipper slicing through its teeth was louder than I'd ever heard before, my pulse thrumming in my ears, deafening me. If I wasn't careful, I'd come before I even buried myself inside her, which wasn't a great first impression. Maddie deserved all of me, for as long as I could muster, so in order to calm the raging need wrapping around me, I took a step back before she was able to shimmy my jeans off.

"Did you change your mind?" She swallowed nervously and moved to cover herself with her hands.

"No. I just need a minute." It was while I worked to regain my bearings, I heard someone shout from out in the common room, drawing my attention to the door and realizing I never locked it. Other than in the ring, I swore I'd never moved so fast before, clicking the lock to make sure no one could barge in on us. Not only would that be embarrassing for Maddie, but I'd never hear the end of it because whoever interrupted us would assume I was taking advantage of her. "Don't want to give anyone a show." I chuckled, wiggling my brows and making her smile.

Not wanting to waste any more precious time, I removed the rest of my clothes, and while I had an impressive physique and was well-endowed, the way she stared at me made me self-conscious. I glanced down at myself before looking back at her.

"Is everything okay?"

"It's not what I expected," she uttered before devouring the sight of me again.

"Is that bad?"

"No. You're... beautiful."

"Beautiful?" I laughed. I'd never been called that before. Sexy, gorgeous, cute, sure, but never beautiful.

She approached me tentatively, looking more nervous than anything, and I thought possibly she was in the middle of changing her mind. But when she touched my chest, trailing her fingers over my skin, it dawned on me that she'd probably never touched a guy like this, which both thrilled and gutted me. I was only too happy to be her first, but because of what they'd stolen from her, she'd never had the opportunity to explore a male, her curiosity evident with the way her eyes danced as she lost herself to her exploration.

"Can I touch it?" She licked her lips, her focus on my dick and not my face.

"Be my guest." I'd had sex with my share of women, but I'd never felt so exposed before, so vulnerable.

"Careful." My laugh morphed into a groan when she gently squeezed me.

"Does it hurt?"

"Hurt? Yeah, but not in the way you might think."

"It's so hard, but it's soft, too." I bit down on my lip as she stroked me from root to tip, sliding her finger over the drop of precum. "Thank you." Her hand fell to her side, and she backed up a step.

"Why are you thanking me?"

"Because you let me touch you."

"Believe me, Maddie, I should be the one thanking you." When she smiled, my heart burst a little more, and I vowed right then and there to make her smile as much as possible. "Wanna move this to the bed?" She nodded, hooking her thumbs into the waistband of her panties. "Leave 'em on." Her hands fell to her sides once more. "I wanna take 'em off."

I positioned her until she was flat on her back, her eyes wide and expectant as she watched me remove the last piece of her clothing. My head became clouded thinking about what she would taste like, feel like wrapped around my cock. If I didn't get myself under control, all this would be over with before it really started.

"I want to touch you now." I climbed in bed next to her. With me on my side and her on her back, our faces were close, closer than our bodies, because I needed the short span of distance to be able to move as freely as I wanted without hindrance. I parted her thighs with my hand, tossing her right leg over my hip so I had better access. When I slid my finger through her folds, her body jerked. "Did I hurt you?" I couldn't see how that was possible because she was drenched, but I needed to be sure.

"No." Her breathy response told me the opposite was true of what I momentarily feared. She reached over and dug her nails into my leg. "That feels good."

Never before did I want to thoroughly take my time, and while I always made sure whoever I was with came before me, it was always a rush to the finish line afterward. There was never slow foreplay, exploring, reveling in the feel of the other person. But with Maddie, I didn't want to stop. I could stay locked away with her like this for days, weeks even, content with discovering every inch of her.

After inserting a finger, I pressed my thumb against her clit, and she nearly shot off the bed. Her moans increased the more pressure I applied, adding a second finger, remaining mindful not to hurt her. I wasn't sure how much was too much, so I needed to go slow.

Dragging the bottom of her earlobe through my teeth, I bit down the same time I curved my fingers inside her. "Do you like that?" She nodded. Her inner muscles clenched, and I assumed she was close, but I asked anyway. "Are you gonna come for me?" She nodded again, her nails digging harder into my thigh. "Good." I withdrew my fingers and quickly repositioned myself with my head between her legs.

"Li..." I had no idea if she was gonna ask me to stop, tell me she was embarrassed with the new position, or what, but her head twisted to the side with the first swipe of my tongue, her arms extending above her head while her lids fluttered closed.

I'd only had one taste of Maddie, and already I was starving for more. Too many emotions battled inside me when it came to her, and although I understood what I felt wasn't purely physical need, I couldn't pinpoint what exactly it was.

But I knew one thing for sure, all the time in the world with her wouldn't be enough.

# Thirty-Three

## Maddie

The moment Lincoln agreed to be with me was the moment I realized I loved him. And although most people would tell me I was crazy, that I couldn't fall in love with someone in such a short amount of time, I felt it in my soul.

The draw toward him the very first time I laid eyes on him was too strong not to be something special. And even though I was in a bad situation and didn't know him, my gut told me he wasn't like the men who belonged to the Reapers, even though it took my head a while to come to the same conclusion. As it turned out, I was right.

"Do you wanna come?" he asked, his voice low and gravelly. I'd been on the verge before he moved to bury his head down below. I couldn't respond, the air in my lungs lacking in order to breathe life to an answer. Lowering my right arm, I gripped his hair and pulled; the sound that erupted from his throat savage. I was shameless in the way I ground against his tongue, but my body took over, my mind flitting away because the pleasure was borderline too much. Then his voice brought me back. "I could eat your pussy forever."

Warmth spread through me, and only a fraction of the heat was due to embarrassment at his words, even though I apparently had no issue with the physical act. How could I still be shy with Lincoln's mouth working me toward release?

I lost myself to the rhythm of his tongue and the way his fingers played me like an instrument. It was as if he knew my body better than I did.

Even though my dad had preached masturbation to be a sin, that didn't stop me from touching myself when I was younger. Hormones would do that to a young girl. I'd take extra-long showers or wait until I knew my parents were asleep before discovering my body, figuring out how to pleasure myself.

Clamping my legs together to alleviate the intensity did nothing but push Lincoln's mouth closer. I was on the brink, the tingling in my belly cresting and pushing me toward an all-consuming orgasm.

"Lincoln!" I shouted, pulling on his hair before letting my legs fall to the side.

"Shhh," he warned, throwing my leg over his shoulder. "I don't want anyone to hear you comin'."

It was late, and while I'd heard some voices earlier, I didn't think there were many people gathered in the other area of the clubhouse. But I didn't know if there was anyone else staying in any of the other rooms, so I tried to control myself. Moan after moan fell from my lips, and when he realized I couldn't be quiet, he moved up my body and covered my mouth with his, his fingers continuing to work me over as he swallowed my screams when he tipped me over.

When I started to come back down, he kissed along my jaw, then beneath my earlobe, which was a ticklish spot I found out.

I laughed when he persisted and tried to move away, but he had me pinned in place.

"Now I know your weakness." He wiggled his brows and his fingers at the same time, which were still inside me, lazily stroking me.

"You're my weakness." My heart ached at the thought of not being with Lincoln. I was an overthinker by nature, and every time I concocted some hypothetical scenario, I swore my heart and mind reeled with the possibilities that someday we'd be separated. While I was young, what I felt for him was the real deal.

"I'm your weakness?" he asked, propping himself up on his forearm, trailing the fingers he had inside me a moment ago along my side, making me flinch. Apparently, I was ticklish in more than one spot.

"Yes." I looked away for a moment to gather my nerve. "Please don't be freaked out, but I need you." I wanted to say so much more but feared he'd reject me and run.

"I know. That's why I'm right here." He looked like he wanted to say something else but kissed me instead. It was moments later when he finally spoke again. "I want you so bad right now, but if you've changed your mind, I'll stop. Just say the word."

His concern for my well-being touched me so deeply I couldn't even put it into words. But instead of being extra mushy, and getting even more emotional than I already was, I said, "I want to be with you."

Lincoln pushed himself back until he sat at the bottom of the bed. He leaned over, reached down and grabbed his jeans, pulling a condom from his back pocket. Standing to his full height, he ripped the foil with his teeth and sheathed himself before covering my body with his once more.

"Wrap your legs around me. Yeah, like that." His hand disappeared between our bodies right before the tip of him pressed into me. I'd seen what he was gifted with, and he was as large as he felt. There was a mild discomfort as he worked himself all the way in, but once I was full, the ache that had resided within me pumped back to full force. "Am I hurting you?"

A tear escaped from the corner of my eye at his question, and it had nothing to do with what he'd asked me. Not really. The last time Griller forced himself on me, he asked me that same question when I was facedown on his mattress. When I answered yes, he laughed but never stopped. He loved my pain, whereas Lincoln would do everything in his power to protect me from it.

"Why are you crying?"

"Because you care."

"I do." He kissed me. "More than I ever have for anyone else before." He pulled back before thrusting forward, slow and gentle, the muscles in his neck straining as he moved back and forth. "Fuck!" he grunted, capturing my mouth and stealing my breath. "I want to stay buried inside you for days."

"Okay." I was serious, but when he chuckled, so did I.

He kissed the sweet spot beneath my lobe, only this time I was too busy enjoying the feel of him to be bothered by the slight tickle of his lips. I ran my hands over his broad shoulders before grasping his arms as he drove into me in long, sure strokes, pinning me to the bed.

I was caged beneath him, but I'd never felt so free.

When Lincoln picked up his pace, the sounds he made were guttural, filled with desire and need, pushing me into a world of sweet torture.

"Maddie." My name was expelled on a ragged breath. He dipped his head and took my nipple into his mouth, teasing the tightened bud with his tongue, then his teeth, careful not to apply too much pressure before releasing me. He moved to my other breast, continuing to torment me with his mouth.

Moments later, with a gruff moan, he rolled us until he was on his back and I sat astride him. "Is this okay?" He barely had the air in his lungs to ask the question, grabbing my hips and moving me back and forth on top of him.

The position allowed me to feel like I was in control, not that I didn't feel that way when I was beneath him, but there was something about this position that lit fire to my confidence.

"Yes, but I'm not sure how to—" He pumped upward, obliterating the rest of what I was gonna say. "Oh... you're so deep this way." I held myself upright by slapping my hands on his chest, the hardness of his muscles eradicating any fear I was hurting him.

"Grab your tits," he ordered, his eyes darkening with lust.

"But I'll fall." I wanted to please him, but I feared I'd topple over if I removed my hands from him.

"I got you." His grip on my waist tightened, but he wasn't hurting me. If anything, the power of his hold thrilled me. "Do it." I moved my hands up my body until I came to my breasts. "Squeeze them. Play with your nipples. Yeah... like that."

Watching the way Lincoln licked his lips as he watched me play with myself was like the best drug. He made me feel desirable, something I'd never felt before him. But it wasn't long before he was commanding me into another position, pulling me toward him.

"Put your hands on the bed." As soon as I complied, he reached around and gripped my ass, moving me so that I was bouncing up and down on him. Then he thrust upward and pulled me down at the same time, rocking me back and forth like before. "Fuck, yeah," he grunted. "I'm gonna come soon." The sounds he made pushed me closer and closer. "Use my cock for what you need, baby." He licked at the seam of my lips. "Are you close?"

"Yes." I could barely breathe. My body was filled by him, as was my heart. "I'm almost there." He rested his forehead against mine, his warm breath fanning my mouth as he struggled to maintain any sort of composure.

Then, without warning, Lincoln flipped me on my back, never breaking stride as he continued driving into me. His hand disappeared between our bodies, finally shoving me over the cliff. With his head buried in my neck, his hand moved to cover my mouth when I started to scream. I ended up biting his finger, but I didn't think he even noticed, grinding into me as he came seconds after me.

Only when our heartbeats slowed, did Lincoln roll onto his back next to me, removing the condom and tossing it in a nearby waste bin. "Come here," he said, pulling me so that my head rested on his chest. "That was—"

"Amazing," I finished for him. "I've never...." My words trailed off because I didn't want to think about what I'd never been able to do before he came into my life. I only wished my virginity hadn't been stolen so I could've given it to him.

Craning my head to look up at him, my heart skidded to a stop when he winked at me, his smile widening when I snuggled closer.

"I love you," I whispered but loud enough for him to hear me clearly because his eyes almost popped out of his head.

"Maddie... I... I don't think what you feel for me is love." He flashed me a strained grin, looking more like a guy who wanted to run for the hills rather than lie here with me.

"But I do," I argued, my heart splintering with every second in which he didn't tell me he felt the same way.

Lincoln shifted, helping me to sit beside him. "I know you believe that, but I think sleeping together has muddied the waters between us."

"You regret it?" I tried to remain as calm as I could, but my damn voice shook. "You think having sex with me was a mistake?"

He reached for my hands, but I yanked them back. "Mad-die. No. Of course, I don't regret it."

"But you said that if we did it, that I would belong to you. And you to me." My bottom lip quivered, and I cursed my emotions for rushing over me.

"I didn't lie about that." He moved into a sitting position as well, reaching for me once more, but again, I moved back. If he touched me, I didn't know what I'd do, too vulnerable right now to trust myself.

All the times I'd been forced to have sex, I'd never once felt this exposed, my heart hanging in the balance. The one person I knew I was meant for didn't love me.

"You don't love me."

"I don't," he quickly responded.

What's the saying?

Like a Band-Aid... right off.

## Lincoln

"Maddie. Come back here."

She told me she loved me, and I told her I didn't feel the same. What was wrong with me? She offered me her body and her heart, and I dumped over the entire experience with my thoughtless words. And now she locked herself in the bathroom.

"Go away," she cried, her voice cracking, devastating me.

*Knock. Knock. Knock.*

"Fuck!" I growled, walking the few feet to get to the bedroom door, glancing behind me to see if Maddie had come out of the bathroom. Of course, she hadn't. She'd probably never come out again.

*Knock. Knock.*

"Linc!" Ace shouted from the hallway.

I swung open the door so fast Ace almost hit me in the face, his fist raised to pound on the wood again.

"What?" My temper had gotten the best of me, and although Ace didn't deserve to be on the receiving end, I didn't have time to mess around. I had to get back to Maddie before my thoughtlessness did any more damage.

"You left your cell on the bar," he answered, handing it to me.

"So?"

"So, it keeps ringing. I think it's Rico, about a fight." He moved to walk past me and into the room, but I blocked him from entering. "Where's Maddie?" Ace looked down and saw that I was naked except for a sheet wrapped around my waist.

"She's in the bathroom."

"Whatcha doin' in there?" His arched brow indicated his disappointment, but the crook of his smile told me he might be amused. I didn't have time to decipher exactly what expression was the one he wanted to portray, so I shoved him back.

"None of your business," I said, slamming the door in his face before he could ask me any more questions or shoot any more confusing looks my way.

I was next to the bathroom two seconds later. "Maddie, please open the door and talk to me."

"There's nothing to talk about." I heard her sniffles, and instead of giving her the time she so obviously needed, I pounded on the door.

"I'm not goin' anywhere, so you better get your ass out here and talk to me." I hit the door with my fist over and over, coming across as annoying more than anything else. But I'd do whatever it took to get her to hear me out.

After another minute with no result, I must've released every curse word known to man, backing up and leaning against the nearest wall. I ran through all the things I wanted to tell her, none of which would soothe the wound I'd created.

Maddie was mine. Undeniably.

Did she make my heart race? Yes.

Did I dream about her? Did I miss her when she wasn't with me? Yes, and yes.

Did I want to give her the world? Yes.

Was there a strange pull dragging me toward her? Another yes.

Could I picture my life without her? No.

Did I love her? Wasn't it too soon?

I didn't have a straightforward answer, which angered me. Why couldn't this be simple? And if it was confusing for me, how was I gonna be able to explain it to her?

The creak of the door opening had me moving forward, meeting Maddie at the threshold of the bathroom. She'd been crying, as I suspected, her eyes red and slightly puffy.

"I'm so sorry, babe." That time when I reached out to touch her, she let me. "It's not that I don't—"

"You don't have to say anything." She shook her head. "I shouldn't have told you that. You're right. I've been through a lot, and I'm just confused. What I feel for you probably isn't love at all, but something else altogether."

I'd been the one to try and convince her of that very thing, so why the hell did her words gut me?

# Maddie

Two days had passed, and the awkwardness between me and Lincoln only seemed to increase. Ever since I told him that what I felt for him wasn't love, although I believed the opposite to be true, he seemed to be distancing himself, acting like I'd been the one to break his heart and not the other way around. He wasn't even sleeping in the same room with me anymore.

My time here was closing in, and although I feared that Griller was still waiting to snatch me back, I had to devise some sort of plan to leave. I couldn't stay here at the clubhouse forever, and now that things between us were strained, I thought it was best to leave.

Losing myself in mindless television did nothing to take my mind off my situation, and it wasn't until Lincoln walked into the bedroom that I perked up. Simply looking at him made my heart thrash inside my chest, so much I sometimes feared I'd have a heart attack.

"Hi," he greeted, rooting through some of the drawers of the dresser until he pulled out a white T-shirt. Turning away from me briefly, he pulled his off and tossed it in the corner. Before he redressed, I saw the handle of a gun in his waistband.

"I don't like guns." I didn't know why I felt the need to say that because I doubted he cared.

"I'm not a fan either, but we need to carry in case somethin' goes down."

"Speaking of which," I said, moving to stand next to him. "I've been thinking and... um... it's for the best if I leave."

"Leave?"

"Yeah. It's because of me that the Reapers might come after you all, and I just think I should go."

"And where do you think you'd go?" He folded his arms over his chest and didn't look pleased to be having this conversation. Was it because he realized I'd need his help? I didn't have any money, so I would need to borrow some from him. I'd pay him back, of course, once I was settled and got a job.

"Back home to Oklahoma. I have an aunt who lives about an hour from where I did. I haven't spoken to her in years, but I'm sure if I reached out, she'd help me."

"No." His response was immediate and curt.

"What do you mean, no?"

"What do you think no means, Maddie? It means you're not goin' anywhere." He unfolded his arms and advanced toward me. "I told you right before you spread your legs for me that if we had sex, you belonged to me, and me to you. Do you remember that?" His tone was angry, some of his word choices crass, but his eyes told me something different.

Was he upset I wanted to leave here?

Leave him?

"Do you remember?" he repeated, grabbing my arms and pulling me into him, his lips an inch from mine.

"Yes."

"So, what makes you think I'll let you go?"

"Are you saying I'm your prisoner now?" My heart skidded to a stop, my mouth dropping open in surprise. Had I been wrong about Lincoln all this time? While he never physically hurt me, nor did any other members of his club, was he going to keep me here against my will?

There was a knock, the handle of the door twisting before he could answer.

"Linc, what the hell ya doin' back here? Let's go." A young guy who looked to be closer to my age walked in, looking to me, then Lincoln. "Hi." He stepped forward and extended his hand. "I'm Zander. Linc's brother." As soon as he introduced himself, I saw the resemblance, although their eye and hair color were different.

"Hi. I'm Maddie." I looked at Lincoln quickly. "I didn't know you had a brother."

"That's probably because he didn't want any competition." Zander was attractive with his dark blond hair and hazel-colored eyes, his hair a bit shorter than Lincoln's. He was tall, but then next to me, most people were. "Do you know he has a sister?"

"Yes. Riley. I met her a couple times. I like her." I smiled to ease the mounting tension in the room. I'd suddenly become uncomfortable with the way Lincoln's eyes bounced between me and his sibling.

"And how do you know my big bro?"

"She's my girlfriend," he answered for me, shocking me half to death.

"Okay." He nodded before inspecting the room. "Are you keeping her locked in here? How come I haven't heard anything about her? No offense, Maddie," he said, before turning his focus back on his brother.

"It's complicated."

*Wasn't that the understatement of the year?*

"Sure, it is. Okay, whatever. You ready to go or what?" Apparently, Zander wasn't going to inquire any more about me or our relationship, which was fine with me.

"Yeah, give me two minutes." His brother huffed. "Zan… two minutes. Go talk to Dad or somethin' until I'm done."

"Where's he at?"

"I don't know, but he's here somewhere because Mom still won't let him come home."

"Those two." Zander sighed, shaking his head. He pointed his finger at his brother. "Hurry up." Then his eyes landed back on me. "Nice to meet you, Maddie." And as quickly as he appeared, he was gone, leaving me with all sorts of new questions.

Once the door closed, my mouth opened. "Why did you tell him I was your girlfriend? And why did you never mention him before?" I was insulted he didn't think me worthy enough to tell me about his other family member. "Do you have any more, other than Riley and Zander?"

"No. Only the two."

"So why did you call me your girlfriend?"

"Because you are."

"Since when?" I wasn't going to get my hopes up because everything pertaining to Lincoln lately confused me.

"I told you. Since we had sex."

"But then I told you I loved you, and you told me you didn't feel the same way."

"So." Anger lit his one-word reply. Why was he getting upset with me? I was only trying to clarify what we were to each other, if that was even possible.

"I don't understand." My head started to hurt.

"Listen, I have to go. We'll talk when I get back, okay?" I gave him a noncommittal half-shrug. "And don't go anywhere."

He walked out before I could ask him how he was gonna

stop me if I tried, which would've been pointless, seeing as I couldn't get far with no money.

Stewing in the room lasted a whole twenty minutes before I decided a drink was in order.

Nothing crazy, just something to help take the edge off until he came back.

## Lincoln

"So, what's the real reason you didn't tell me about Maddie? You hidin' her away for some reason?" Zander's curiosity riled me, and although he hadn't said anything wrong, his assessment of the situation was spot on, pissing me off because there wasn't a fuckin' thing I could do otherwise. I had to keep her at the clubhouse until further notice, or until Marek told me she had to go someplace else.

I couldn't take her out to eat, or to go see a goddamn movie because the threat against her, against us, was still prevalent, even though those bastards still hadn't made a move. Yet.

"It's complicated," I finally replied, tapping the steering wheel to the beat of the song on the radio to distract myself. It wasn't working.

"Yeah, you said that before." He looked out the window. "I hope it gets better as we get older."

"If Mom and Dad are any indication of what's to come, we're fucked." Zander's only response was a halfhearted grunt. "What's goin' on, man? Everything okay?"

"Kim's been texting me. I think she wants to get back together."

"Do you want that?"

"I don't know. She messed me up pretty bad when she broke up with me, and over text, which was... I deserved better than that. I don't think I can trust her, but...."

"But what?" He didn't answer, so I did it for him. "But you still love her."

Love was an annoying concept, one that screwed up a lot of people, giving some a reason to act stupid.

"Yeah, I think so."

I hated that with everything goin' on at the club and life in general, Zander and I hadn't gotten much time to hang out, something I was set on changing very soon. I missed him. He was a cool dude, calm, hardly letting anything bother him. His resemblance to our father was uncanny, but thankfully, he didn't inherit the ol' man's temper.

"Then you have some stuff to think about. If you do give her another shot, make sure it's what you want. Don't let her pressure you into anything because you feel some type of way toward her." I offered my advice, but it was up to him to make his own decisions. Zander was nineteen, only a couple of years younger than me, but he was certainly old enough to make his own decisions. One of them being moving in with Luke, who had recently returned home. He'd been staying in Seattle with his ex-girlfriend, Aubrey, but shit went south when her grandmother died. She'd taken off on him, and he hadn't heard from her since. That was months ago.

Looked like relationships weren't any of our strong suits.

"I'll figure it out." He changed the station, tapping his hand on his thigh when he came to a country song he liked. "So gettin' back to my original question." I kept my focus on the road ahead even though I knew he was looking at me. "What's the deal with Maddie?"

"I thought I already said it was complicated."

"So? We have some time before we get to the house. Out with it." I finally turned toward him, his smile easing my anxiousness.

I'd never hidden anything from my brother before, and I wasn't about to start now. "The Reapers were keepin' her against her will, doing things to her..." I needed to take a breath because referencing what happened was enough to enrage me all over again. "Anyway, after one of my fights, we got into it with them, and she was there. And now she's with us."

"Is that how you got that scrape on the side of your head?"

"Mom told you what happened?"

"Yeah, and she wasn't happy at all. More worried than anything, though." He punched me on the arm. "Glad you're okay."

"Me too."

"Ya know, they probably didn't take too kindly to you snatching her from them, but I'm glad you did." Zander knew a bit about the Savage Reapers and the dealings between our clubs, more so in the recent past than as of lately. He never showed any interest in joining the Knights, preferring to go to school instead. He was finishing up his first year at a local college before deciding where to go next. "I don't know her, obviously, but from the few minutes I spent with you two, I could see there's a connection between you."

"What?" How did he know that?

"Anyone with eyes can see it." He smiled at my shocked expression. "You definitely don't have a poker face. It's why I win whenever we play cards."

"Fucker." I laughed after he hit my arm again, shaking my head because he was right. I wasn't as good at hiding my emotions as I thought. It was probably the reason Maddie felt comfortable telling me she loved me. She probably picked up on my feelings toward her, believing I felt the same way. *Don't you?*

"She's hot."

"Who?"

"Maddie." My grip on the steering wheel tightened. "Don't get any ideas," I growled.

"Why would I hit on your girlfriend?"

Oh shit! That's right. I called her my girlfriend, more in anger and annoyance than anything else, without a doubt confusing her more than she already was.

"You wouldn't."

"Exactly. But you better get your head out of your ass because if you don't man up, someone else will."

"What makes you think my head's up my ass?"

"Because I've known you forever." He tapped his window. "Turn right up there."

"What did Mom say about you movin' out?" A change in subject was necessary.

"She asked me why I wasn't takin' you with me." He chuckled, which in turn, spurred my own laughter.

"She probably did."

"Speaking of, why the hell are you still living at home? It's not like you can't afford a place of your own."

"I dunno. Never had a reason to before."

"Now you do."

"What do you mean?"

"Don't tell me you want to stay at the clubhouse with Maddie forever."

"It won't be forever. Only until the threat is gone."

"Then what? You bring her home, where you still live with your parents?" I pulled into the driveway of a single house, the place that Zander and Luke would call home for the foreseeable future. Turning in my seat after I threw my truck in Park, I caught the moment my brother rolled his eyes at me. "I'm sure she'll love that."

Instead of making up some excuse, I responded with, "Maybe you're right." That was the extent of mental energy I was givin' the topic right now, too much other stuff running through my head to give it the proper amount of weight it deserved.

"Damn right I am. Now, come on. I wanna show you the place." Our parents, as well as Luke's, Tripp and Reece, had splurged on furnishing their house with whatever they needed, which basically meant a house full of new stuff.

Instead of a porch, there was a small stoop in front with an overhead covering, two white pillars on each side. The front door was a rich mahogany color, the maroon shutters on the white-sided house a nice contrast. A small foyer was what we walked into, the staircase off to the right. Hardwood floors spread throughout all the rooms, which was perfect because these two could be messy sometimes, and it was easier to clean floors than carpet.

"Zan, that you?" Luke yelled from somewhere else in the house. The place wasn't huge, but it wasn't tiny either. There was a nice-size living room, which was all decked out with a comfy-looking sectional, as well as curtains, lamps, a large-screen television hung on the wall, and a few other pieces of furniture.

"When did you move in here?" The house looked like it had been inhabited for years.

"Two days ago," he answered, walking ahead of me toward the kitchen.

Luke removed dishes from a moving box and put them right into the dishwasher. "Hey, man," he greeted, stepping forward and clasping my hand before giving me a side hug.

Luke was only two months younger than me, and while I

hadn't seen him as much as I'd wanted over the past year, we picked up right where we left off.

While Luke took after Reece in the looks department, he'd inherited Tripp's height. He wasn't quite six four, but he was a couple inches taller than me, putting him around six two. Where I was lean and ripped, Luke was bigger. Again, not as big as his dad, but he had the potential to be so if he spent his life in the gym, which I doubted he had interest in.

Lightly tapping him on the back of the head, I said, "You need a haircut." His ash-brown strands hit the top of his collar, waving out and looking like he just got out of bed. "Call Riley. Tell her to hook you up."

"Call me for what?" My sister walked into the kitchen, Kaden two feet behind her. She gave Zander a hug before greeting Luke. We'd all seen each other at Roman's birthday party a couple weeks ago, but it seemed like life was getting back in the way again, so any time to spend with each other was always welcome.

"Linc says I need to get it cut," Luke answered, pushing his fingers through his hair and making it stick up in places.

"He's right," my sister agreed. Kaden leaned into her ear and said something, her eyes darting around the room before her face turned a light shade of red. My eyes connected with Kaden's right after he said whatever he did, and he winked.

"Gross."

He laughed as did I. I didn't even want to imagine what he'd told my sister, so I focused on getting a tour of Zander and Luke's new place. But before I could ask to see more, Reece and Tripp came walking around the corner. "Where did you two come from?"

"Upstairs," Tripp answered, his arm slung over his wife's shoulders and pulling her close.

"Doin' what?" Luke's eyes narrowed as he looked at his parents.

"Putting up the rest of your curtains." Reece adjusted her ponytail to include the chestnut-colored pieces that had somehow come loose. I wanted to believe she was a tiny bit disheveled because of hanging drapes, like she said, but one look at Tripp, and I could guess other reasons were to blame.

"Among other things," Tripp added. His wife slapped his chest and smiled. "What?"

"You better not have done anything up there?" Luke sighed and rubbed his hand over his face.

"Stop being so dramatic, sweetheart." Reece broke free from Tripp and hugged her son. "Your dad's kidding."

"He better be."

When Tripp caught my eye, he shrugged then winked, much like Kaden had done. While I dealt with my own issues, at least the other people in my life seemed to be happy. Maybe I'd get to the same place, hopefully sooner rather than later.

After finally touring the rest of the new place, we all hung out in the kitchen, snacking on chips and dip as well as a cheese and cracker plate Reece had brought.

This was the first time since Maddie had come to be with us that I was able to relax and enjoy myself without being bombarded with a thousand what-ifs.

That was until my phone started blowing up. The first time it rang, Ace's name came across my screen. Deciding to call him back in a bit, I let the call ring out until it went to voice mail. Seconds later, it rang again. Then again.

"You wanna answer that?" Tripp asked, looking more concerned than curious. He walked up next to me while everyone else continued to chat away.

"Hello?"

"Fuck, man," Ace hurried to say. "You gonna be long?"

"No. Why?"

"It's Maddie."

I reached for the handle of the gun tucked inside my waistband, my heart skidding to a stop. "What's wrong?" I looked to Tripp as I asked the question, his own posture straightening, much like mine.

"She's safe." Air escaped my mouth in a slow trickle. "But she's drunk, ramblin' on about you. She even cried. I think you better get back here."

"I'm on my way."

"Everything okay?" Tripp rested his hand on my shoulder.

"Ace said Maddie's drunk… and emotional."

"Don't the two go hand in hand?" He laughed, but I didn't, too worried about her state of mind, especially after all that went down between us.

"I gotta go." I said my goodbyes, asked Riley to give Zander a ride back to his car, rushed out to my truck, and sped back toward the clubhouse.

What the hell was I gonna walk into when I got there?

## Lincoln

The moment I stepped inside, I saw her sitting at the bar with Ace. Instead of focusing on how much I didn't appreciate him being so close to her, I strode toward them with purpose, attempting to tamp down the anger bursting to life inside me.

Maddie swiveled in her chair to face me once I was a few feet from her.

"There's the guy who doesn't love me," she whisper-shouted, tugging on Ace's arm, as if he didn't see me walk up behind them.

*She certainly came out of her shell.*

Instead of responding to her comment, I stared a hole right through Ace. "Who the hell let her drink so much?"

"She was like this when I got here. I think she snatched the tequila from behind the bar."

"Tequila?" He pointed to the bottle, which was almost empty. "How much was in there when she started?"

"Beats me. Hawke is the only one I've seen touch that garbage."

"Great." I walked around Maddie and stood on her other side. "Do you know how much you've had to drink?"

"A lot," she slurred.

"Why?"

"'Cause I'm sadnfused." Her words slammed together, but I understood her.

"Why don't we get you back to the room?" I touched her arm, but she shrugged away from me.

"Why? So you can have sex with me again? Kiss me as if you like me? Then kill my heart? No, thank you."

"What is she talkin' about?" Ace rose from his stool. Before I answered, I saw Brick walking toward us, followed by Trigger, both of whom were talking amongst themselves until they heard Ace's raised voice.

"Mind your business, man."

"Did you fuck her?"

"No," Maddie answered for me. "He made love to me." She slapped the bar before reaching for the almost empty bottle of nasty tequila. "But he doesn't love me."

"What's goin' on here?" Brick walked up in front of me, his attention bouncing between Ace, Maddie, and me. Trigger walked behind the bar and grabbed the alcohol from Maddie's hand, tutting and shaking his head at the same time.

"Apparently, our boy here had sex with Maddie."

"What?" Brick and Trigger shouted simultaneously.

"The fuck is wrong with you?" Brick asked, shoving me backward. I tripped over my feet but steadied myself before I fell on my ass.

"Don't hurt him," Maddie cried, turning in her seat, barely able to sit upright. "I love him. He's my girlfriend."

No one corrected her misspeak.

"You shouldn't waste your time on him, sweetheart." Ace stood close to her. Too close. And I couldn't unhear him calling her sweetheart. I didn't like it one bit. Ace glared at me. "He shouldn't have led you on."

How did everything go south so fast? Not only had I hurt Maddie, but she was tellin' everyone what happened between us, and now they were lookin' at me like I was an asshole. Maybe I was. Or maybe my only fault was that I hadn't been stronger at resisting Maddie when she told me she wanted me.

"Come on," I said, reaching for her hand. "You need to lie down."

"She might have alcohol poisoning," Brick growled, clenching his fists at his sides. I was man enough to admit having Brick's anger pointed toward me was a bit terrifying. I could get in a few good shots if we were to fight, but his sheer size would work to his advantage. And the guy was much quicker than he looked.

"She should be fine," Trigger chimed in. "She didn't drink too much to be hazardous." He pointed toward the line on the bottle. "It was right here when she snatched it."

"That's still too much," I said, angry I left with Zander instead of staying with her to try and work through our issue. Well, my issue.

"I agree." Trigger uncapped a bottled water and pushed it toward Maddie. "Drink up."

She made a face but did as she was told. Now, if only she'd listen to me, we could get away from the three men shootin' daggers at me. If the roles were reversed, would I have assumed the worst about Ace or Brick? Would I have condemned them for having sex with a chick they saved from the Reapers, knowing she was emotionally fragile?

The simple answer was yes.

However, although Maddie had suffered greatly, she was strong, stronger than anyone knew, including herself. My gut told me so.

Water droplets dripped off her chin, and when I moved to wipe them away, she leaned into me. "I missed you." She grabbed on to my arm, her hand skating down until her fingers entwined with mine.

"Better?" I asked, flashing her a tight smile.

"Yes."

"Wanna go lie down for a bit?"

"Will you stay with me?" The hopeful look in her eyes sealed the deal. There was no way I could leave her alone after all this.

"Of course." I helped her from her seat, holding on to her waist and assisting her back to the room, all while ignoring the grumbling erupting behind us. She wobbled a few times and even tripped over a raised section of the carpet in the hallway, but otherwise, we made it back without incident.

Once inside, I locked the door. I didn't need anyone getting any bright ideas and storming in here. And while I appreciated they were all looking out for Maddie's best interests, I didn't like that they looked at me like I was the devil for something that was supposed to have been kept private between me and her.

"I can't get these off." She collapsed on the bed, fiddling with the button to her jeans, but to no avail.

"I'll help you." After popping the button and pulling on the zipper, I shimmied them down her legs, discarding them in the corner of the room, the patience to fold them nonexistent.

"Are you mad at me?" Her voice was soft, unsure.

"Why would I be mad at you?" I lifted the bottom of her shirt. "Raise your hands." After the fabric cleared her head, I tossed it next to her jeans.

"Because I told them we made love." She reached behind her and unclasped her bra. My dick jumped at seeing her topless, but I ignored him, focusing on her and nothing else. Or at least, trying to. The only piece of clothing she had on now was her panties. Thankfully, she didn't remove them before lying flat on her back, her arms stretched out at her sides.

"I'm not mad, babe. Now, why don't you get some rest." Because she barely weighed anything at all, I was able to tuck her underneath the covers without effort.

"Lie with me." She reached for me, but her arm fell and hit the bed seconds later. Then she was out cold. I promised to stay with her, but I needed to talk to someone before the situation between us got any more complicated or stressful. Maddie had shown me her heart, and I needed to reciprocate.

Gently closing the door behind me, I headed back toward the bar area, looking for one man in particular. I prayed he was still here, although the chances he'd gone home were pretty high.

As luck would have it, he was still on the premises, walking toward his bike.

"Prez!" I shouted, jogging toward him while I tried to figure out exactly what I wanted to ask him.

"What's up?" He grabbed his helmet off his seat and swung his leg over his Harley.

"Got a sec?"

"Yeah." He checked his phone quick before looking back to me. "Before I forget, did you talk to Rico yet?"

"No."

"Call and tell him you're not fighting for a couple weeks. That should give us enough time to devise whatever plan we need."

"Okay." I shuffled my feet, lost inside my own thoughts while trying to figure out how to start what it was I wanted to talk to him about.

"I ain't got all day, Linc." His impatience had me tripping over my words when I finally opened my mouth.

"Sorry. Um... so I got this thing with Maddie. Uh... and I feel something, but I'm not sure what to say. I didn't tell her what she wanted before, and I don't... I don't know what to do." I barely made any sense to myself, so I could only imagine what he thought of my barrage of words.

"What the hell are you goin' on about?"

"Me and Maddie."

"Isn't there someone else you can talk to about this?"

"Not really. You're the only one who's been through something like this. You know... with Sully." His intense gaze studied me, and for a moment, I didn't know if he was gonna ignore me and take off, or punch me, his expression one I couldn't read well.

"What exactly happened?" He held his hand up before I started to speak. "And make sense this time."

What I was about to reveal could make him angry or disappointed in me, but I had to tell the truth in order to get his true take on things.

"We had sex. She told me she loved me afterward, and I told her I didn't feel the same way. I tried to explain it to her that what she feels for me probably isn't love but more like appreciation or something like that. I'm paraphrasing."

"Okay." He raised his brows, waiting for me to continue.

"Some of the other guys think I took advantage of her, but I swear to you I didn't. She was the one who kept telling me she wanted to, ya know." I shrugged, feeling guiltier with every word I spoke. Marek remained quiet, probably waiting for me to get to the point. So, I hurried things along by asking, "Did Sully tell you she loved you soon after she met you? How long did it take for you to realize you loved her?"

Silence ensued, and the longer he stared at me, the more I thought it was a mistake for me to single him out and ask him such intimate questions.

But then he sighed and flashed me the tiniest smirk.

"It wasn't that long after she came here that I told Sully I loved her. I was the first to say it, and she freaked out. Said no one ever told her that before. She thought I was lying."

"Oh."

"There's a possibility that what Maddie feels for you is something other than love. You're the guy who saved her from them. It could be deep-seated gratitude. It could be some form of hero shit. I don't know. Or it could be actual love. How do you feel about her?"

"I don't think I love her. It's too soon."

"Listen, if I know anything, it's that time isn't a factor. Don't worry about how long you've known her. You were trying to protect her before you even met her." He pulled his helmet on and clicked the strap under his chin. "Do you think about her all the time? Do you worry about her? Do you miss her when you're not with her? Does your chest hurt when she looks at you? Does the world make sense when you're near her, when you touch her?"

"Yeah."

"You love her."

"I do?" I took a moment and ran through his questions one more time in my head. "I do," I said definitively. "But I hurt her."

"Join the fuckin' club. Do you have any idea how many times I've put my foot in my mouth with Sully over the years? Too many to count. But, God love her, she continues to put up with my ass." Marek laughed, the sound working to soothe some of my worry.

He kicked over the engine and threw on his shades. "Tell her the truth. I'm not a sentimental or emotional man, Linc, but when it comes to the women in our lives, you have to lay it out on the line and hope for the best. Don't waste time. Don't fuck around. Life is way too short for any of that." I took a step back from his bike. "Got it?"

"Got it. Thanks, Prez."

He nodded before taking off toward the end of the clubhouse lot, leaving me standing there, contemplating exactly what I'd say to Maddie as soon as she was sober enough to remember.

## Maddie

I'd like to say that I didn't have any more nightmares about Griller or any of the other guys in the Reapers, but that would be a lie. They'd lessened since Lincoln came into my life, but I still sometimes found myself trapped in them. Only my dreams were more memories than my subconscious throwing together a concoction of thoughts and images.

Startling awake, my breaths heavy and uneven, I searched my surroundings all without moving a muscle, relaxing only when I remembered where I was. Then I felt warm breath on my neck, and an arm slung over my midsection, holding me close.

Three seconds passed before my brain registered that Lincoln was the person behind me. This was the first time we'd actually slept in the same bed together, and even through everything that had happened between us in the past couple days, I couldn't think of a more perfect way to wake up.

I needed to use the toilet, but I didn't want to leave the comfort of his soothing embrace. When he moved his arm lower and pressed closer, however, I realized if I didn't empty my bladder, I'd end up having a mess to clean up.

Pushing on his arm did nothing but make him grip me tighter. "Lincoln," I croaked, my mouth void of any moisture. "I gotta... pee." Barely able to talk, I hoped he heard me. Several seconds passed, but nothing happened. I tried to move his arm again, and he groaned.

"What are you doin', woman?" he grunted.

"Pee" was the only word that came out clearly.

He mumbled something before rolling onto his back, releasing me. I scrambled to the edge of the bed, threw my feet over the side, and stood. My head spun, and I almost fell back onto the mattress but caught myself at the last second. Shuffling forward, I finally made it the few feet to the bathroom, did my business, then stopped at the sink to wash my hands. I glanced into the mirror and saw someone who'd had too much alcohol the night before. But my reflection wasn't the same one I gazed upon last time in this room, which was only a shell of a person. I had more life in my eyes, even though they were glassy and red, and while I was heartbroken Lincoln didn't love me like I did him, I didn't live in constant fear anymore.

"Be thankful you're free," I murmured to my likeness. "Your heart might hurt, but your body doesn't." Splashing some cold water on my face, I felt remotely better, but not by much. I curved my hand under the faucet and drank several mouthfuls from the tap, the cotton feeling in my mouth finally dissipating. Then, after a quick brush of my teeth, I wiped my face, sucked in a fortifying breath and released it slowly, giving me a couple extra seconds before I laid eyes on the guy who had turned my world upside down, both good and bad.

When I reentered the room, his eyes were on me, and it was then it dawned on me I wore nothing more than a pair of panties. The way his heated gaze traveled over me made the buzzing beneath my skin erupt, and all I wanted to do was crawl back into his arms and lose myself—emotionally as well as physically. But there was still one big issue between us.

Lincoln reached out his hand. "Come here, Maddie." I didn't think I'd ever tire of hearing him say my name, his morning voice groggy yet undeniably sexy.

I slid my palm into his, and he moved back, guiding me in front of him so he could snuggle behind me.

"Lincoln, I wanna—"

"How come you don't call me Linc?"

I shrugged. "I don't know. I guess I figured only your friends and family called you that."

His lips pressed against my shoulder, the slight flick of his tongue on my skin making me want to turn around and ravage his mouth. But I kept still.

"That's silly. You're my woman. You can certainly call me by my nickname. If you want to, of course. Or you can call me babe or whatever you're comfortable with." He kissed my shoulder once more, cuddling closer, his excitement pressing into my backside.

My mind raced with why he acted so differently this morning. He seemed relaxed, happy even, whereas before he left with his brother yesterday, he was irritated with me. I couldn't recall much of our interaction after he returned to the clubhouse because my inebriated state didn't allow me to retain much of a memory.

I turned to ask him what changed, but he was off the bed and rushing toward the bathroom. "Be right back." Two minutes later, he stood beside me, looking down at me like I was the eighth wonder of the world. "You're so beautiful. You know that?"

"Even looking as hungover as I do?" Instead of waiting for his answer, I took in the state of him standing there in nothing but his boxer briefs, his impressive bulge doing a great job of stretching the fabric. When he moved his hand toward his hair, my eyes traveled up the length of him, appreciating every hard plane of his body. Lincoln was built to fight, and as it turned out, he fought to save me. Now all I had to do was come to terms with the fact that while I believed he desired me, his heart hadn't taken the plunge yet.

"You look perfect," he finally answered, tossing the covers from me and pinning me to the bed. Instinctually, I spread my legs so he could rest atop of me, most of his weight held up by his forearms. His face was inches from mine, and while I wanted to dwell on my heartache, all I could do was hope for one kiss. "Maddie, I... I want to tell you something."

Oh no! Was he going to break it off with me? Was he going to tell me I had to leave, that he thought maybe it was best if I went back home? Holding my breath in anxiousness did nothing but make my lungs burn, so I tried my best to breathe regularly and remain calm, but all the while, my pulse thrummed so fast, I was sure he heard it.

He pulled us into a sitting position, his finger tracing the length of my thigh as he looked at me, brushing away the hair that had fallen over my eye. I was so in love with him even though I suspected he was about to shatter the remaining fragments of my heart, which prompted me to say the only thing I could think of to protect myself.

"I don't love you," I blurted, swallowing hard when his expression tightened.

"You don't?" His eyebrow lifted as he leaned in, looking more puzzled than hurt or angry.

Then suddenly, I found myself more confused than ever. One moment I was studying his face, and the next, I was kissing him back with every ounce of love and desire tightly wound inside me, feeding off his need to stroke my tongue with his. "I think you're lying," he said when he finally broke away.

"I'm... I'm not."

"Then that's a shame." His bottom lip jutted forward right before he tsked.

"It is?"

"Yeah."

"Why?"

Resting his hand in the center of my chest, he slowly pushed me until I was on my back again, hovering over me, confusing me, until he parted his lips and confessed, "Because I love you."

"You do?" I was surprised I had enough brainpower to form those two words, let alone speak them out loud. "But you told me you didn't."

Lincoln trailed his finger from my temple to my jaw, down my neck, and over my collarbone until he rested his hand over my heart. His touch was intimate, sensual, loving. The way his eyes bore into mine made me feel cherished and revered.

"I didn't know."

"What changed overnight?"

"Someone made me see the light." He smiled, and it was the best sight I'd ever seen. More glorious than the most colorful sunset. Perhaps I was overly sentimental, but I didn't care how corny I sounded inside my head.

"Do you mind if I ask you another question?"

"Ask away, babe." *I love it when he calls me that.*

"How did you know I was lying?"

Instead of answering me right away, he traced my nipple with the tip of his tongue, capturing the tight bud between his teeth and gently pulling before wrapping his lips around me. A quiver of excitement churned through me, heightening all my senses. Releasing my breast, he hurriedly removed my panties and tossed them behind him, nestling back between my legs.

"Because I see the way you look at me."

"And how do I look at you?"

"Probably the same way I look at you," he responded.

I sighed, digging my nails into his biceps and wrapping my legs over his. My heart was full, but my body was on edge. All he had to do was pull himself free and he'd be inside me.

"Lincoln?"

"Still not gonna use my nickname?" He laughed but stopped when I wriggled beneath him.

"Will you make love to me now?"

"I thought you'd never ask." There was that glorious smile once again. He tried to move back, but I held on to him. "I have to get a condom."

"Oh. Okay." I'd almost forgotten about protection. That was exactly how people ended up with a surprise nine months later. And while I'd never gotten pregnant before, I didn't want to chance it. "Can you ask your mom to set up the appointment for me so I can go on the pill? That way we won't have to worry about condoms."

He nodded emphatically, looking like I just told him he'd won the lottery. "Consider it done."

As Lincoln shed his last piece of clothing, I was mesmerized. Every inch of his body fascinated me, some parts more than others. I blushed thinking about the way he felt inside me, even as I blatantly stared at his nakedness.

"You like what you see?" he asked, smirking when all I could do was nod. "Good. 'Cause it's all yours." After he finished putting on the condom, he crawled up the bed and nudged my legs apart, running a finger through my folds. "Wanna make sure you're ready for me."

"Always." My breathless reply made the corners of his mouth kick upward again.

Before I could form another thought or take a breath, he breached my opening, moving slowly until he was all the way in. My body locked up from an overwhelming sense of fullness, the ache budding inside me becoming stronger and more intense as he started to move.

"Feel good?" he murmured next to my ear, his wicked tone spellbinding me. I didn't think it possible that someone's voice could make me feel shy, empowered, and vulnerable all at the same time. I wanted to scream his name. I wanted to bombard him with demands and entice him to fuck me deeper with a flick of my hips. But I didn't do anything except answer him, allowing him to work me into a frenzy.

"Yes," I moaned, tangling my fingers into his thick hair and clutching him to me.

"I love being inside you. I don't wanna exist anywhere else." He pumped his hips, switching from slow to fast and back again before exploring the depths of my mouth with his tongue. I was thrilled Lincoln had been my first kiss, and as it turned out, my first love. Correction… first and only love. I had no idea what the future held for us, but I couldn't imagine my life without him, and I definitely couldn't imagine ever feeling this way about another living soul. He had officially ruined me for all others.

## Lincoln

Her moans drove me wild, her eyes searching mine, screaming for me to tip her over, all without saying a single word.

Hooking her leg over the crook of my arm, I thrust so deep I pushed her up the bed.

"Linc!" she cried. "Keep doing that."

"That's what it takes to get you to call me Linc?" Her smile fell when I repeated the motion. She bunched the sheet in her hands, her body rocking into rhythm with mine.

"I don't ever wanna stop," I huffed, my muscles tightening, the familiar swirl of need cresting over me. "I love your pussy, baby." I sucked her bottom lip into my mouth and bit down before plunging my tongue inside. The way she kissed me erased the memory of everyone who came before her. I couldn't believe her lips had never touched another's before me. She truly was a gift in every sense of the word.

During the short time since Maddie had come into my life, my feelings had morphed from curiosity to protectiveness to love, the latter emotion scaring me. Not because I was a commitment-phobe or didn't want to settle down, though. I feared losing her.

Her breathing came short and fast. She was close. But instead of rushing to the finish line, I pulled out and turned her on her side, cradling her from behind, pushing her leg forward before reentering her quick and hard.

She sucked in a lungful of air at the intrusion.

"Did I hurt you?"

"No. Do it again." She reached back and grabbed a handful of my hair, turning her face so she could kiss me. "Do it," she demanded, licking at my mouth.

Withdrawing until only the tip remained, I slammed back into her in one motion. Her mouth dropped open before she pleaded with me to do it again.

Circling her clit with my finger, I stole her mouth while I fucked her, swallowing her moans, which only intensified the closer she got.

"Are you gonna—"

"Yes!" she shouted. "Yes, keep... right there...." I applied more pressure, and she clenched around me, rocking back and forth as she claimed her orgasm. When she was on her way back down, I moved my hand to seize her waist, anchoring her in position.

"I'm gonna come," I grunted. The buildup was more intense than ever before, and the moment everything clicked, and I finally tipped over, it was pure bliss. Not that every orgasm wasn't spectacular in its own right, but after owning my feelings and telling Maddie I loved her, and knowing she felt the same about me, my release had been so powerful I couldn't breathe. I'd never cared this much about anyone before, and while I was still trying to sort my emotions, I tried not to overthink everything I felt. Sharing my feelings with her terrified me, but also made me feel invincible. I wanted to open up more, but I also didn't want to overshare too much at the same time.

"And... I'm spent." I chuckled, kissing her once more before rolling onto my back, discarding the condom and pulling her close. "Are you happy?" She snuggled in closer but didn't give me a verbal answer. "Babe?"

She crawled up my body until her lips were an inch from mine. "I never thought I'd be able to say this again, but yes, I'm happy. So much so it kinda scares me."

"Me too," I confessed, lazily running my fingers up and down her back, smiling when I'd hit the perfect spot which made her twitch. "I have another very important question to ask you." My expression turned serious.

"You hungry?"

She sighed before playfully slapping my chest. "I'm starving."

"Okay, give me a few minutes, and I'll scrounge up something for us to eat." With my breathing starting to regulate, I worked up the courage to ask her something else I'd been contemplating.

"I was thinkin' about moving out of my parents' house and into my own place. What do you think?"

She rested her hands on my chest, propping up her chin as she looked at me. "I think if you want to move out, you should. It'd be nice to have your own space, right?"

"Our own space," I corrected, waiting for my response to hit its mark. I didn't have to wait long, her beautiful eyes widening.

"You want me to move in with you?"

"Yes. I can't very well leave you here."

Her mouth turned down. "So, it's only because I can't stay here that I'd be living with you?"

"Well... yeah. It wouldn't make any sense for me to have a place and for you to still be holed up in this room." Maddie moved back until she was sitting beside me. I reached for her hand, but she pulled back. "What's wrong?"

"I don't want you to feel obligated. I can find a place of my own."

"Absolutely not. You're not living by yourself. I need to know where you are at all times."

"You do?" Her brows pinched together, and I thought she'd never looked more beautiful, her confusion amusing me a little.

"Until we can make sure no one is comin' after you, you'll be with me."

"And then what?"

"Then you'll still be with me, only I won't have to worry as much." Her slight resistance urged me to keep going. "I could stay at home and you here, but I don't want that. I want us to have our own space. Privacy to do what we want, when we want." I leaned up and pressed my lips to hers. "I want you to move in with me, babe."

"I like when you call me that."

"Good. So do I."

"But what about the times you're gone, and I'm alone. Won't you be worried about me?"

"Of course, but wherever we go, we'll have a state-of-the-art security system, and I'll check in with you often. That or I'll post Brick outside the place. No one is gonna mess with him."

"He's better than a guard dog." She laughed. "Let's go with that option."

"You better not be gettin' any ideas about him," I teased, but a twinge of jealousy fired off inside me.

"I only have eyes for you." She fell onto her back, tugging me to come with her. With our chests flush together, she cradled my face in her hands. "I love you."

"I think I've heard something about that." I pecked her lips, then moved to suck her neck, making her squirm because I'd hit another one of her ticklish spots. After several seconds of her trying to get away from me, she pushed at my shoulder.

"Say it again." Her voice was timid at first, but when I

frowned, acting like I had no idea what she was talking about, she smacked me on the arm. "Please. Say it."

"Say what?"

"You know." Maddie dipped her head, stealing her eyes from me for a second too long.

"That I love your pussy?" A beautiful pink flushed over her cheeks.

"No."

"No? Hmm... let me think." I made a clicking noise with my tongue before saying, "That I want you to move in with me?"

"That's not it either, although that one makes me happy, too."

"That I love your tits?"

That one earned me another gentle slap. "No. Besides, you've never told me that."

"I didn't? Because I do." I kissed the tip of her nose. "Is it... I love you?"

She nodded, biting her bottom lip. "Do you mean it?"

"I wouldn't say it if I didn't." I wasn't sure if it was the conviction of my answer or that she didn't want to push, but she didn't argue. "Wanna go again?" My hand disappeared between her legs, and she hissed as soon as I made contact.

"After we eat?"

"Oh, sorry," I laughed, hopping off the bed and throwing my jeans on. "I think we might have some eggs. Want an omelet?"

"Please." Maddie lounged on the bed, naked and satiated, a slow smile lifting the corners of her mouth while she watched me dress. I was gonna saunter out there with only my jeans on but then thought better of it. No one needed to know what was goin' on between us anymore than they already did.

I pulled my shirt over my head. "Be back soon."

Several minutes later and I was cracking eggs and whipping them in a bowl. The only other ingredients we had in the fridge were cheese and milk, which would do the trick for a nice thick omelet.

"Hey, that smells good." My ol' man walked in, scratching the top of his head before stretching his arms in the air. "Got enough to make me one?"

He leaned against the counter, wearing nothing but his jeans. The man kept himself in top shape, and covered in ink, he drew the attention of plenty of females. I noticed the way women looked at my ol' man, appreciative glances thrown his way whenever we were out together, and while he pretended not to notice, there was no way he was that blind. Right then, I was thankful Maddie had stayed in the room and hadn't come in the kitchen with me. Not that she would hit on my dad, but I didn't want her lookin' at anyone's body other than mine. Oh no! If this was me bein' crazy over my ol' man, how was I gonna feel when she was around other guys our age? She drank with Ace and Brick, but they were clothed at the time.

Shaking my head, realizing I might be goin' crazy, I flipped the omelet and moved it toward the back of the pan to make room for my dad's breakfast.

"Sure." I wanted to hurry up and get back to Maddie, but he was goin' through something with my mom, so the least I could do was help him out by making him somethin' to eat. "You ever gonna go home?" I asked, cracking more eggs. "Where did you even sleep?"

"In the back bedroom."

My hand froze mid whisk. "Where?"

"You can't hear so well in the morning? The back bedroom?"

"O... oh." I fumbled over my next question. "Are these walls thin?"

"I dunno." He peered over my shoulder. "You makin' something for Maddie?"

"Yeah." I really didn't know what to do or say. If he'd just come out of his room, which was right next to the one Maddie and I were in, there was no way he didn't hear everything. My ol' man was a light sleeper. It was how I'd always gotten caught breaking curfew in high school.

"Why you so tense?" he asked, slapping me on the back.

"No reason."

"Are you wonderin' if I heard you two havin' sex?"

My lungs deflated, and I hung my head. "You heard that?"

"Hey, at least one of us is gettin' it." He chuckled.

"Ew. Don't make me think about you and Mom."

"How do you think you, Riley, and Zander got here?"

"You guys only had sex three times. That's it." We shared a laugh, but I seriously didn't want to think about him and my mom together, so I switched the subject. "How long are you gonna hide out here before goin' home?"

"That's up to your mother."

"No. That's up to you," I reminded him, pointing the spatula at him. "You gotta let this thing go with Ry and Kaden."

"Don't talk to me about them," he growled. "He's lucky I haven't killed him yet." I tilted my head and raised my brows. "What? He is."

I never called him Dad while at the club or while dealing with club business, but I needed him to hear me. "Dad. Kaden is a good guy. You once loved him like he was your own son."

"Not anymore. He went behind my back for years like he wasn't...." Rubbing his hand down his face, he grabbed his beard and tugged. "What he did was unforgivable."

"You could look at it like he saved her from dating assholes who might've taken advantage of her, or broke her heart, or one of a hundred other things."

"You can look at it any way you want. But the only thing that's gonna happen is me punching that fucker again the first chance I get."

"Don't be surprised if he hits you back this time." He

shrugged, not a care for the thought that he might get into a brawl with his best friend's son. My ol' man took stubbornness to a whole other level for sure. "You're never goin' home, are ya?"

He didn't answer, instead grabbing a plate from the cupboard and handing it to me. After I gave him his omelet, he thanked me and turned to leave, and that's the exact moment when Kaden walked into the kitchen.

## Lincoln

I grumbled under my breath, tending to Maddie's food and distracting myself because the tension between these two was thick. More so my father's anger toward Kaden than the other way around, although with each verbal assault and threat of another fight, Kaden was close to boiling over as well.

"Marek said not here," I reminded him. He didn't say a word before walking past Kaden, knocking into his shoulder before he left.

Kaden crossed the small space until he was next to me. "Stone is lucky I have respect for my elders, because I would've put him on his ass the first time he hit me."

"You could've tried."

He scoffed. "You don't think I can take him?"

"I dunno. He wants to rip your head off, so he's got rage on his side."

"Yeah, but I got youth."

"How about both of you keep your hands to yourself."

"Tell him. It doesn't matter anyway. Even if I could take him, it's not like I'd hurt him. Lucky bastard." Kaden moved around me, opened the fridge and groaned. "Did you eat the last of the eggs?" he asked, easily switching from one subject to another as he turned and looked at the omelet in my hands. "I'll give you twenty bucks to split that with me. I didn't grab anything, and I don't work the best on an empty stomach. I got two trucks and a bike to fix before I can even think about grabbing lunch." He reached for the plate, but I pulled it back at the last second.

"No can do. This is for Maddie. Call Riley and ask her to bring you something. Or better yet, take your lazy ass to the restaurant. I'm sure Kena will whip somethin' up for you." Jagger's wife ran her family's restaurant, and since it was only a few miles away, it was the perfect solution for him, given there was no more food left.

"Maybe I'll go the restaurant route. I don't need any more shit from Stone this morning." He leaned against the counter, almost in the exact spot my ol' man had been in. "How're things with Maddie?"

I placed another plate on top of the one holding the food to keep it warm. "We're movin' in together as soon as I find a place."

"What the hell?"

"I know. We haven't known each other long at all, but I can't keep her here much longer, and it's about time I moved out into my own space. If Zander left the nest, as well as Riley, then so should I, right? Anyway, there's nowhere else for her to go other than with me. Plus, I want her with me." Kaden stood there, staring at me in shock. "You gonna say anything?"

"How did you convince her to move in with you? I've been trying everything I can on your sister, and she won't budge, even though she stays at my house five out of seven nights."

"You can't convince Riley to do anything she doesn't want to or isn't ready for, so good luck. And besides, our situations are completely different."

Kaden scratched the side of his jaw, his beard looking a bit scruffier than usual. "I guess you're right." He eyed up my plate again. "You sure you can't spare some of that."

"You wanna take food out of Maddie's mouth?"

"You're right." He groaned like a kid. "I'm just so hungry."

"Call Kena," I yelled over my shoulder as I walked out, almost running right into Marek.

"How are things?" He looked down at the plate, then back up at me. "Everything good?"

"Couldn't be better." I swore if I smiled any bigger, my face would crack.

Marek slapped my back. "Good man."

As I walked back down the hall, many thoughts plagued me, slowing every step I took even though I wanted to rush back to her.

What was gonna happen with Tag when we went to the safe house?

Whenever I did return to the ring, would the Reapers be there, waiting to exact revenge for having taken Maddie from them?

Would I be able to fulfill my promise and keep her safe?

While I didn't know any of these answers, I did know one thing for sure.

I'd do anything to protect the woman I loved, and while that knowledge gave me comfort, it also gave me pause because the probability of bloodshed in the very near future was high.

# Epilogue

## Lincoln

"What was that?" Maddie asked, pressing her finger to my lips. I'd been in the middle of reading her a description of the house I'd found that would be prefect for us when she interrupted me. "Shh…." I nipped her finger and made a move to tackle her on the bed, but she pressed back against me. "Seriously. I think something's goin' on."

I strained to listen but could only hear a faint noise, thinking it was possibly the television out by the bar, but then the noise suddenly erupted.

Someone shouted my name, but I couldn't tell who it was until they were closer to the room. Then came the incessant pounding. "Open up! Now!"

I hopped off the bed and threw on my jeans in record time, making sure Maddie was decent before pulling open the door. Brick's face stared back at me. "What's goin' on?" I asked, my pulse quickening in anticipation of bad news.

"Fuckin' Reaper, man. One of 'em is here, and he's askin' for you."

"Fuck!"

"Yeah, you can say that again. Hawke's got him on the ground with a gun to his head."

"Is he alone?"

"Yep. He's a prospect for them. Saw it on his cut before Hawke hit him."

I turned around to look at Maddie, and her eyes went wide. "Don't even fuckin' think about it. Stay here."

"But if it's Pike...."

"I don't care. He deserves what he gets coming here." My eyes locked on Brick's. "Make sure she stays put. Don't let her out of your sight." I snatched my gun from the dresser, checked the clip, and held it at my side.

"You got it." Brick moved into the room as Maddie jumped off the bed. I didn't have any time to check on her, trusting he'd keep her here as instructed and out of harm's way.

She shouted something after me, but I was too amped up to make out what it was, completely focused on why one of them would come here. I mean, I know why they would, but I never thought they'd have the balls to show up. Whoever Hawke had on the ground was as good as dead. I only prayed I wouldn't have to be the one to pull the trigger. I heard that shit stays with a man, but I'd do whatever was necessary to protect Maddie.

Whatever. Was. Necessary.

Because it was dark out, I only saw shadows on the other side of the lot, closer to the gate. It wasn't until I was practically on them, under the lighting, did I see who was present.

Hawke was yelling at the guy on the ground, pointing his gun at the man's head, like Brick said. Ace and Kaden stood next to the nomad with their weapons drawn as well.

"What the hell is goin' on?" I asked, rushing forward.

The guy lying on the ground had been beaten badly, the side of his face covered in blood, his one eye swollen shut.

There was no way Hawke could've caused all that damage in this short amount of time.

Kaden kicked the guy in the side, and he grunted. When he finally lifted his head enough to look up at me, I saw that it was indeed Pike, the Reaper prospect who'd shoved Maddie at me during the fight and told me to take her. She'd told me some things about the guy, and while she painted him to not be as bad as the rest of them, that he tried to help her as much as he could, he still had a hand in mistreating her. She claimed he was forced to rape her, but he raped her just the same.

A garbled barrage of words spewed from his mouth, but none of us could make out anything he said. Kaden kicked him again, which only made his speech worse when he tried a second time.

"Hey, maybe don't kick him so we can understand what the fuck he's tryin' to tell us." Kaden looked more annoyed than pissed off at the request, taking a step back.

"Why are you here?"

"War... warn you." He spit on the ground, a string of bloody saliva dangling from his mouth. "They're co... comin'."

"Who?" Hawke shouted, bending over and pressing the barrel of the gun to the guy's temple. "Your fuckin' buddies?"

The prospect nodded.

Then just like in a movie, I saw Maddie running toward us in slow motion, Brick a few feet behind her, reaching out but not quite making the connection to snatch her back.

She skidded to a stop and fell to the ground next to his bloodied form. "Cody," she cried, running her hands all over him. She looked up at me with pleading eyes. "Please don't kill him."

"You have a soft spot in your heart for the guys who raped you?" Hawke asked, sneering at her as if she disgusted him.

"He's not like that. He tried to help me," she hiccupped, her tears and concern for the bastard making me insanely jealous and angry. I barely had enough time to reel it in before Hawke's words finally registered, incensing me on a whole other level.

I was furious at Maddie for disobeying me and giving Brick the slip, which he'd hear about, of course, and for also trying to protect a Reaper. Help or no help.

"Brick, get her outta here," I shouted, tapping the gun against my thigh.

He reached down and scooped her up with no effort at all, his hand wrapped around her waist as he carted her off. She wore a thin top and short shorts, and while I hated that anyone had seen her like that, I doubted they were paying much attention with what was goin' down.

"Lincoln! Please don't do it," she bawled, beating her tiny fists against Brick's arms to try and get down. "Please..." Her voice faded the further away he took her, leaving the rest of us to focus on this guy.

"Now, why exactly did you come here to warn us?" I asked. "Did they send you in as bait?" I looked to the other guys. "Is there anyone else around. Did you check?"

"Yeah," Hawke answered. "This isn't my first rodeo."

I wanted to shout "It is for me," but that comment was unnecessary. We were in it now, my decision to take Maddie that night the catalyst to what was happening right at our feet... literally.

Pike shook his head as best he could in response to my question, his breathing coming in shallow spurts.

"Who fucked you up?" I asked him.

"Griller."

"Why?"

"Be... because I tried to..." He coughed, spitting up more blood onto the gravel. His hands clenched into fists while he struggled to take air into his lungs. "Convince them to leave Maddie alone. Get new pussy."

His reference to her made my blood boil, the inferno

erupting inside me set to blow any second. Trying to remain calm was difficult, but I somehow succeeded, albeit barely.

"When are they comin' for her? For us?" Ace asked, running his hand over the top of his head, his other holding his weapon steady.

"Soon."

Contemplating what to do with him, I teetered between gettin' rid of him, in whatever way that entailed I wasn't sure yet, and keeping him around for more questioning.

I crouched down so I could see him better. "Did you guys set the fire at Indulge?" A crease formed between his eyes. "One of our strip clubs," I clarified, guessing the answer before he gave it with a nod... then fell unconscious.

"What are we gonna do with him?" Kaden asked, walking in a circle while glancing down at the Reaper every few seconds. "We can't leave him here."

"We can dump him where we've discarded the others." Hawke pulled out his cell and dialed a number, allowing his words to sink in. Ace, Kaden, and I exchanged glances before I closed my eyes and pushed out a breath.

"And where is that?" The more I learned about the dealings of the club in the old days, the more hesitant I was to ask questions, but I supposed it had become a necessary evil as of late.

"'Bout an hour from here." He walked away as soon as his call connected.

"What the fuck?" Ace griped, pacing around the Reaper and mumbling to himself. "I've never been involved in a murder before, and now the count is gonna be up to two." He explained further when Kaden and I kept staring at him. "Tag and now this guy."

"We don't know Tag is gonna be killed," I said.

"What else do you think is gonna happen?" Kaden shook his head and took a few steps back.

Before I could even think of a reply, Hawke came walking

back over, shoving his phone in his pocket. "Prez said to bring him to the safe house. He's givin' Miles, Rez, and Nash a heads-up we're comin'. I'll grab the van." He walked away without another word.

"I'll be right back." I tucked the gun into the back of my waistband and jogged toward the clubhouse. While I continued to deal with twinges of jealousy and anger toward Maddie, I still didn't want to leave her. But it looked like I had no other choice in the matter.

She was sitting at the bar, Brick caging her in her seat. While I didn't appreciate how close he was to her, or that he'd had his hands on her before, I trusted him to not be inappropriate or cross any lines where she was concerned.

The moment she saw me, she hopped off the stool and rushed toward me, throwing her hands around my neck. "Please tell me you didn't kill him." She sobbed, her concern for this guy making my stomach roll.

I pushed her back so I could see her face, hating every one of her tears that were being shed for another man. "He is none of your concern."

"Lincoln, please..." Her body trembled as she looked up at me with her imploring stare. "Please don't—"

"Maddie, listen to me. Whatever happens to him is not on you." She opened her mouth to interrupt, but I shook my head before continuing to speak. "He knew what could happen by showing up here." More tears stained her cheeks. "What he did to you is unforgiveable. I know you believe he's not a bad guy because he was nice to you sometimes, but he's a coward. He took you to his club knowing what type of men they are. And you can argue with me until you're blue in the face, but that piece of shit out there," I said, raising my voice and pointing toward the door, "is not someone who deserves your tears. And don't think for a second he won't lure another unsuspecting girl back to his buddies." Even as the words left my mouth, I became conflicted with the suspected truth of them. Pike had come here to warn us, but as of this moment, I couldn't figure out if he told us the truth or if this was part of a setup.

When her tears slowed, I looked over her head to Brick. "We gotta go. Can you stay here and watch her?"

"Of course," he responded right away, alleviating some of my worry.

Maddie clutched on to my shirt, the fabric stretching when I tried to pull away. Gently but firmly unfurling her fingers, I passed her back to him.

As I walked away, I couldn't help the overwhelming feeling of dread that passed through me over what was to come.

Do you want more? Are you excited to find out what happens next? Well, you won't have to wait long for Ace, book 3 in the KCMC Next Generation series, which will be released in early July 2020.

Do you want to be the first to know when Ace goes live? Then make sure to sign up here:

www.subscribepage.com/snelsonnewsletter

HAVE YOU READ THE ORIGINAL KNIGHTS CORRUPTION SERIES WHERE IT ALL BEGAN? IF YOU'RE LOOKING FOR A BINGE WORTHY MC READ THAT WILL CONSUME YOU, THEN START TODAY WITH MAREK

With the weight of the club on his shoulders, Cole Marek, president of the Knights Corruption MC, had only one choice: Turn their livelihood legit.
Everything was falling into place until one unexpected, fateful night. With an attack on his fellow brothers, Marek had no choice but to retaliate against their sworn enemy.
Swarming their compound, he comes face-to-face with the daughter of his rival club, making an astonishing decision which would change his life forever.

Did you enjoy Lincoln?

Want to find out about S. Nelson's next novel?

Each month she sends out updates on upcoming books, sales, cover reveals, and awesome giveaways.

Get her FREE monthly newsletter by going to:

www.subscribepage.com/snelsonnewsletter

WANT A STORY THAT WILL LEAVE YOU BREATHLESS? THEN GRAB YOUR COPY OF ADDICTED, BOOK ONE IN THE ADDICTED TRILOGY

She intrigues him.
She challenges him.
She threatens the secret he's been hiding for years.
Will a promise made long ago be the very same thing that destroys their chance for happiness?

S. Nelson grew up with a love of reading and a very active imagination, never putting pen to paper, or fingers to keyboard until 2013.

Her passion to create was overwhelming, and within a few months she'd written her first novel. When she isn't engrossed in creating one of the many stories rattling around inside her head, she loves to read and travel as much as she can. She lives in the Northeast with her husband and two dogs, enjoying the ever changing seasons.

If you would like to follow or contact her please feel free to do so at the following:

Website: www.snelsonauthor.com
Email: snelsonauthor8@gmail.com

Also on Facebook, Goodreads, Amazon, Instagram and Twitter

# Note to Reader

If you are a new reader of my work, thank you so much for taking a chance on me. If I'm old news to you, thank you for continuing to support me. It truly means the world to me.

If you've enjoyed this book, or any of my other stories, please consider leaving a review. It doesn't have to be long at all. A sentence or two will do just fine. Of course, if you wish to elaborate, feel free to write as much as you want.

To my husband, thank you for always holding down the fort so that I can pursue my dream. I love you!

Clarise (CT Cover Creations), you are so freakin' talented, woman! Lincoln's cover is AMAZING! You've done a brilliant job and I cannot wait to work with you on my next project.

To Becky, my editor, your suggestions and comments have really helped to polish the second book in the KCMC Next Gen series. I don't know what I'd do without you.

Ruth, I'm so excited to have you in my corner. You've been my rock, especially when I feel like pulling my hair out. I look forward to our chats and love that you love my men as much as I do. I can't believe book two in this series is already done!

Elmarie, thank you so much for taking the time to beta read yet another book for me, although something tells me you were looking forward to finding out what happened in this one. I can't wait to chat with you about the next one.

To all of the bloggers who have shared my work, I'm forever indebted to you. You ladies are simply wonderful!

To all of you who have reached out to me to let me know how much you loved my stories, I am beyond humbled. Thank you so much, and I'll continue to do my best to bring you stories you can lose yourself in, even if it's only for a few hours.

And last but not least, I would like to thank you, the reader. If this is the first book you've read from me, I hope you enjoy it. If this is yet another story from me you've taken a chance on... THANK YOU from the bottom of my heart!

**Standalones**

Stolen Fate

Redemption

Torn

Blind Devotion

**Massey Security Duet**

The Assignment

The Score

**Addicted Trilogy**

Addicted

Shattered

Wanted

**Knights Corruption MC Series**

Marek

Stone

Jagger

Tripp

Ryder

**Knights Corruption Complete Series (all five original MC books in one)**

**Knights Corruption MC Series-Next Generation**

Kaden

Lincoln

Stolen
FATE
When betrayal is the only path to love
S. NELSON

a light in the darkness
REDEMPTION
S. NELSON

TORN
S. NELSON

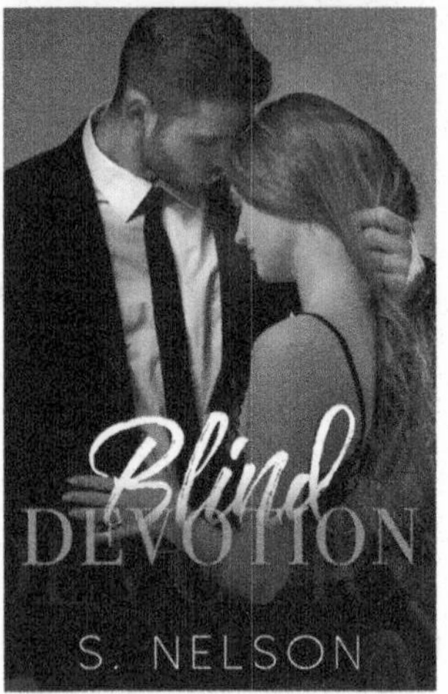
Blind
DEVOTION
S. NELSON

THE
ASSIGNMENT
S. NELSON
THE
SCORE
MASSEY SECURITY DUET BOOK TWO
S. NELSON

ADDICTED TRILOGY BOOK ONE
addicted
S. NELSON
ADDICTED TRILOGY BOOK TWO
shattered
S. NELSON
ADDICTED TRILOGY BOOK THREE
wanted
S. NELSON

MAREK
KNIGHTS CORRUPTION MC SERIES
S. NELSON

KNIGHTS
CORRUPTION

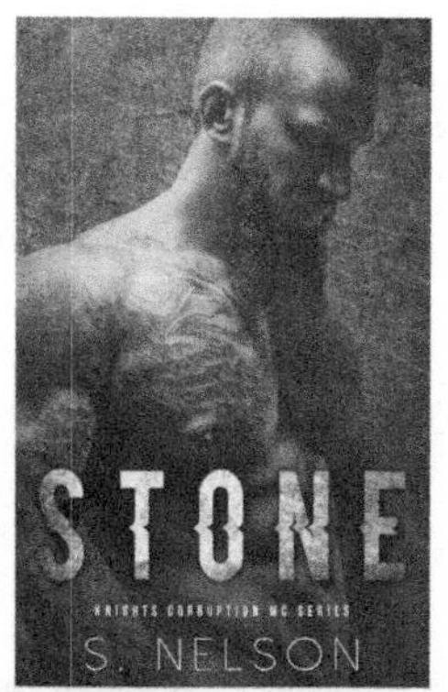
STONE
KNIGHTS CORRUPTION MC SERIES
S. NELSON

JAGGER
KNIGHTS CORRUPTION MC SERIES
S. NELSON

TRIPP
KNIGHTS CORRUPTION MC SERIES
S. NELSON

RYDER
KNIGHTS CORRUPTION MC SERIES
S. NELSON

KNIGHTS CORRUPTION

COMPLETE SERIES

S. NELSON

KADEN
KNIGHTS CORRUPTION MC SERIES
S. NELSON

LINCOLN
KNIGHTS CORRUPTION MC SERIES
S. NELSON

Made in the USA
Coppell, TX
10 November 2022